PENGUI

TWELVE STORIES BY
AMERICAN WOMEN

ARIELLE ZIBRAK is professor of English and gender and women's studies at the University of Wyoming. She is the editor of *Edith Wharton's* The Age of Innocence: *New Centenary Essays* (Bloomsbury, 2019) and the author of *Avidly Reads Guilty Pleasures* (New York University Press, 2021) and *Writing Against Reform: Aesthetic Realism in the Progressive Era* (University of Massachusetts Press, 2024). She is currently at work on a video streaming series for The Great Courses called "A Literary Tour of the United States" and two books: a public history of consumer feminism and New Age philosophy in America titled *The Image of Desire* and a memoir that examines how we process trauma both individually and collectively called *The Ghost in the Mirror.*

Twelve Stories by American Women

Edited with an Introduction by
ARIELLE ZIBRAK

PENGUIN BOOKS

PENGUIN BOOKS

An imprint of Penguin Random House LLC
1745 Broadway, New York, NY 10019
penguinrandomhouse.com

Introduction, selection, and suggestions for further reading
copyright © 2025 by Arielle Zibrak

LIBRARY OF CONGRESS CATALOGING-IN-PUBLICATION DATA
Names: Zibrak, Arielle, editor.
Title: Twelve stories by American women / edited with an introduction by
Arielle Zibrak.
Other titles: 12 stories by American women
Description: New York : Penguin Books, 2025. | Series: Penguin classics |
Includes bibliographical references.
Identifiers: LCCN 2024043275 (print) | LCCN 2024043276 (ebook) | ISBN
9780143138174 (paperback) | ISBN 9780593512319 (ebook)
Subjects: LCSH: Short stories, American. | American fiction—Women authors.
| American fiction—19th century. | American fiction—20th century.
Classification: LCC PS647.W6 T84 2025 (print) | LCC PS647.W6 (ebook) |
DDC 813/.01089287—dc23/eng/20241021
LC record available at https://lccn.loc.gov/2024043275
LC ebook record available at https://lccn.loc.gov/2024043276

Printed in the United States of America
1st Printing

The authorized representative in the EU for product safety and
compliance is Penguin Random House Ireland, Morrison Chambers,
32 Nassau Street, Dublin D02 YH68, Ireland,
https://eu-contact.penguin.ie.

Contents

TWELVE STORIES BY AMERICAN WOMEN

Introduction

THE SHORT STORY

Women writers in the almost hundred-year period this anthology spans—1830 to 1926—turned to the short story for many reasons. In 1830, the short story was a relatively new genre and the first genre that we might consider to have been born in the United States. By 1926, it was a highly popular form that could be found in periodicals, anthologies, and collections by individual authors all over the world. The development of the techniques and characteristics of the American short story can be traced throughout the works that have been selected here—from sentimental satires to political fables to supernatural tales to mysteries to realistic portrayals rooted in the particularities of their regional settings.

Most literary historians date the emergence of the short story to the tales that appeared in Washington Irving's *The Sketch Book*, which was published in installments between 1819 and 1820 and included the story "The Legend of Sleepy Hollow." Edgar Allan Poe, one of the genre's earliest theorists, surmised that the strength of short stories was to be found in what he called their "totality"—a singular purpose and plot that carry the reader propulsively forward until the ending's final blow.[1] For this reason, short stories also offered an ideal format for using fiction to make an urgent sociopolitical point.

Works in this anthology like Charlotte Perkins Gilman's "The Yellow Wall-paper," Rebecca Harding Davis's "Life in the Iron-Mills," and Zitkála-Šá's "The Widespread Enigma Concerning Blue-Star Woman" raise awareness about different forms of injustice by highlighting the fictionalized experiences of individual women despite the fact that women's publicly expressed political views had a tendency to ignite controversy. The short story form had a service to offer there too. Short fiction was more likely to reach readers while escaping the notice of censorious reviewers and commentators. In the preface to a collection of ghost stories written between 1902 and 1937, Edith Wharton reflected that "most purveyors of fiction will agree with me that the readers who pour out on the author of the published book such floods of interrogatory ink pay little heed to the isolated tale in a magazine."[2] The downside of this equation was that, for the first half of the nineteenth century, short stories were not highly profitable endeavors for writers.

As the periodical market expanded in the second half of the century, however, writers could more easily sell one-off tales to editors, tiding themselves over financially while they labored at more lucrative long-form projects. This was especially appealing to female writers, who often had both less time and less money than their male counterparts, as short stories could be produced and read within the disconnected intervals of free time that made up most women's lives. In 1899, the writer Kate Chopin, who was a single mother to six children, told the *St. Louis Post-Dispatch*:

> When do I write? I am greatly tempted here to use slang and reply "any old time," bet that would lend a tone of levity to this bit of confidence, whose seriousness I want to keep intact if possible. So I shall say I write in the morning, when not too strongly drawn to struggle with the intricacies of a pattern, and in the afternoon, if the temptation to try a new furniture polish on an old table leg is not too powerful to be denied; sometimes at night, though as I grow older I am more and more inclined to believe that night was made for sleep.[3]

Chopin's claim that her writing fits in at "any old time" like a hobby rather than an occupation should be taken both seriously and with a grain of salt. Chopin was a dedicated writer who worked at a constant pace and recorded the sales of her stories in a ledger, keeping tabs on what themes and formats won her the highest prices. But she was also a single mother and a woman living at the end of the nineteenth century, when the public nature of professional writing was still a somewhat dicey prospect for female writers who wanted to maintain their esteem in social circles. So, the paradoxical nature of Chopin's statement and status as an artist (both serious and not serious) in many ways mirrors the central paradox of the emergence of female authorship in the United States: American women have played a significant role in the creation of an American culture of letters for as long as that role has been minimized. In large part this is because writing is a profession, and while women needed no encouragement to take up their pens, the United States has long had an aversion to female professionalism.

FEMALE LITERARY PROFESSIONALISM IN THE UNITED STATES

In some ways, the idea of an "emergence" of female authorship in the United States makes no sense. It was never the case that women were barred from authorship or relegated to the sidelines of the creation of an American literature. It is simply that their contributions have been so insistently overlooked, discredited, or left out of sweeping literary historical narratives when, in fact, women have been at the forefront of print culture in the United States since its beginnings. The 1650 collection of poetry *The Tenth Muse, Lately Sprung Up in America* by Anne Bradstreet was one of the earliest publications distributed in colonial America. Years later, Bradstreet publicly claimed to have had the work published against her will in a poem, "The Author to her Book," which includes the self-deprecating lines, "Thou ill-form'd offspring of my feeble brain, / Who after birth didst by my side remain, / Till snatched from thence by friends, less wise then true / Who thee abroad, expos'd to publick view."[4] Ostensibly, Bradstreet denies any serious intention of trying to become a published author. Such a masculine aspiration, especially in her historical moment, would subject a woman to scorn and ostracism. Even two hundred years later, when the novelist Harriet Beecher Stowe had become the most famous woman in America for writing *Uncle Tom's Cabin*, a book that nearly every literate American read, she claimed to not have written it at all, stating instead that God spoke through her pen. Stowe would also refuse to read publicly, preferring to observe popular prohibitions against female orators by sitting silently on stage while her husband, Calvin, read her words for her.

Despite these pretenses toward modesty and disinterestedness, American women would continue to write prolifically and with a purpose. Phillis Wheatley, a young woman kidnapped from Gambia as a child and brought to Boston to work as an enslaved domestic laborer, published the first volume of poetry by an African American in 1773. In it, she condemned the Atlantic slave trade and subtly criticized the racist hypocrisy of abolitionist Bostonians. One of the first bestsellers to be printed in the United States was the 1797 epistolary novel *The Coquette* by Hannah Webster Foster. Published anonymously, it was a fictionalized account of a woman who died at a roadside tavern after giving birth to a child out of wedlock. Foster's work drew attention to the double standard of sexual propriety that destroyed so many women's lives in her time, setting a precedent for women writers who transcended confinement to the domestic sphere by voicing their opinions in print.

Nineteenth-century women not only rose to prominence as writers, they also shaped the literary marketplace and the public's tastes for textual entertainment and edification. The most widely circulated periodical in the United States prior to the Civil War was *Godey's Lady's Book*, which began printing bimonthly issues in Philadelphia in 1830. During the forty years that it was edited by the poet Sarah Josepha Hale—of "Mary Had a Little Lamb" fame—it published dress patterns, recipes, poetry, fiction, and essays on the issues of the day by both male and female writers, but Hale had an overarching vision for the magazine as a space where female readers and writers could engage in public discourse. At a time when the middle- and upper-class white women who were Hale's primary readership were most often relegated to the "separate sphere" of the home, the magazine culture envisioned by Hale eased their isolation and gave them a place to think about and engage with the broader world without compromising the mandates that women be domestic, submissive, and private.

Though Hale was the most successful and visible editor of her time, male or female, she was hardly alone. The literary scholar Patricia Okker has identified more than six hundred nineteenth-century women editors who published periodicals ranging from children's magazines to law reviews to medical journals to political papers.[5] Women were so professionally active in the literary sphere that their presence there became something of a joke among women writers themselves. The first story in this volume is Catharine Maria Sedgwick's "Cacoethes Scribendi." (The title is Latin for "mania for writing.") Sedgwick was a literary power broker herself, albeit on a slightly smaller scale than a figure like Hale. Her 1827 historical novel, *Hope Leslie*, created a sensation in nineteenth-century America and her fiction enjoyed a wide readership throughout the middle of the century. In "Cacoethes Scribendi," she depicts an all-female town possessed with the desire to turn every recipe, experience, and idea they encounter into publishable material. Taken up with the notion that professional writing is a sort of alchemy whereby women can transform ideas into money without leaving the comfort of their own homes, the mother of the young protagonist, Alice, tries to encourage her daughter to embark on a literary career. Alice is ultimately uninterested in sullying her name with printer's ink and chooses instead to marry.

At first glance, the story may seem to condemn women writers wholesale, but it's more accurately seen as a document of just how successful the project of female authorship was in nineteenth-century America. The target of Sedgwick's satire isn't female writers in general but the increasingly consumerist nature of the literary marketplace that their success as producers of literary commodities engendered. In another story

published two years later, "A Sketch of a Bluestocking," Sedgwick paints a far more charitable portrait of a female professional writer. The significant difference is that the Bluestocking,
unlike the hack writers of "Cacoethes Scribendi," is possessed
of "the most ardent devotion to knowledge and talent" and is,
furthermore, "the most honored and beloved of wives; the
most tender and capable of mothers; the most efficient and
least bustling of housewives; the truest of friends; and the
most attractive of women."[6] High standards, to be sure, but
Sedgwick's point here seems to be that writing has no neces-
sarily derogatory impact on a woman's feminine virtues.

Many nineteenth-century women who became writers had
to put virtue aside precisely because they had no husband or
male relatives who could support them financially, and these
were inevitably the writers whose works were the most harshly
critical of the laws and social practices that still so dramati-
cally restricted women's ability to achieve independence through
work. The writer Sara Payson Willis Parton, who published as
Fanny Fern (the name itself was a parody of the frilly feminine
noms de plume that populated the kinds of popular periodicals
Sedgwick satirized), also found herself unable to support her
family as a young widow. She remarried hastily under familial
pressure and her family withdrew financial support altogether
when she left her abusive second husband. Motivated by equal
measures of financial desperation and literary talent, Fanny
Fern's 1854 novel, *Ruth Hall*, was a thinly veiled autobiographical account of her desertion and her rise to fame as a popular
columnist. Nathaniel Hawthorne enjoyed the novel, writing to
his editor that "the woman writes as if the devil was in her."[7]
In an article in the *New York Ledger*, Fern succinctly stated
the nature of that devil:

> There are few people who speak approbatively of a woman who
> has a smart business talent or capability. No matter how iso-
> lated or destitute her condition, the majority would consider it
> more "feminine" would she unobtrusively gather up her thimble,
> and, retiring into some out-of-the-way place, gradually scoop
> out her coffin with it, than to develop that smart turn for busi-

ness which would lift her at once out of her troubles; and which, in a man so situated, would be applauded as exceedingly praiseworthy.[8]

The most radical thing about the novel *Ruth Hall* may be that it ends in financial independence—not marriage—as the bringer of safety and salvation.

MARRIAGE AND INDEPENDENCE

Marriage is such a pervasive theme in American women's fiction not primarily because women delighted in telling and reading love stories, but because marriage was the site of their survival or dissolution, variously their hope for salvation or the repeated scene of their oppression. Many writers were pressured by audiences and editors to marry off their heroines to appeal to more traditional values. During the serial publication of her 1868 novel, *Little Women*, Louisa May Alcott wrote in her diary, "Girls write to ask who the little women marry, as if that was the only end and aim of a woman's life. I won't marry Jo to Laurie to please any one."[9] And while she did eventually succumb to the pressure to marry her heroine off, albeit to another character, Alcott herself would never choose to marry. The history of the lived experiences of the writers in this volume and the themes within their fictions tell a complex story about what it meant for women to tie their lives and livelihoods to men.

Though Rebecca Harding Davis wrote in 1886 that "marriage, provided it to be based on pure, strong affection, is better for a woman, even under the worst circumstances, than a single life under the best,"[10] her 1861 short story, "Life in the Iron-Mills," included here, features a disabled female character living in dire poverty and working as a "picker" in a cotton mill whose salvation comes not through her romantic union with the cousin she loves but through her rescue by a Quaker activist fighting to improve labor conditions for workers like Deb. Davis herself did not marry until she was thirty-two, and her choice of husband was an editor who admired—and therefore would support—her professional career. Charlotte Perkins Gilman left her husband and child to pursue a full-time career as a writer and activist, inciting a controversy that would follow her throughout her life.

Frances Ellen Watkins Harper was one of the first of many women writers to dramatize the choice between a potentially oppressive marriage and an independent life devoted to art or good works. Her 1859 short story, "The Two Offers," included here, is thought to be the first short story published by an African American woman. The two cousins in the story—Janette Alston and Laura Lagrange—choose two different paths. Laura marries a man whose drinking renders her life a misery, while Janette struggles to support herself and faces social prejudice as a "spinster." But the story looks charitably on Janette's choice:

> No husband brightened her life with his love, or shaded it with his neglect. No children nestling lovingly in her arms called her mother. No one appended Mrs. to her name; she was indeed an old maid, not vainly striving to keep up an appearance of girlishness, when departed was written on her youth [. . .] and as old age descended peacefully and gently upon her, she had learned one of life's most precious lessons, that true happiness consists not so much in the fruition of our wishes as in the regulation of desires and the full development and right culture of our whole statures (p. 28).

Harper married only briefly and later in life. She published nine books and numerous stories, essays, and poems throughout her career and donated the majority of the proceeds of these works, along with her earnings from a rigorous lecturing schedule, to the antislavery cause. In addition to her writing, she worked to organize a boycott of goods sold by enslavers, aided with the organization of the Underground Railroad, and was active in the women's suffrage movement despite its often-exclusionary attitude toward women of color. Harper did not reject the institution of marriage altogether. But, like Janette in "The Two Offers," she would choose to devote her own life to bettering society rather than subjugating herself to a husband.

Barbara Pope's story "The New Woman" offers a more hopeful vision of the possibilities for an equitable union between a man and a woman. The title references a popular figure in the period literary critics and historians have more often associated with modern, liberated white women, but Pope's main character is a talented and independent Black woman who gradually reasons with her husband to disabuse him of his sexist expectations for their marriage by convincing him to let her clerk for him in his law office, as she did for her father. "The bargain was that you would practice law and I take charge of the home," she tells him, "but neither of us must be selfish, and each will call on the other for assistance when needed" (p. 117). Pope, who grew up in a progressive family in Georgetown's thriving free Black community, worked as a teacher at Booker T. Washington's Tuskegee Institute and as an educational reformer in the district's colored school system. Her life was devoted to her fiction and political activism; she would never marry.

Edith Wharton, who as a young woman was considered unmarriageable on account of her bookishness, divorced the husband she was convinced to settle for after twenty-eight unhappy years together, moved to France, and never married again. Her novels continued to be bestsellers, beloved by readers and critics alike, and she even asked her publisher to subsidize the meager royalty statements of her good friend Henry James from the profits of her own robust sales. Her 1899 story "Souls Belated," included here, follows a woman who has traveled to Europe with her lover to evade scandal while awaiting the arrival of her divorce papers. Their secret is inevitably guessed by their fellow hotel patrons and, cover blown, they must come to terms with the social reality of their situation.

No-fault divorces weren't introduced into the US legal code until 1969, a development that began in 1899 with the formation of the feminist National Association of Women Lawyers, which lobbied for marriage laws that would give women rights to their own property and legal recourse when subjected to domestic abuse. Since divorce laws were determined on a state-by-state basis, migratory divorce was a common practice in the late nineteenth and early twentieth centuries. Couples from the East would travel to and temporarily reside in a divorce-friendly state in the West to obtain their legal separation. So, while many women found themselves coerced into marriage by their families, their prospective partners, or their financial circumstances, extracting oneself from an undesirable marriage was a complicated and expensive ordeal that was, for most, impossible.

Zora Neale Hurston's 1937 novelistic masterpiece, *Their Eyes Were Watching God*, tells the story of a woman who must marry three times before she can find a partner who sees her as worthy of his respect. The protagonist of her story in this volume, "Sweat," supports herself and her husband through her grueling home laundry business, laboring in the same space where she is repeatedly abused. Her husband brings home a snake to taunt her only to find himself the victim of its fangs. It's a revenge fantasy for survivors of abuse to be sure, but also one that gestures toward the senselessness of misogyny. The snake of the husband's animosity bites him in the end, after all.

It's not difficult to understand, given these circumstances, why some women writers in the period this volume addresses lived in "Boston marriages," a popular term for the arrangement where two unmarried women would split the costs and responsibilities of managing a household with each other. These arrangements provided companionship and support outside of the legally and socially oppressive conditions of heterosexual marriage. Other women writers either lived openly or semi-covertly under the guise of a Boston marriage within romantic partnerships with other women. One such writer was Madelene Yale Wynne, whose story "The Little Room" appears in this volume.

Wynne was the daughter of a successful engineer and entrepreneur who became wealthy after inventing the Yale cylinder lock we still use today. At the age of eighteen, she married Senator Henry Winn and began a life as a society wife. In 1873, her mother wrote a friend that Madeline "has had a sad winter, all Mr. Winn's most trying qualities having culminated in what I consider tyrannies and persecutions of an unendurable nature."[11] In 1874, Madeline moved in with her mother and the following year, Winn filed a claim for desertion. Madeline defaulted on the warrant summoning her to appear in court, so Winn got his divorce and Madeline got nothing but her children and her freedom. She would subsequently change the spelling of her first name to "Madelene" and her last name to "Wynne" and devote her life to the American Arts and Crafts Movement—an aesthetic and social project that championed the production of handmade, rather than manufactured, goods and the social uplift of women and the working classes. The movement brought her into contact with the craftsperson Annie Cabot Putnam, who became her romantic and professional partner for the remainder of her life.

Together, the couple divided their time between Chicago—where they contributed to the settlement house movement begun by their friend and collaborator Jane Addams at Hull House—and Deerfield, Massachusetts—where they founded a female artists' colony and taught skills like basket weaving and metalwork. Wynne's 1895 "The Little Room" was so popular it inspired the creation of "Little Room Societies" across the country where participants would discuss the socialist ideas that were important to Wynne and her colleagues. But "The Little Room" also offers a sly critique of heterosexual marriages wherein the normative superiority of the male partner is unquestioned. While a case of disputed reality within the story creates conflict for all the couples who encounter it, only the same-sex couple in the story—Cousin Nan and her "friend" Rita Lash—come to mutual resolution. Within heterosexual marriage, the story implies, women can never have an equal voice.

Many of the happiest romantic relationships among women writers within this period seem to have been with other women. In April 1881, when her editor, James Fields, died, the Maine writer Sarah Orne Jewett paid a condolence visit to his

wife, Annie, in Boston. The visit lasted three months and culminated in the two taking a trip together to Europe. From that
time onward, they lived openly as a couple and exchanged love
letters when apart, using their pet names for one another like
Pinny, Mouse, and Fuss.

Jewett's stories are primarily set in Dunnet Landing, a fictional town on the Maine coast populated by sailors, farmers,
and a curious number of single old women. These stories were
a part of the regionalist movement in literature, also sometimes called "local color" fiction, which highlighted setting,
dialect, and the particularities of the many distinct regions of
the Americas. Prominent regionalist writers included Jewett
and Mary Wilkins Freeman in the Northeast; Kate Chopin,
Ruth McEnery Stuart, and Ellen Glasgow in the South; Rebecca
Harding Davis and Mary Noailles Murfree in Appalachia;
and Mary Hunter Austin and Zona Gale in the West. Jewett's
brand of literary regionalism was marked by a deep love and
concern for the natural environment that was intertwined
with the social concerns of her contemporaries.

THE POLITICAL WORK
OF WOMEN'S FICTION

Sarah Orne Jewett understood the natural world to be under
threat by the same forces that the young women protagonists
who visit their elders in Dunnet Landing faced. In "A White
Heron," Jewett's story in this volume, the grandmother of the
young protagonist, Sylvia, reflects, "there never was such a
child for straying about out-of-doors since the world was
made!" (p. 70). Sylvia's love for the out-of-doors is connected
to her pastoral innocence, and when an ornithologist appears
near her grandmother's property in search of a white heron to
kill and study, Sylvia is thrust between competing desires. The
ornithologist's drive to order and control the natural world
through violence is contrasted with Sylvia's more sympathetic
way of existing within it. Nevertheless, her incipient romantic

desire for the ornithologist as a specimen of adult masculinity causes her to briefly question her loyalty to the heron. In the end, she chooses the bird over the man.

The women of Jewett's fiction are typically pre- or post-marrying age, a gesture that sets her stories apart from the dramas of courtship and marriage that animate so much women's fiction. This attention to children and, especially, the old has long been seen as one of the radical qualities in Jewett's work. The literary critic Sari Edelstein points out that the old age of many of Jewett's characters is a queer or "backward-oriented" status that protests capitalist ideas of success. Jewett's older female characters assert a right to live freely outside of a capitalist system motivated by productivity and consumption—to simply *exist* like the heron of the story. At the same time, such portrayals of older white women have been seen by some critics as evidence of the period's nativist concerns with "race suicide"— the fear that people of color would continue to reproduce while the white race allowed itself to die out.

Coined by Edward A. Ross, the term "race suicide" came to stand for what the critic and historian Holly Jackson has called "the ultimate fear underlying this apocalyptic mix of anti-feminist and anti-immigration ideologies" that swirled around the dominant discourse of the period.[12] There is no smoking-gun evidence to suggest that Jewett herself adopted these beliefs, but the same cannot be said for Charlotte Perkins Gilman.

Gilman is an important case study for this volume because of both the radical nature of her feminism for the period and the radical nature of her nativist beliefs. Her 1898 nonfiction work, *Women and Economics*, raised concerns recognized today as some of feminism's most urgent demands—such as the need for professionalized child care, universal health care, communal living situations, and frank conversations about sexuality. Her famous short story included here, "The Yellow Wall-paper," made an early intervention in mental health care reform and inaugurated a conversation about gaslighting we're still having today. But her commitment to the racist eugenics movement and her belief in the unquestioned superiority of the white race, evinced in articles like the 1908 "A Suggestion on the Negro Problem," remain troubling pills to swallow when surveying her career as a whole.[13]

Edith Wharton's fiction likewise contains still-vital critiques of the marginalization of female voices and the double standards that keep women from succeeding personally or professionally, and yet it also offers many glimpses of the author's considerable classism, racism, and anti-Semitism. These are by no means reasons to stop reading these authors, but it is important that we acknowledge their shortcomings as we celebrate their vision.

For many years, our concept of American women's literature in this period was shaped by a small cadre of wealthy white women from the Northeast like Jewett, Gilman, and Wharton. There are many reasons for this, but primary among them is the fact that such women were more likely to have the education, resources, free time, and social connections that made publication a possibility. Women of color who published in the United States in this period had to overcome extraordinary barriers and leverage extraordinary advantages in order to do so. While many poor and working-class African American storytellers continued to create and circulate stories within an oral literary tradition, the African American women who published fiction during this period in volumes and periodicals, like Harper and Pope, most often came from families that had been free for more than one generation and who had financial resources and access to education. The genres that would allow such writers to place their work in the mainstream periodicals of the day belonged to a written literary tradition that typically had to be learned within the context of formal schooling. Likewise, while Indigenous oral traditions allowed tribal communities to record their own cultures and histories through storykeepers, Native American women who published in mainstream venues during this time had been previously subjected to the conventions of white educational systems.

In 1884, Zitkála-Šá was taken from her mother's home on the Yankton Reservation in South Dakota and brought to

White's Indiana Manual Labor Institute, an integrated school
for children of color and poor whites, by Quaker missionaries.
Her description of this educational experience is one of deep
cultural violence. In a short autobiographical work called
"The School Days of an Indian Girl," she describes,

> I remember being dragged out, though I resisted by kicking and
> scratching wildly. In spite of myself, I was carried downstairs
> and tied fast in a chair. I cried aloud, shaking my head all the
> while until I felt the cold blades of the scissors against my neck,
> and heard them gnaw off one of my thick braids. Then I lost my
> spirit. Since the day I was taken from my mother I had suffered
> extreme indignities. People had stared at me. I had been tossed
> about in the air like a wooden puppet. And now my long hair
> was shingled like a coward's! In my anguish I moaned for my
> mother, but no one came to comfort me. Not a soul reasoned
> quietly with me, as my own mother used to do; for now I was
> only one of many little animals driven by a herder.[14]

After she finished her own schooling, Zitkála-Šá taught
music at the Carlisle Indian Industrial School in Pennsylvania,
where she was eventually dismissed for protesting its assimila-
tionist curriculum. She would go on to produce a significant
number of written works in fiction and nonfiction, to compose
an opera based on the Lakota Sun Dance, and to work as the
Secretary of the Society of American Indians. Her story in this
collection, "The Widespread Enigma Concerning Blue-Star
Woman," uses the plight of a single female elder to illustrate
the clash between Native and white ideas of care and sover-
eignty. Like most of Zitkála-Šá's stories, "Blue-Star Woman"
draws upon the Yankton legends of her childhood as it lever-
ages her knowledge of essayistic and fictional forms to make
compelling political arguments marketable within the mainstream press.

Hurston's "Sweat" also draws upon inherited oral tales as it
intervenes in the tradition of the modern short story. She studied anthropology at Barnard College and Columbia under the
direction of Franz Boas, the founder of the discipline in the

United States, and three of her book-length works (*Every Tongue Got to Confess* [published posthumously in 2001], *Mules and Men* [1935], and *Tell My Horse* [1938]) are the results of her ethnographic studies of African American folklore. In "Sweat," she not only utilizes the animal imagery popular in such tales but also turns her folklorist's eye to a racist US cultural tradition she then satirizes. By inserting her protagonists into stock roles often wielded as stereotypes—the beleaguered washwoman and the wastrel husband—she upturns readerly expectations and takes back the static portrayals of the minstrel tradition.

Writers who found themselves at the intersection of more than one cultural and literary tradition had a careful line to walk when writing as representatives of a nondominant group for predominantly white audiences. María Cristina Mena was the daughter of a Spanish mother and a Mexican father whose business profited under the corrupt rule of Mexican president Porfirio Díaz. For her education, Mena was sent to a convent school for the daughters of the Mexican elite and then to an English boarding school. Her first published stories were written and appeared while she was living in New York City, where she was sent amidst rising political tensions in Mexico. Mena's 1914 short story, "The Vine-Leaf," included here, first appeared in the popular *Century Magazine*. She was considered, like Jewett, a local color writer, and scholars today have debated how to position the complex attitudes toward race that appear in her fiction.

The scholar and cultural theorist Gloria Anzaldúa writes of Mena as a "new mestiza," arguing that "she has a plural personality, she operates in a pluralistic mode—nothing is thrust out, the good, the bad and the ugly, nothing rejected, nothing abandoned. Not only does she sustain contradictions, she turns ambivalence into something else."[15] Other critics identify the contradictions in her work as a desire to appeal to white audiences in order to secure publication.[16] What remains clear through extant letters to her publishers is that it was important to Mena to advocate for Mexico's Indigenous citizens and advance an early position of Chicana women's rights.

In "The Vine-Leaf," Mena rewrites Nathaniel Hawthorne's 1843 "The Birth-Mark," the story of a scientist so obsessed with a birthmark on his wife's face that he winds up killing her during the removal surgery. Mena's story recasts many of its themes from a woman of color's perspective. The quest for female aesthetic perfection at the cost of female life is racialized in Mena's telling, as the vine leaf birthmark is described as "staining a surface as pure as the petal of any magnolia" (p. 171).

Like Mena, Sui Sin Far was a mixed-race writer who made significant inroads in the representation of non-white protagonists in the popular fiction of the period. Born Edith Maude Eaton in England in 1865, she was the daughter of an English merchant father and a Chinese mother. "Mrs. Spring Fragrance," Sui Sin Far's story included here and the title story in her first published collection, is set in the thriving Chinatowns of San Francisco and Seattle. Her protagonist enjoys the relative freedoms of the women in her urban American context but remains rooted in traditional Chinese cultural values. It could be argued that, like the heroine of Pope's story, Mrs. Spring Fragrance is a "new woman" who trains her husband to respect her independence.

Along with her sister, Winnifred Eaton, who wrote under the name Onoto Watanna, Sui Sin Far was one of the first writers to represent Asian American life from an Asian American perspective. In her work, she at times relied on stereotyped depictions that present-day readers may identify with the orientalism of white writers during her period. Her writing was, however, deeply critical of US anti-Chinese policy and, as the literary scholar Mary Chapman has shown, the exclusionary whiteness of the women's suffrage movement.[17]

READING THE STORIES IN CONTEXT

In the early twenty-first century, when feminist movements are thankfully becoming more intersectional and concerned with how the various identities of female people contribute to their unique perspectives as well as their privileges and oppressions, it may be tempting to see this volume as a representative study of women's lives during the period it covers. But a collection of published short stories can offer only a more complete survey of the period's literature—not its lived reality for all. Then, as now, unequal access to education, health care, and child care severely delimited those whose works of creative expression could be professionalized and who would be exposed to the liberatory frameworks they may need in order to find their voice in the first place.

Students and scholars of literature alike have a tendency to privilege writers whom they can identify as having been ahead of their time, and the recovery of American women writers initially proceeded by first attending to the nineteenth- and early twentieth-century writers whose views looked a little bit more like late twentieth-century ideas of feminism. Praising a writer for being ahead of their time is, after all, the same as saying we like them because they are more like us. But one of the most important things reading can do for us is to teach us more about the thoughts, feelings, and circumstances of those who are *not* like us. This can mean reading texts written in our own time by writers whose identities are very different from our own. But it can also mean looking to literature to give us a more multifaceted understanding of the past. The writers in this volume, like most great writers in the history of literature, are probably better described as "of" rather than "ahead" of their times. But this only means that in reading their words, we can understand the past in a more nuanced way, which, in turn, gives us insight into our own short-comings.

How many of us, truly, would be considered ahead of our time if our thoughts were to be read a hundred and fifty years from now? It is impossible to say from our present vantage point if the people of the future would be horrified by how we understand race, gender, and sexuality, the environment, or wage labor. We cannot look to these writers, who were simi-larly embedded in the prejudices and specific material condi-tions of their own historical moment, to solve the problems we face today. But they are our ancestors, all, and they have much to offer us beyond solutions. These stories are the work of the women who turned to literature themselves to try to better understand their own world, and by turning to them now, we assert the value of learning the past as a part of our own story. It is in this way that these writers can still guide us—by showing us where we came from.

ARIELLE ZIBRAK

Suggestions for Further Reading

MORE WRITING BY THESE AUTHORS AND THEIR CONTEMPORARIES

Bendixen, Alfred, ed. *Charlotte Perkins Gilman: Novels, Stories, and Poems.* New York: Modern Library, 2022.

Chapman, Mary, ed. *Becoming Sui Sin Far.* Montreal: McGill-Queen's University Press, 2016.

Chopin, Kate. *The Awakening and Other Writings by Kate Chopin.* Edited by Suzanne L. Disheroon, Barbara C. Ewell, Pamela Glenn Menke, and Susie Scifres. Peterborough: Broadview Press, 2011.

Correas de Zapata, Celia, ed. *Short Stories by Latin American Women: The Magic and the Real.* New York: Modern Library, 2003.

Edmundson, Melissa, ed. *Women's Weird: Strange Stories by Women, 1890–1940.* Bath: Handheld Classics, 2019.

Fern, Fanny. *Ruth Hall.* New York: Penguin, 1997.

Harper, Frances Ellen Watkins. *A Brighter Coming Day: A Frances Ellen Watkins Harper Reader.* Edited by Frances Smith Foster. New York: Feminist Press, 1990.

———. *Iola Leroy.* New York: Penguin Classics, 2010.

Hopkins, Pauline Elizabeth. *Of One Blood Or, the Hidden Self.* Edited by Eurie Dahn and Brian Sweeney. Peterborough, ON: Broadview, 2022.

Hopkins, Sarah Winnemucca. *Life Among the Piutes: Their Wrongs and Claims.* Reno: University of Nevada Press, 1994.

Howe, Julia Ward. *The Hermaphrodite.* Edited by Gary Williams. Lincoln: University of Nebraska Press, 2004.

Hurston, Zora Neale. *Hitting a Straight Lick with a Crooked Stick: Stories from the Harlem Renaissance.* New York: Amistad, 2020.

Jewett, Sarah Orne. *The Country of the Pointed Firs.* New York: Penguin, 1995.

Koppelman, Susan, ed. *Two Friends and Other 19th-Century American Lesbian Short Stories*. New York: Penguin, 1994.

Looby, Christopher, ed. *"The Man Who Thought Himself a Woman" and Other Queer Nineteenth-Century Short Stories*. Philadelphia: University of Pennsylvania Press, 2018.

Mena, María Cristina. *The Collected Stories of María Cristina Mena*. Houston: Arte Público, 1997.

Pfaelzer, Jean, ed. *A Rebecca Harding Davis Reader*. Pittsburgh: University of Pittsburgh Press, 1995.

Robbins, Hollis, and Henry Louis Gates, Jr., eds. *The Portable Nineteenth-Century African American Women Writers*. New York: Penguin, 2017.

Showalter, Elaine, ed. *Scribbling Women: Short Stories by 19th-Century American Women*. New Brunswick: Rutgers, 1996.

Southworth, E.D.E.N. *The Hidden Hand*. New Brunswick: Rutgers University Press, 1988.

Stoddard, Elizabeth. *The Morgesons*. New York: Penguin Classics, 1997.

Ward, Elizabeth Stuart Phelps. *The Story of Avis*. New Brunswick: Rutgers University Press, 1985.

Wharton, Edith. *The Collected Stories of Edith Wharton*. Boston: De Capo, 2002.

Zitkála-Šá. *American Indian Stories, Legends, and Other Writings*. New York: Penguin, 2003.

SECONDARY WORKS OF LITERARY CRITICISM, THEORY, AND HISTORY

Allen, Paula Gunn. *The Sacred Hoop: Recovering the Feminine in American Indian Traditions*. Boston: Beacon, 1986.

Ammons, Elizabeth. *Conflicting Stories: American Women Writers at the Turn into the Twentieth Century*. Oxford and New York: Oxford University Press, 1991.

Berlant, Lauren. *The Female Complaint*. Durham, NC: Duke University Press, 2008.

Boyd, Anne E. *Writing for Immortality: Women and the Emergence of High Literary Culture in America*. Baltimore: Johns Hopkins University Press, 2004.

Cane, Aleta Feinsod, and Susan Alves, eds. *"The Only Efficient Instrument": American Women Writers and the Periodical, 1837–1916*. Iowa City: University of Iowa Press, 2001.

Davis, Cynthia. *Charlotte Perkins Gilman: A Biography.* Palo Alto: Stanford University Press, 2010.

Fleissner, Jennifer. *Women, Compulsion, Modernity: The Moment of American Naturalism.* Chicago: University of Chicago Press, 2004.

Foote, Stephanie. *The Parvenu's Plot: Gender, Culture, and Class in the Age of Realism.* Durham: University of New Hampshire Press, 2014.

Foreman, P. Gabrielle. *Activist Sentiments: Reading Black Women in the Nineteenth Century.* Champaign: University of Illinois Press, 2009.

Gilbert, Sandra M., and Susan Gubar. *The Madwoman in the Attic: The Woman Writer and the Nineteenth-Century Literary Imagination.* New Haven: Yale University Press, 1979.

Halpern, Faye. *Sentimental Readers: The Rise, Fall, and Revival of a Disparaged Rhetoric.* Iowa City: University of Iowa Press, 2013.

Hartman, Saidiya V. *Wayward Lives, Beautiful Experiments: Intimate Histories of Social Upheaval.* New York: W. W. Norton, 2019.

Kilcup, Karen L. *Fallen Forests: Emotion, Embodiment, and Ethics in American Women's Environmental Writing, 1781–1924.* Athens: University of Georgia, 2013.

Kilcup, Karen L., ed. *Nineteenth-Century American Women Writers: A Critical Reader.* Malden, MA: Blackwell, 1998.

Merish, Lori. *Sentimental Materialism: Gender, Commodity Culture, and Nineteenth-Century American Literature.* Durham, NC: Duke University Press, 2000.

Noble, Marianne. *The Masochistic Pleasures of Sentimental Literature.* Princeton: Princeton University Press, 2000.

Romero, Lora. *Home Fronts: Domesticity and Its Critics in the Antebellum United States.* Durham, NC: Duke University Press, 1997.

Sheffer, Jolie A. *The Romance of Race: Incest, Miscegenation, and Multiculturalism in the United States, 1880–1930.* New Brunswick: Rutgers University Press, 2013.

ONLINE ARCHIVES AND RESOURCES

Archives of Women's Political Communication, https://awpc.cattcenter.iastate.edu/.

Carlisle Indian School Digital Resource Center, https://carlisleindian
    .dickinson.edu/.
Cassey & Dickerson Friendship Album Project, https://lcpalbum
    project.org/.
Colored Conventions Project, https://coloredconventions.org/.
Native American Authors, https://www.ipl.org/div/natam/.
Rebecca Harding Davis Archive, https://www.rebeccahardingdavis
    archive.org/.
Wheatley Peters Project, https://wheatleypetersproject.weebly.com/.
Winnifred Eaton Archive, https://www.winnifredeatonarchive.org/.
Zora Neale Hurston Digital Archive, https://chdr.cah.ucf.edu
    /hurstonarchive/?p=_home.

A Note on the Text

Spelling and punctuation have been Americanized; however, the overall punctuation style has been maintained and reflects the conventions of the time in which the pieces were written. Negligible spelling and typographical errors have been corrected. The following versions were used for the generation of this text:

Catharine Maria Sedgwick, "Cacoethes Scribendi," *Atlantic Souvenir* (Philadelphia: Carey, Lea & Carey, 1830), 17–38.

Frances Ellen Watkins [Harper], "The Two Offers," *Anglo-African Magazine* 1 (June and July 1859): 288–91 and 339–45.

[Anonymous], "Life in the Iron-Mills," *Atlantic*, April 1861, 430–51.

Sarah Orne Jewett, "A White Heron," *A White Heron and Other Stories* (Boston: Houghton, Mifflin, and Company, 1886), 1–22.

Charlotte Perkins Stetson, "The Yellow Wall-paper. A Story," *New England Magazine* 11.5 (January 1892): 647–56.

Charlotte Perkins Stetson, "Why I Wrote the Yellow Wallpaper?" *Forerunner* 4 (October 1913): 271.

Madelene Yale Wynne, "The Little Room," *Harper's New Monthly Magazine* 91 (April 1895): 467–73.

Barbara Pope, "The New Woman," *Waverley Magazine*, July 18, 1896, in *Storiettes* (Paris: Paris Exposition Universelle,

1900), microfilm, Class P Miscellaneous Monographs & Pamphlets, reel 74771 PZ, Library of Congress, Washington, DC.

Edith Wharton, "Souls Belated," *The Greater Inclination* (New York: Charles Scribner's Sons, 1899), 83–128.

Sui Sin Far, "Mrs. Spring Fragrance," *Mrs. Spring Fragrance* (Chicago: A. C. McClurg & Co., 1912), 1–20.

María Cristina Mena, "The Vine-Leaf," *Century Magazine*, December 1914, 289–92.

Zitkála-Šá, "The Widespread Enigma Concerning Blue-Star Woman," *American Indian Stories* (Washington, DC: Hayworth Publishing House, 1921), 159–82.

Zora Neale Hurston, "Sweat," *Fire!! A Quarterly Devoted to Younger Negro Artists* 1.1 (November 1926): 40–45.

Twelve Stories by American Women

"CACOETHES SCRIBENDI"

by Catharine Maria Sedgwick,
1830[1]

Glory and gain the industrious tribe provoke.

—Pope[2]

The little secluded and quiet village of H. lies at no great distance from our "literary emporium." It was never remarked or remarkable for anything, save one mournful preeminence, to those who sojourned within its borders—it was duller even than common villages. The young men of the better class all emigrated. The most daring spirits adventured on the sea. Some went to Boston; some to the south; and some to the west; and left a community of women who lived like nuns, with the advantage of more liberty and fresh air, but without the consolation and excitement of a religious vow. Literally, there was not a single young gentleman in the village—nothing in manly shape to which these desperate circumstances could give the form and quality and use of a beau. Some dashing city blades, who once strayed from the turnpike to this sequestered spot, averred that the girls stared at them as if, like Miranda, they would have exclaimed—

> "What is't? a spirit?
> Lord, how it looks about! Believe me, sir,
> It carries a brave form:—But 'tis a spirit."[3]

A peculiar fatality hung over this devoted place. If death seized on either head of a family, he was sure to take the husband; every woman in H. was a widow or maiden; and it is a sad fact, that when the holiest office of the church was celebrated, they were compelled to borrow deacons from an adjacent village. But, incredible as it may be, there was no great diminution of happiness in consequence of the absence of the nobler sex. Mothers were occupied with their children and housewifery, and the young ladies read their books with as much interest as if they had lovers to discuss them with, and worked their frills and capes as diligently, and wore them as complacently, as if they were to be seen by manly eyes. Never were there pleasanter gatherings or parties (for that was the word even in their nomenclature) than those of the young girls of H. There was no mincing—no affectation—no hope of passing for what they were not—no envy of the pretty and fortunate—no insolent triumph over the plain and demure and neglected,—but all was good will and good humor. They were a pretty circle of girls—a garland of bright fresh flowers. Never were there more sparkling glances,—never sweeter smiles—nor more of them. Their present was all health and cheerfulness; and their future, not the gloomy perspective of dreary singleness, for somewhere in the passage of life they were sure to be mated. Most of the young men who had abandoned their native soil, as soon as they found themselves *getting along*, loyally returned to lay their fortunes at the feet of the companions of their childhood.

The girls made occasional visits to Boston, and occasional journeys to various parts of the country, for they were all enterprising and independent, and had the characteristic New England avidity for seizing a "privilege"; and in these various ways, to borrow a phrase of their good grandames, "a door was opened for them," and in due time they fulfilled the destiny of women.

We spoke strictly, and à la lettre, when we said that in the village of H. there was not a single *beau*. But on the outskirts of the town, at a pleasant farm, embracing hill and valley, upland and meadow land; in a neat house, looking to the south, with true economy of sunshine and comfort, and overlooking the prettiest winding stream that ever sent up its sparkling beauty to the eye, and flanked on the north by a rich maple grove, beautiful in spring and summer, and glorious in autumn, and the kindest defense in winter;—on this farm and in this house dwelt a youth, to fame unknown, but known and loved by every inhabitant of H., old and young, grave and gay, lively and severe. Ralph Hepburn was one of nature's favorites. He had a figure that would have adorned courts and cities; and a face that adorned human nature, for it was full of good humor, kindheartedness, spirit, and intelligence; and driving the plough or wielding the scythe, his cheek flushed with manly and profitable exercise, he looked as if he had been molded in a poet's fancy—as farmers look in Georgics and Pastorals.[4] His gifts were by no means all external. He wrote verses in every album in the village, and very pretty album verses they were, and numerous too—for the number of albums was equivalent to the whole female population. He was admirable at pencil sketches; and once with a little paint, the refuse of a house painting, he achieved an admirable portrait of his grandmother and her cat. There was, to be sure, a striking likeness between the two figures, but he was limited to the same colors for both; and besides, it was not out of nature, for the old lady and her cat had purred together in the chimney corner, till their physiognomies bore an obvious resemblance to each other. Ralph had a talent for music too. His voice was the sweetest of all the Sunday choir, and one would have fancied, from the bright eyes that were turned on him from the long line and double lines of treble and counter singers, that Ralph Hepburn was a note book, or that the girls listened with their eyes as well as their ears. Ralph did not restrict himself to psalmody. He had an ear so exquisitely susceptible to the "touches of sweet harmony," that he discovered, by the stroke of his axe, the musical capacities of certain species of wood, and he made himself a violin of chestnut, and drew strains from it, that if they could not create a soul under the ribs of death, could make the prettiest feet and the lightest hearts dance, an achievement far more to Ralph's taste than the

aforesaid miracle. In short, it seemed as if nature, in her love
of compensation, had showered on Ralph all the gifts that are
usually diffused through a community of beaux. Yet Ralph
was no prodigy; none of his talents were in excess, but all in
moderate degree. No genius was ever so good humored, so
useful, so practical; and though, in his small and modest way,
a Crichton,[5] he was not, like most universal geniuses, good for
nothing for any particular office in life. His farm was not a
pattern farm—a prize farm for an agricultural society, but in
wonderful order considering—his miscellaneous pursuits. He
was the delight of his grandfather for his sagacity in hunting
bees—the old man's favorite, in truth his only pursuit. He was
so skilled in woodcraft that the report of his gun was as certain a signal of death as the tolling of a church bell. The fish
always caught at his bait. He manufactured half his farming
utensils, improved upon old inventions, and struck out some
new ones; tamed partridges—the most untamable of all the
feathered tribe; domesticated squirrels; rivaled Scheherazade
herself in telling stories, strange and long—the latter quality
being essential at a country fireside; and, in short, Ralph made
a perpetual holiday of a life of labor.

Every girl in the village street knew when Ralph's wagon or
sleigh traversed it; indeed, there was scarcely a house to which
the horses did not, as if by instinct, turn up while their master
greeted its fair tenants. This state of affairs had continued for
two winters and two summers since Ralph came to his majority and, by the death of his father, to the sole proprietorship of
the "Hepburn farm,"—the name his patrimonial acres had
obtained from the singular circumstance (in our *moving* country) of their having remained in the same family for four gen-
erations. Never was the matrimonial destiny of a young lord,
or heir just come to his estate, more thoroughly canvassed than
young Hepburn's by mothers, aunts, daughters, and nieces. But
Ralph, perhaps from sheer good heartedness, seemed reluctant
to give to one the heart that diffused rays of sunshine through
the whole village.

With all decent people he eschewed the doctrines of a certain erratic female lecturer on the odious monopoly of mar-

riage,[6] yet Ralph, like a tender hearted judge, hesitated to place on a single brow the crown matrimonial which so many deserved, and which, though Ralph was far enough from a coxcomb,[7] he could not but see so many coveted.

Whether our hero perceived that his mind was becoming elated or distracted with this general favor, or that he observed a dawning of rivalry among the fair competitors, or whatever was the cause, the fact was, that he by degrees circumscribed his visits, and finally concentrated them in the family of his Aunt Courland.

Mrs. Courland was a widow, and Ralph was the kindest of nephews to her, and the kindest of cousins to her children. To their mother he seemed their guardian angel. That the five lawless, daring little urchins did not drown themselves when they were swimming, nor shoot themselves when they were shooting, was, in her eyes, Ralph's merit; and then "he was so attentive to Alice, her only daughter—a brother could not be kinder." But who would not be kind to Alice? she was a sweet girl of seventeen, not beautiful, not handsome perhaps,—but pretty enough—with soft hazel eyes, a profusion of light brown hair, always in the neatest trim, and a mouth that could not but be lovely and loveable, for all kind and tender affections were playing about it. Though Alice was the only daughter of a doting mother, the only sister of five loving boys, the only niece of three single, fond aunts, and, last and greatest, the only cousin of our only beau, Ralph Hepburn, no girl of seventeen was ever more disinterested, unassuming, unostentatious, and unspoiled. Ralph and Alice had always lived on terms of cousinly affection—an affection of a neutral tint that they never thought of being shaded into the deep dye of a more tender passion. Ralph rendered her all cousinly offices. If he had twenty damsels to escort, not an uncommon case, he never forgot Alice. When he returned from any little excursion, he always brought some graceful offering to Alice.

He had lately paid a visit to Boston. It was at the season of the periodical inundation of annuals.[8] He brought two of the prettiest to Alice. Ah! little did she think they were to prove Pandora's box to her. Poor simple girl! she sat down to read them, as if an annual were meant to be read, and she was honestly interested and charmed. Her mother observed her delight. "What have you there, Alice?" she asked. "Oh the prettiest story, mamma!—two such tried faithful lovers, and married at last! It ends beautifully: I hate love stories that don't end in marriage."

"And so do I, Alice," exclaimed Ralph, who entered at the moment, and for the first time Alice felt her cheeks tingle at his approach. He had brought a basket, containing a choice plant he had obtained for her, and she laid down the annual and went with him to the garden to see it set by his own hand.

Mrs. Courland seized upon the annual with avidity. She had imbibed a literary taste in Boston, where the best and happiest years of her life were passed. She had some literary ambition too. She read the North American Review[9] from beginning to end, and she fancied no conversation could be sensible or improving that was not about books. But she had been effectually prevented, by the necessities of a narrow income, and by the unceasing wants of five teasing boys, from indulging her literary inclinations; for Mrs. Courland, like all New England women, had been taught to consider domestic duties as the first temporal duties of her sex. She had recently seen some of the native productions with which the press is daily teeming, and which certainly have a tendency to dispel our early illusions about the craft of authorship. She had even felt some obscure intimations, within her secret soul, that she might herself become an author. The annual was destined to fix her fate. She opened it—the publisher had written the names of the authors of the anonymous pieces against their productions. Among them she found some of the familiar friends of her childhood and youth.

If, by a sudden gift of second sight, she had seen them enthroned as kings and queens, she would not have been more astonished. She turned to their pieces, and read them, as perchance no one else ever did, from beginning to end—faithfully. Not a sentence—a sentence! not a word was skipped. She paused to consider commas, colons, and dashes. All the art and magic of authorship were made level to her comprehension, and when she closed the book, she *felt a call* to become an author, and before she retired to bed she obeyed the call, as if it had been, in truth, a divinity stirring within her. In the morning she presented an article to *her* public, consisting of her own family and a few select friends. All applauded, and every voice, save one, was unanimous for publication—that one was Alice. She was a modest, prudent girl; she feared failure, and feared notoriety still more. Her mother laughed at her childish scruples. The piece was sent off, and in due time graced the pages of an annual. Mrs. Courland's fate was now decided. She had, to use her own phrase, started in the career of letters, and she was no Atalanta[10] to be seduced from her straight onward way. She was a social, sympathetic, good hearted creature too, and she could not bear to go forth in the golden field to reap alone.

She was, besides, a prudent woman, as most of her country-women are, and the little pecuniary equivalent for this delightful exercise of talents was not overlooked. Mrs. Courland, as we have somewhere said, had three single sisters—worthy women they were—but nobody ever dreamed of their taking to authorship. She, however, held them all in sisterly estimation. Their talents were magnified as the talents of persons who live in a circumscribed sphere are apt to be, particularly if seen through the dilating medium of affection.

Miss Anne, the oldest, was fond of flowers, a successful cultivator, and a diligent student of the science of botany. All this taste and knowledge, Mrs. Courland thought, might be turned to excellent account; and she persuaded Miss Anne to write a little book entitled "Familiar Dialogues on Botany." The second sister, Miss Ruth, had a turn for education ("bachelor's wives and maid's children are always well taught"), and Miss Ruth undertook a popular treatise on that subject. Miss Sally, the youngest, was the saint of the family, and she doubted about the propriety of a literary occupation, till her scruples were overcome by the fortunate suggestion that her coup d'essai[11] should be a Saturday night book[12] entitled "Solemn Hours,"—and solemn hours they were to their unhappy readers. Mrs. Courland next besieged her old mother. "You know,

mamma," she said, "you have such a precious fund of anec-
dotes of the revolution and the French war, and you talk just
like the 'Annals of the Parish,'[13] and I am certain you can write
a book fully as good."

"My child, you are distracted! I write a dreadful poor hand,
and I never learned to spell—no girls did in my time."

"Spell! that is not of the least consequence—the printers
correct the spelling."

But the honest old lady would not be tempted on the cru-
sade, and her daughter consoled herself with the reflection
that if she would not write, she was an admirable subject to be
written about, and her diligent fingers worked off three distinct stories in which the old lady figured.

Mrs. Courland's ambition, of course, embraced within its
widening circle her favorite nephew Ralph. She had always
thought him a genius, and genius in her estimation was the
philosopher's stone. In his youth she had labored to persuade
his father to send him to Cambridge,[14] but the old man uni-
formly replied that Ralph "was a smart lad on the farm, and
steady, and by that he knew he was no genius." As Ralph's
character was developed, and talent after talent broke forth,
his aunt renewed her lamentations over his ignoble destiny.
That Ralph was useful, good, and happy—the most difficult
and rare results achieved in life—was nothing, so long as he
was but a farmer in H. Once she did half persuade him to turn
painter, but his good sense and filial duty triumphed over her
eloquence, and suppressed the hankerings after distinction
that are innate in every human breast, from the little ragged
chimneysweep that hopes to be a *boss*, to the political aspirant
whose bright goal is the presidential chair.

Now Mrs. Courland fancied Ralph might climb the steep of
fame without quitting his farm; occasional authorship was
compatible with his vocation. But alas! she could not persuade
Ralph to pluck the laurels that she saw ready grown to his
hand. She was not offended, for she was the best natured
woman in the world, but she heartily pitied him, and seldom
mentioned his name without repeating that stanza of Gray's,
inspired for the consolation of hopeless obscurity:

"Full many a gem of purest ray serene," &c.[15]

Poor Alice's sorrows we have reserved to the last, for they were heaviest. "Alice," her mother said, "was gifted; she was well educated, well informed; she was everything necessary to be an author." But Alice resisted; and, though the gentlest, most complying of all good daughters, she would have resisted to the death—she would as soon have stood in a pillory as appeared in print. Her mother, Mrs. Courland, was not an obstinate woman, and gave up in despair. But still our poor heroine was destined to be the victim of this *cacoethes scribendi*; for Mrs. Courland divided the world into two classes, or rather parts—authors and subjects for authors; the one active, the other passive. At first blush one would have thought the village of H. rather a barren field for such a reaper as Mrs. Courland, but her zeal and indefatigableness worked wonders. She converted the stern scholastic divine of H. into as much of a La Roche[16] as she could describe; a tall wrinkled bony old woman, who reminded her of Meg Merrilies,[17] sat for a witch; the school master for an Ichabod Crane;[18] a poor half witted boy was made to utter as much pathos and sentiment and wit as she could put into his lips; and a crazy vagrant was a Godsend to her. Then every "wide spreading elm," "blasted pine," or "gnarled oak," flourished on her pages. The village church and school house stood there according to their actual dimensions. One old *pilgrim* house was as prolific as haunted tower or ruined abbey. It was surveyed outside, ransacked inside, and again made habitable for the reimbodied spirits of its founders.

The most kind hearted of women, Mrs. Courland's interests came to be so at variance with the prosperity of the little community of H., that a sudden calamity, a death, a funeral, were fortunate events to her. To do her justice she felt them in a twofold capacity. She wept as a woman, and exulted as an author. The days of the calamities of authors have passed by. We have all wept over Otway and shivered at the thought of Tasso.[19] But times are changed. The lean sheaf is devouring the full one. A new class of sufferers has arisen, and there is nothing more touching in all the memoirs Mr. D'Israeli[20] has collected, than the trials of poor Alice, tragi-comic though they were. Mrs. Courland's new passion ran most naturally in the worn channel of maternal affection. Her boys were too purely boys for her art—but Alice, her sweet Alice, was preeminently lovely in the new light in which she now placed every object. Not an incident of her life but was inscribed on her mother's memory, and thence transferred to her pages, by way of precept, or example, or pathetic or ludicrous circumstance. She regretted now, for the first time, that Alice had no lover whom she might introduce among her dramatis personae.[21] Once her thoughts did glance on Ralph, but she had not quite merged the woman in the author; she knew instinctively that Alice would be particularly offended at being thus paired with Ralph. But Alice's *public life* was not limited to her mother's productions. She was the darling niece of her three aunts. She had studied botany with the eldest, and Miss Anne had recorded in her private diary all her favorite's clever remarks during their progress in the science. This diary was now a mine of gold to her, and faithfully worked up for a circulating medium. But, most trying of all to poor Alice, was the attitude in which she appeared in her aunt Sally's "solemn hours." Every aspiration of piety to which her young lips had given utterance was there *printed*. She felt as if she were condemned to say her prayers in the market place. Every act of kindness, every deed of charity, she had ever performed, were produced to the public. Alice would have been consoled if she had known how small that public was; but, as it was, she felt like a modest country girl when she first enters an apartment hung on every side with mirrors, when, shrinking from observation, she sees in every direction her image multiplied and often distorted; for, notwithstanding Alice's dutiful respect for her good aunts, and her consciousness of their affectionate intentions, she could not but perceive that they were unskilled painters. She grew afraid to speak or to act, and from being the most artless, frank, and, at home, social little creature in the world, she became as silent and as stiff as a statue. And, in the circle of her young associates, her natural gaiety was constantly checked by their winks and smiles, and broader al-lusions to her multiplied portraits; for they had instantly rec-ognized them through the thin veil of feigned names of persons and places. They called her a blue stocking[22] too; for they had the vulgar notion that every body must be tinged that lived under the same roof with an author. Our poor victim was afraid to speak of a book—worse than that, she was afraid to touch one, and the last Waverley[23] novel actually lay in the house a month before she opened it. She avoided wearing even a blue ribbon, as fearfully as a forsaken damsel shuns the color of green.[24]

It was during the height of this literary fever in the Cour-land family, that Ralph Hepburn, as has been mentioned, con-centrated all his visiting there. He was of a compassionate disposition, and he knew Alice was, unless relieved by him, in solitary possession of their once social parlor, while her mother and aunts were driving their quills in their several apartments.

Oh! what a changed place was that parlor! Not the tower of Babel,[25] after the builders had forsaken it, exhibited a sadder reverse; not a Lancaster school,[26] when the boys have left it, a more striking contrast. Mrs. Courland and her sisters were all "talking women" and too generous to encroach on one anoth-er's rights and happiness. They had acquired the power to hear and speak simultaneously. Their parlor was the general gath-ering place, a sort of village exchange, where all the innocent gossips, old and young, met together. "There are tongues in trees," and surely there seemed to be tongues in the very walls of that vocal parlor. Everything there had a social aspect. There was something agreeable and conversable in the litter of netting and knitting work, of sewing implements, and all the signs and shows of happy female occupation.

Now, all was as orderly as a town drawing room in com-pany hours. Not a sound was heard there save Ralph's and Al-ice's voices, mingling in soft and suppressed murmurs, as if afraid of breaking the chain of their aunt's ideas, or, per-chance, of too rudely jarring a tenderer chain. One evening, after tea, Mrs. Courland remained with her daughter, instead

of retiring, as usual, to her writing desk.—"Alice, my dear,"
said the good mother, "I have noticed for a few days past that
you look out of spirits. You will listen to nothing I say on that
subject; but if you would try it, my dear, if you would only try
it, you would find there is nothing so tranquilizing as the occupation of writing."

"I shall never try it, mamma."

"You are afraid of being called a blue stocking. Ah! Ralph,
how are you?"—Ralph entered at this moment.—"Ralph, tell
me honestly, do you not think it a weakness in Alice to be so
afraid of blue stockings?"

"It would be a pity, aunt, to put blue stockings on such
pretty feet as Alice's."

Alice blushed and smiled, and her mother said—"Nonsense,
Ralph; you should bear in mind the celebrated saying of the
Edinburgh wit—'no matter how blue the stockings are, if the
petticoats are long enough to hide them.'"[27]

"Hide Alice's feet! Oh aunt, worse and worse!"

"Better hide her feet, Ralph, than her talents—that is a sin
for which both she and you will have to answer. Oh! you and
Alice need not exchange such significant glances! You are
doing yourselves and the public injustice, and you have no idea
how easy writing is."

"Easy writing, but hard reading, aunt."

"That's false modesty, Ralph. If I had but your opportuni-
ties to collect materials"—Mrs. Courland did not know that
in literature, as in some species of manufacture, the most exquisite productions are wrought from the smallest quantity of
raw material—"There's your journey to New York, Ralph,"
she continued, "you might have made three capital articles out
of that. The revolutionary officer would have worked up for
the 'Legendary'; the mysterious lady for the 'Token'; and the
man in black for the 'Remember Me';—all founded on fact, all
romantic and pathetic."[28]

"But mamma," said Alice, expressing in words what Ralph's
arch smile expressed almost as plainly, "you know the officer
drank too much; and the mysterious lady turned out to be a
runaway milliner; and the man in black—oh! what a theme

for a pathetic story!—the man in black was a widower, on his way to Newhaven, where he was to select his third wife from three *recommended* candidates."

"Pshaw! Alice: do you suppose it is necessary to tell things precisely as they are?"

"Alice is wrong, aunt, and you are right; and if she will open her writing desk for me, I will sit down this moment, and write a story—a true story—true from beginning to end; and if it moves you, my dear aunt, if it meets your approbation, my destiny is decided."

Mrs. Courland was delighted; she had slain the giant, and she saw fame and fortune smiling on her favorite. She arranged the desk for him herself; she prepared a folio sheet of paper, folded the ominous margins; and was so absorbed in her bright visions, that she did not hear a little by-talk between Ralph and Alice, nor see the tell-tale flush on their cheeks, nor notice the perturbation with which Alice walked first to one window and then to another, and finally settled herself to that best of all sedatives—hemming a ruffle. Ralph chewed off the end of his quill, mended his pen twice, though his aunt assured him "printers did not mind the penmanship," and had achieved a single line when Mrs. Courland's vigilant eye was averted by the entrance of her servant girl, who put a packet into her hands. She looked at the direction, cut the string, broke the seals, and took out a periodical fresh from the publisher. She opened at the first article—a strangely mingled current of maternal pride and literary triumph rushed through her heart and brightened her face. She whispered to the servant a summons to all her sisters to the parlor, and an intimation, sufficiently intelligible to them, of her joyful reason for interrupting them.

Our readers will sympathize with her, and with Alice too, when we disclose to them the secret of her joy. The article in question was a clever composition written by our devoted Alice when she was at school. One of her fond aunts had preserved it; and aunts and mother had combined in the pious fraud of giving it to the public, unknown to Alice. They were perfectly aware of her determination never to be an author.

But they fancied it was the mere timidity of an unfledged bird; and that when, by their innocent artifice, she found that her opinions could soar in a literary atmosphere, she would realize the sweet fluttering sensations they had experienced at their first flight. The good souls all hurried to the parlor, eager to witness the coup de théâtre. Miss Sally's pen stood emblematically erect in her turban; Miss Ruth, in her haste, had overset her inkstand, and the drops were trickling down her white dressing, or, as she now called it, writing gown; and Miss Anne had a wild flower in her hand, as she hoped, of an undescribed species, which, in her joyful agitation, she most unluckily picked to pieces. All bit their lips to keep impatient congratulation from bursting forth. Ralph was so intent on his writing, and Alice on her hemming, that neither noticed the irruption; and Mrs. Courland was obliged twice to speak to her daughter before she could draw her attention.

"Alice, look here—Alice, my dear."

"What is it, mamma? something new of yours?"

"No; guess again, Alice."

"Of one of my aunts, of course?"

"Neither, dear, neither. Come and look for yourself, and see if you can then tell whose it is."

Alice dutifully laid aside her work, approached and took the book. The moment her eye glanced on the fatal page, all her apathy vanished—deep crimson overspread her cheeks, brow, and neck. She burst into tears of irrepressible vexation, and threw the book into the blazing fire.

The gentle Alice! Never had she been guilty of such an ebullition of temper. Her poor dismayed aunts retreated; her mother looked at her in mute astonishment; and Ralph, struck with her emotion, started from the desk, and would have asked an explanation, but Alice exclaimed—"Don't say anything about it, mamma—I cannot bear it now."

Mrs. Courland knew instinctively that Ralph would sympathize entirely with Alice, and quite willing to avoid an éclaircissement,[29] she said—"Some other time, Ralph, I'll tell you the whole. Show me now what you have written. How have you begun?"

Ralph handed her the paper with a novice's trembling hand.

"Oh! how very little! and so scratched and interlined! but never mind—'c'est le premier pas qui coute.'"[30]

While making these general observations, the good mother was getting out and fixing her spectacles, and Alice and Ralph had retreated behind her. Alice rested her head on his shoulder, and Ralph's lips were not far from her ear. Whether he was soothing her ruffled spirit, or what he was doing, is not recorded. Mrs. Courland read and re-read the sentence. She dropped a tear on it. She forgot her literary aspirations for Ralph and Alice—forgot she was herself an author—forgot everything but the mother; and rising, embraced them both as her dear children, and expressed, in her raised and moistened eye, consent to their union, which Ralph had dutifully and prettily asked in that short and true story of his love for his sweet cousin Alice.

In due time the village of H. was animated with the celebration of Alice's nuptials: and when her mother and aunts saw her the happy mistress of the Hepburn farm, and the happiest of wives, they relinquished, without a sigh, the hope of ever seeing her an AUTHOR.

"THE TWO OFFERS"

by Frances Ellen Watkins Harper,
1859

"What is the matter with you, Laura, this morning? I have
been watching you this hour, and in that time you have commenced a half dozen letters and torn them all up. What matter
of such grave moment is puzzling your dear little head, that
you do not know how to decide?"

"Well, it is an important matter: I have two offers for marriage, and I do not know which to choose."

"I should accept neither, or to say the least, not at present."

"Why not?"

"Because I think a woman who is undecided between two
offers, has not love enough for either to make a choice; and in
that very hesitation, indecision, she has a reason to pause and
seriously reflect, lest her marriage, instead of being an affinity
of souls or a union of hearts, should only be a mere matter of
bargain and sale, or an affair of convenience and selfish interest."

"But I consider them both very good offers, just such as
many a girl would gladly receive. But to tell you the truth, I do
not think that I regard either as a woman should the man she
chooses for her husband. But then if I refuse, there is the risk
of being an old maid, and that is not to be thought of."

"Well, suppose there is, is that the most dreadful fate that
can befall a woman? Is there not more intense wretchedness in
an ill-assorted marriage—more utter loneliness in a loveless
home, than in the lot of the old maid who accepts her earthly
mission as a gift from God, and strives to walk the path of life
with earnest and unfaltering steps?"

"Oh! what a little preacher you are. I really believe that you were cut out for an old maid; that when nature formed you, she put in a double portion of intellect to make up for a deficiency of love; and yet you are kind and affectionate. But I do not think that you know anything of the grand, over-mastering passion, or the deep necessity of woman's heart for loving."

"Do you think so?" resumed the first speaker; and bending over her work she quietly applied herself to the knitting that had lain neglected by her side, during this brief conversation; but as she did so, a shadow flitted over her pale and intellectual brow, a mist gathered in her eyes, and a slight quivering of the lips, revealed a depth of feeling to which her companion was a stranger.

But before I proceed with my story, let me give you a slight history of the speakers. They were cousins, who had met life under different auspices. Laura Lagrange, was the only daughter of rich and indulgent parents, who had spared no pains to make her an accomplished lady. Her cousin, Janette Alston, was the child of parents, rich only in goodness and affection. Her father had been unfortunate in business, and dying before he could retrieve his fortunes, left his business in an embarrassed state. His widow was unacquainted with his business affairs, and when the estate was settled, hungry creditors had brought their claims and the lawyers had received their fees, she found herself homeless and almost penniless, and she who had been sheltered in the warm clasp of loving arms, found them too powerless to shield her from the pitiless pelting storms of adversity. Year after year she struggled with poverty and wrestled with want, till her toil-worn hands became too feeble to hold the shattered chords of existence, and her tear-dimmed eyes grew heavy with the slumber of death. Her daughter had watched over her with untiring devotion, had closed her eyes in death, and gone out into the busy, restless world, missing a precious tone from the voices of earth, a beloved step from the paths of life. Too self reliant to depend on the charity of relations, she endeavored to support herself by her own exertions, and she had succeeded. Her path for a while was marked with struggle and trial, but instead of uselessly repining, she met them bravely, and her life became not a thing of ease and indulgence, but of conquest, victory, and accomplishments. At the time when this conversation took place, the deep trials of her life had passed away. The achievements of her genius had won her a position in the literary world, where she shone as one of its bright particular stars. And with her fame came a competence of worldly means, which gave her leisure for improvement, and the riper development of her rare talents. And she, that pale intellectual woman, whose genius gave life and vivacity to the social circle, and whose presence threw a halo of beauty and grace around the charmed atmosphere in which she moved, had at one period of her life, known the mystic and solemn strength of an all-absorbing love. Years faded into the misty past, had seen the kindling of her eye, the quick flushing of her cheek, and the wild throbbing of her heart, at tones of a voice long since hushed to the stillness of death. Deeply, wildly, passionately, she had loved. Her whole life seemed like the pouring out of rich, warm and gushing affections. This love quickened her talents, inspired her genius, and threw over her life a tender and spiritual earnestness. And then came a fearful shock, a mournful waking from that "dream of beauty and delight." A shadow fell around her path; it came between her and the object of her heart's worship; first a few cold words, estrangement, and then a painful separation; the old story of woman's pride—digging the sepulchre of her happiness, and then a new-made grave, and her path over it to the spirit world; and thus faded out from that young heart her bright, brief and saddened dream of life. Faint and spirit-broken, she turned from the scenes associated with the memory of the loved and lost. She tried to break the chain of sad associations that bound her to the mournful past; and so, pressing back the bitter sobs from her almost breaking heart, like the dying dolphin, whose beauty is born of its death anguish, her genius gathered strength from suffering and wondrous power and brilliancy from the agony she hid within the desolate chambers of her soul. Men hailed her as one of earth's strangely gifted children, and wreathed the garlands of fame for her brow, when it was throbbing with a wild and fearful unrest. They breathed her name with applause, when through the lonely halls of her stricken spirit, was an earnest cry for peace, a deep yearning for sympathy and heart-support.

But life, with its stern realities, met her; its solemn responsibilities confronted her, and turning, with an earnest and shattered spirit, to life's duties and trials, she found a calmness and strength that she had only imagined in her dreams of poetry and song. We will now pass over a period of ten years, and the cousins have met again. In that calm and lovely woman, in whose eyes is a depth of tenderness, tempering the flashes of her genius, whose looks and tones are full of sympathy and love, we recognize the once smitten and stricken Janette Alston. The bloom of her girlhood had given way to a higher type of spiritual beauty, as if some unseen hand had been polishing and refining the temple in which her lovely spirit found its habitation; and this had been the fact. Her inner life had grown beautiful, and it was this that was constantly developing the outer. Never, in the early flush of womanhood, when an absorbing love had lit up her eyes and glowed in her life, had she appeared so interesting as when, with a countenance which seemed overshadowed with a spiritual light, she bent over the death-bed of a young woman, just lingering at the shadowy gates of the unseen land.

"Has he come?" faintly but eagerly exclaimed the dying woman. "Oh! how I have longed for his coming, and even in death he forgets me."

"Oh, do not say so, dear Laura, some accident may have detained him," said Janette to her cousin; for on that bed, from whence she will never rise, lies the once-beautiful and light-hearted Laura Lagrange, the brightness of whose eyes has long since been dimmed with tears, and whose voice had become like a harp whose every chord is turned to sadness—whose faintest thrill and loudest vibrations are but the variations of agony. A heavy hand was laid upon her once warm and bounding heart, and a voice came whispering through her soul, that she must die. But, to her, the tidings was a message of deliverance—a voice, hushing her wild sorrows to the calmness of resignation and hope. Life had grown so weary upon her head—the future looked so hopeless—she had no wish to tread again the track where thorns had pierced her feet, and clouds overcast her sky; and she hailed the coming of death's angel as the footsteps of a welcome friend. And yet, earth had one object so very dear to her weary heart. It was her absent and recreant husband; for, since that conversation, she had accepted one of her offers, and become a wife. But, before she married, she learned that great lesson of human experience and woman's life, to love the man who bowed at her shrine, a willing worshipper. He had a pleasing address, raven hair, flashing eyes, a voice of thrilling sweetness, and lips of persuasive eloquence; and being well versed in the ways of the world, he won his way to her heart, and she became his bride, and he was proud of his prize. Vain and superficial in his character, he looked upon marriage not as a divine sacrament for the soul's development and human progression, but as the title-deed that gave him possession of the woman he thought he loved. But alas for her, the laxity of his principles had rendered him unworthy of the deep and undying devotion of a pure-hearted woman; but, for awhile, he hid from her his true character, and she blindly loved him, and for a short period was happy in the consciousness of being beloved; though sometimes a vague unrest would fill her soul, when, overflowing with a sense of the good, the beautiful, and the true, she would turn to him, but find no response to the deep yearnings of her soul—no appreciation of life's highest realities—its solemn grandeur and significant importance. Their souls never met, and soon she found a void in her bosom, that his earth-born love could not fill. He did not satisfy the wants of her mental and moral nature—between him and her there was no affinity of minds, no intercommunion of souls.

Talk as you will of woman's deep capacity for loving, of the strength of her affectional nature. I do not deny it; but will the mere possession of any human love, fully satisfy all the demands of her whole being? You may paint her in poetry or fiction, as a frail vine, clinging to her brother man for support, and dying when deprived of it; and all this may sound well enough to please the imaginations of school-girls, or love-lorn maidens. But woman—the true woman—if you would render her happy, it needs more than the mere development of her affectional nature. Her conscience should be enlightened, her faith in the true and right established, and scope given to her Heaven-endowed and God-given faculties. The true aim of female education should be not a development of one or two, but all the faculties of the human soul, because no perfect womanhood is developed by imperfect culture. Intense love is often akin to intense suffering, and to trust the whole wealth of a woman's nature on the frail bark of human love, may often be like trusting a cargo of gold and precious gems, to a bark that has never battled with the storm, or buffeted the waves. Is it any wonder, then, that so many life-barks go down, paving the ocean of time with precious hearts and wasted hopes? that so many float around us, shattered and dismasted wrecks? that so many are stranded on the shoals of existence, mournful beacons and solemn warnings for the thoughtless, to whom marriage is a careless and hasty rushing together of the affections? Alas that an institution so fraught with good for humanity should be so perverted, and that state of life, which should be filled with happiness, become so replete with misery. And this was the fate of Laura Lagrange. For a brief period after her marriage her life seemed like a bright and beautiful dream, full of hope and radiant with joy. And then there came a change—he found other attractions that lay beyond the pale of home influences. The gambling saloon had power to win him from her side, he had lived in an element of unhealthy and unhallowed excitements, and the society of a loving wife, the pleasures of a well-regulated home, were enjoyments too tame for one who had vitiated his tastes by the pleasures of sin. There were charmed houses of vice, built upon dead men's loves, where, amid the flow of song, laughter, wine, and careless mirth, he would spend hour after hour, forgetting the cheek that was paling through his neglect, heedless of the tear-dimmed eyes, peering anxiously into the darkness, waiting, or watching his return.

The influence of old associations was upon him. In early life, home had been to him a place of ceilings and walls, not a true home, built upon goodness, love and truth. It was a place where velvet carpets hushed its tread, where images of loveliness and beauty invoked into being by painter's art and sculptor's skill, pleased the eye and gratified the taste, where magnificence surrounded his way and costly clothing adorned his person; but it was not the place for the true culture and right development of his soul. His father had been too much engrossed in making money, and his mother in spending it, in striving to maintain a fashionable position in society, and shining in the eyes of the world, to give the proper direction to the character of their wayward and impulsive son. His mother put beautiful robes upon his body, but left ugly scars upon his soul; she pampered his appetite, but starved his spirit. Every mother should be a true artist, who knows how to weave into her child's life images of grace and beauty, the true poet capable of writing on the soul of childhood the harmony of love and truth, and teaching it how to produce the grandest of all poems—the poetry of a true and noble life. But in his home, a love for the good, the true and right, had been sacrificed at the shrine of frivolity and fashion. That parental authority which should have been preserved as a string of precious pearls, unbroken and unscattered, was simply the administration of chance. At one time obedience was enforced by authority, at another time by flattery and promises, and just as often it was not enforced at all. His early associations were formed as chance directed, and from his want of home-training, his character received a bias, his life a shade, which ran through every avenue of his existence, and darkened all his future hours. Oh, if we would trace the history of all the crimes that have o'ershadowed this sin-shrouded and sorrow-darkened world of ours, how many might be seen arising from the wrong home influences, or the weakening of the home ties. Home should always be the best school for the affections, the birthplace of high resolves, and the altar upon which lofty aspirations are kindled, from whence the soul may go forth strengthened, to act its part aright in the great drama of life with conscience enlightened, affections cultivated, and reason and judgment dominant. But alas for the young wife. Her husband had not been blessed with such a home. When he entered the arena of life, the voices from home did not linger around his path as angels of guidance about his steps; they were not like so many messages to invite him to deeds of high and holy worth. The memory of no sainted mother arose between him and deeds of darkness; the earnest prayers of no father arrested him in his downward course: and before a year of his married life had waned, his young wife had learned to wait and mourn his frequent and uncalled-for absence. More than once had she seen him come home from his midnight haunts, the bright intelligence of his eye displaced by the drunkard's stare, and his manly gait changed to the inebriate's stagger; and she was beginning to know the bitter agony that is compressed in the mournful words, a drunkard's wife. And then there came a bright but brief episode in her experience; the angel of life gave to her existence a deeper meaning and loftier significance; she sheltered in the warm clasp of her loving arms, a dear babe, a precious child, whose love filled every chamber of her heart, and felt the fount of maternal love gushing so new within her soul. That child was hers. How overshadowing was the love with which she bent over its helplessness, how much it helped to fill the void and chasms in her soul. How many lonely hours were beguiled by its winsome ways, its answering smiles and fond caresses. How exquisite and solemn was the feeling that thrilled her heart when she clasped the tiny hands together and taught her dear child to call God "Our Father."

What a blessing was that child. The father paused in his headlong career, awed by the strange beauty and precocious intellect of his child; and the mother's life had a better expression through her ministrations of love. And then there came hours of bitter anguish, shading the sunlight of her home and hushing the music of her heart. The angel of death bent over the couch of her child and beaconed it away. Closer and closer the mother strained her child to her wildly heaving breast, and struggled with the heavy hand that lay upon its heart. Love and agony contended with death, and the language of the mother's heart was,

> "Oh, Death, away! that innocent is mine;
> I cannot spare him from my arms
> To lay him, Death, in thine.
> I am a mother, Death; I gave that darling birth
> I could not bear his lifeless limbs
> Should molder in the earth."

But death was stronger than love and mightier than agony and won the child for the land of crystal founts and deathless flowers, and the poor, stricken mother sat down beneath the shadow of her mighty grief, feeling as if a great light had gone out from her soul, and that the sunshine had suddenly faded around her path. She turned in her deep anguish to the father of her child, the loved and cherished dead. For awhile his words were kind and tender, his heart seemed subdued, and his tenderness fell upon her worn and weary heart like rain on perishing flowers, or cooling waters to lips all parched with thirst and scorched with fever; but the change was evanescent, the influence of un-hallowed associations and evil habits had vitiated and poisoned the springs of his existence. They had bound him in their meshes, and he lacked the moral strength to break his fetters, and stand erect in all the strength and dignity of a true manhood, making life's highest excellence his ideal, and striving to gain it.

And yet moments of deep contrition would sweep over him, when he would resolve to abandon the wine-cup forever, when he was ready to forswear the handling of another card, and he would try to break away from the associations that he felt were working his ruin; but when the hour of temptation came his strength was weakness, his earnest purposes were cobwebs, his well-meant resolutions ropes of sand, and thus passed year after year of the married life of Laura Lagrange. She tried to hide her agony from the public gaze, to smile when her heart was almost breaking. But year after year her voice grew fainter and sadder, her once light and bounding step grew slower and faltering. Year after year she wrestled with agony, and strove with despair, till the quick eyes of her brother read, in the paling of her cheek and the dimming eye, the secret anguish of her worn and weary spirit. On that wan, sad face, he saw the death-tokens, and he knew the dark wing of the mystic angel swept coldly around her path. "Laura," said her brother to her one day, "you are not well, and I think you need our mother's tender care and nursing. You are daily losing strength, and if you will go I will accompany you." At first, she hesitated, she shrank almost instinctively from presenting that pale sad face to the loved ones at home. That face was such a telltale; it told of heart-sickness, of hope deferred, and the mournful story of unrequited love. But then a deep yearning for home sympathy woke within her a passionate longing for love's kind words, for tenderness and heart-support, and she resolved to seek the home of her childhood and lay her weary head upon her mother's bosom, to be folded again in her loving arms, to lay that poor, bruised and aching heart where it might beat and throb closely to the loved ones at home. A kind welcome awaited her. All that love and tenderness could devise was done to bring the bloom to her cheek and the light to her eye; but it was all in vain; hers was a disease that no medicine could cure, no earthly balm would heal. It was a slow wasting of the vital forces, the sickness of the soul. The unkindness and neglect of her husband, lay like a leaden weight upon her heart, and slowly oozed away its life-drops. And where was he that had won her love, and then cast it aside as a useless thing, who rifled her heart of its wealth and spread bitter ashes upon its broken altars? He was lingering away from her when the death-damps were gathering on her brow, when his name was trembling on her lips! lingering away! when she was watching his coming, though the death films were gathering before her eyes, and earthly things were fading from her vision.

"I think I hear him now," said the dying woman, "surely that is his step"; but the sound died away in the distance.

Again she started from an uneasy slumber, "That is his voice! I am so glad he has come." Tears gathered in the eyes of the sad watchers by that dying bed, for they knew that she was deceived. He had not returned. For her sake they wished his coming. Slowly the hours waned away, and then came the sad,

soul-sickening thought that she was forgotten, forgotten in the
last hour of human need, forgotten when the spirit, about to
be dissolved, paused for the last time on the threshold of existence, a weary watcher at the gates of death. "He has forgotten me," again she faintly murmured, and the last tears she
would ever shed on earth sprung to her mournful eyes, and
clasping her hands together in silent anguish, a few broken
sentences issued from her pale and quivering lips. They were
prayers for strength and earnest pleading for him who had
desolated her young life, by turning its sunshine to shadows,
its smiles to tears. "He has forgotten me," she murmured
again, "but I can bear it, the bitterness of death is passed, and
soon I hope to exchange the shadows of death for the brightness of eternity, the rugged paths of life for the golden streets
of glory, and the care and turmoils of earth for the peace and
rest of heaven." Her voice grew fainter and fainter, they saw
the shadows that never deceive flit over her pale and faded
face, and knew that the death angel waited to soothe their
weary one to rest, to calm the throbbing of her bosom and
cool the fever of her brain. And amid the silent hush of their
grief the freed spirit, refined through suffering, and brought
into divine harmony through the spirit of the living Christ,
passed over the dark waters of death as on a bridge of light,
over whose radiant arches hovering angels bent. They parted
the dark locks from her marble brow, closed the waxen lids
over the once bright and laughing eye, and left her to the
dreamless slumber of the grave. Her cousin turned from that
death-bed a sadder and wiser woman. She resolved more earnestly than ever to make the world better by her example,
gladder by her presence, and to kindle the fires of her genius
on the altars of universal love and truth. She had a higher and
better object in all her writings than the mere acquisition of
gold, or acquirement of fame. She felt that she had a high and
holy mission on the battle-field of existence, that life was not
given her to be frittered away in nonsense, or wasted away in
trifling pursuits. She would willingly espouse an unpopular
cause but not an unrighteous one. In her the down-trodden
slave found an earnest advocate; the flying fugitive remembered

her kindness as he stepped cautiously through our Republic, to gain his freedom in a monarchial land, having broken the chains on which the rust of centuries had gathered. Little children learned to name her with affection, the poor called her blessed, as she broke her bread to the pale lips of hunger. Her life was like a beautiful story, only it was clothed with the dignity of reality and invested with the sublimity of truth. True, she was an old maid. No husband brightened her life with his love, or shaded it with his neglect. No children nestling lovingly in her arms called her mother. No one appended Mrs. to her name; she was indeed an old maid, not vainly striving to keep up an appearance of girlishness, when departed was written on her youth. Not vainly pining at her loneliness and isolation: the world was full of warm, loving hearts, and her own beat in unison with them. Neither was she always sentimentally sighing for something to love, objects of affection were all around her, and the world was not so wealthy in love that it had no use for her's; in blessing others she made a life and benediction, and as old age descended peacefully and gently upon her, she had learned one of life's most precious lessons, that true happiness consists not so much in the fruition of our wishes as in the regulation of desires and the full development and right culture of our whole statures.

"LIFE IN THE IRON-MILLS"

by Rebecca Harding Davis,
1861

> "Is this the end?
> O Life, as futile, then, as frail!
> What hope of answer or redress?"[1]

A cloudy day: do you know what that is in a town of iron-works? The sky sank down before dawn, muddy, flat, immovable. The air is thick, clammy with the breath of crowded human beings. It stifles me. I open the window, and, looking out, can scarcely see through the rain the grocer's shop opposite, where a crowd of drunken Irishmen are puffing Lynchburg tobacco in their pipes. I can detect the scent through all the foul smells ranging loose in the air.

The idiosyncrasy of this town is smoke. It rolls sullenly in slow folds from the great chimneys of the iron-foundries, and settles down in black, slimy pools on the muddy streets. Smoke on the wharves, smoke on the dingy boats, on the yellow river,—clinging in a coating of greasy soot to the house-front, the two faded poplars, the faces of the passers-by. The long train of mules, dragging masses of pig-iron[2] through the narrow street, have a foul vapor hanging to their reeking sides. Here, inside, is a little broken figure of an angel pointing upward from the mantel-shelf; but even its wings are covered with smoke, clotted and black. Smoke everywhere! A dirty canary chirps desolately in a cage beside me. Its dream of green fields and sunshine is a very old dream,—almost worn out, I think.

From the back-window I can see a narrow brick-yard sloping

down to the river-side, strewed with rain-butts and tubs.³ The river, dull and tawny-colored, (*la belle rivière!*)⁴ drags itself sluggishly along, tired of the heavyweight of boats and coal-barges. What wonder? When I was a child, I used to fancy a look of weary, dumb appeal upon the face of the negro-like river slavishly bearing its burden day after day. Something of the same idle notion comes to me to-day, when from the street window, I look on the slow stream of human life creeping past, night and morning, to the great mills. Masses of men, with dull, besotted faces bent to the ground, sharpened here and there by pain or cunning; skin and muscle and flesh be-grimed with smoke and ashes; stooping all night over boiling caldrons of metal, laired by day in dens of drunkenness and infamy; breathing from infancy to death an air saturated with fog and grease and soot, vileness for soul and body. What do you make of a case like that, amateur psychologist? You call it an altogether serious thing to be alive: to these men it is a drunken jest, a joke,—horrible to angels perhaps, to them commonplace enough. My fancy about the river was an idle one: it is no type of such a life. What if it be stagnant and slimy here? It knows that beyond there waits for it odorous sunlight,—quaint old gardens, dusky with soft, green foliage of apple-trees, and flushing crimson with roses,—air, and fields, and mountains. The future of the Welsh puddler⁵ passing just now is not so pleasant. To be stowed away, after his grimy work is done, in a hole in the muddy graveyard, and after that,—*not* air, nor green fields, nor curious roses.

Can you see how foggy the day is? As I stand here, idly tapping the window-pane, and looking out through the rain at the dirty back-yard and the coal-boats below, fragments of an old story float up before me,—a story of this old house into which I happened to come to-day. You may think it a tiresome story enough, as foggy as the day, sharpened by no sudden flashes of pain or pleasure.—I know: only, the outline of a dull life, that long since, with thousands of dull lives like its own, was vainly lived and lost: thousands of them,—massed, vile, slimy lives, like those of the torpid lizards in yonder stagnant water-butt.—Lost? There is a curious point for you to settle, my friend, who study psychology in a lazy, *dilettante* way. Stop a moment. I am going to be honest. This is what I want you to do. I want you to hide your disgust, take no heed to your clean clothes, and come right down with me,—here, into the thickest of the fog and mud and foul effluvia. I want you to hear this story. There is a secret down here, in this nightmare fog, that has lain dumb for centuries: I want to make it a real thing to you. You, Egoist, or Pantheist, or Arminian,[6] busy in making straight paths for your feet on the hills, do not see it clearly,—this terrible question which men here have gone mad and died trying to answer. I dare not put this secret into words. I told you it was dumb. These men, going by with drunken faces, and brains full of unawakened power, do not ask it of Society or of God. Their lives ask it; their deaths ask it. There is no reply. I will tell you plainly that I have a great hope; and I bring it to you to be tested. It is this: that this terrible dumb question is its own reply; that it is not the sentence of death we think it, but, from the very extremity of its darkness, the most solemn prophecy which the world has known of the Hope to come. I dare make my meaning no clearer, but will only tell my story. It will, perhaps, seem to you as foul and dark as this thick vapor about us, and as pregnant with death; but if your eyes are free as mine are to look deeper, no perfume-tinted dawn will be so fair with promise of the day that shall surely come.

My story is very simple,—only what I remember of the life of one of these men,—a furnace-tender in one of Kirby & John's rolling-mills,—Hugh Wolfe.[7] You know the mills? They took the great order for Lower Virginia railroads there last winter; run usually with about a thousand men. I cannot tell why I choose the half-forgotten story of this Wolfe more than that of myriads of these furnace-hands. Perhaps because there is a secret underlying sympathy between that story and this day with its impure fog and thwarted sunshine,—or perhaps simply for the reason that this house is the one where the Wolfes lived. There were the father and son,—both hands, as I said, in one of Kirby & John's mills for making railroad-iron,—and Deborah, their cousin, a picker in some of the cotton-mills.[8] The house was rented then to half a dozen families. The Wolfes had two of the cellar-rooms. The old man, like many of the puddlers and feeders of the mills, was Welsh,—had spent half of his life in the Cornish tin-mines.[9] You may pick the Welsh emigrants, Cornish miners, out of the throng passing the windows, any day. They are a trifle more filthy; their muscles are not so brawny; they stoop more. When they are drunk, they neither yell, nor shout, nor stagger, but skulk along like beaten hounds. A pure, unmixed blood, I fancy: shows itself in the slight angular bodies and sharply-cut facial lines. It is nearly thirty years since the Wolfes lived here. Their lives were like those of their class: incessant labor, sleeping in kennel-like rooms, eating rank pork and molasses, drinking—God and the distillers only know what; with an occasional night in jail, to atone for some drunken excess. Is that all of their lives?—of the portion given to them and these their duplicates swarming the streets to-day?—nothing beneath?—all? So many a political reformer will tell you,—and many a private reformer, too, who has gone among them with a heart tender with Christ's charity, and come out outraged, hardened.

One rainy night, about eleven o'clock, a crowd of half-clothed women stopped outside of the cellar-door. They were going home from the cotton-mill.

"Good-night, Deb," said one, a mulatto, steadying herself against the gas-post. She needed the post to steady her. So did more than one of them.

"Dah's a ball to Miss Potts' tonight. Ye'd best come."

"Inteet, Deb, if hur'll come, hur'll hef fun," said a shrill Welsh voice in the crowd.

Two or three dirty hands were thrust out to catch the gown of the woman, who was groping for the latch of the door.

"No."

"No? Where's Kit Small, then?"

"Begorra![10] on the spools. Alleys behint, though we helped her, we dud. An wid ye! Let Deb alone! It's ondacent frettin' a quite body. Be the powers, an' we'll have a night of it! There'll be lashin's o' drink,—the Vargent[11] be blessed and praised for 't!"

They went on, the mulatto inclining for a moment to show

fight, and drag the woman Wolfe off with them; but, being pacified, she staggered away.

Deborah groped her way into the cellar, and, after considerable stumbling, kindled a match, and lighted a tallow dip, that sent a yellow glimmer over the room. It was low, damp,—the earthen floor covered with a green, slimy moss,—a fetid air smothering the breath. Old Wolfe lay asleep on a heap of straw, wrapped in a torn horse-blanket. He was a pale, meek little man, with a white face and red rabbit-eyes. The woman Deborah was like him; only her face was even more ghastly, her lips bluer, her eyes more watery. She wore a faded cotton gown and a slouching bonnet. When she walked, one could see that she was deformed, almost a hunchback. She trod softly, so as not to waken him, and went through into the room beyond. There she found by the half-extinguished fire an iron saucepan filled with cold boiled potatoes, which she put upon a broken chair with a pint-cup of ale. Placing the old candlestick beside this dainty repast, she untied her bonnet, which hung limp and wet over her face, and prepared to eat her supper. It was the first food that had touched her lips since morning. There was enough of it, however: there is not always. She was hungry,—one could see that easily enough,—and not drunk, as most of her companions would have been found at this hour. She did not drink, this woman,—her face told that, too,—nothing stronger than ale. Perhaps the weak, flaccid wretch had some stimulant in her pale life to keep her up,— some love or hope, it might be, or urgent need. When that stimulant was gone, she would take to whiskey. Man cannot live by work alone. While she was skinning the potatoes, and munching them, a noise behind her made her stop.

"Janey!" she called, lifting the candle and peering into the darkness. "Janey, are you there?"

A heap of ragged coats was heaved up, and the face of a young girl emerged, staring sleepily at the woman.

"Deborah," she said, at last, "I'm here the night."

"Yes, child. Hur's welcome," she said, quietly eating on.

The girl's face was haggard and sickly; her eyes were heavy with sleep and hunger: real Milesian[12] eyes they were, dark, delicate blue, glooming out from black shadows with a pitiful fright.

"I was alone," she said, timidly.

"Where's the father?" asked Deborah, holding out a potato, which the girl greedily seized.

"He's beyant,—wid Haley,—in the stone house." (Did you ever hear the word *jail* from an Irish mouth?) "I came here. Hugh told me never to stay me-lone."

"Hugh?"

"Yes."

A vexed frown crossed her face. The girl saw it, and added quickly,—

"I have not seen Hugh the day, Deb. The old man says his watch lasts till the mornin'."

The woman sprang up, and hastily began to arrange some bread and flitch[13] in a tin pail, and to pour her own measure of ale into a bottle. Tying on her bonnet, she blew out the candle.

"Lay ye down, Janey dear," she said, gently, covering her with the old rags. "Hur can eat the potatoes, if hur's hungry."

"Where are ye goin', Deb? The rain's sharp."

"To the mill, with Hugh's supper."

"Let him bide till th' morn. Sit ye down."

"No, no,"—sharply pushing her off. "The boy'll starve."

She hurried from the cellar, while the child wearily coiled herself up for sleep. The rain was falling heavily, as the woman, pail in hand, emerged from the mouth of the alley, and turned down the narrow street that stretched out, long and black, miles before her. Here and there a flicker of gas lighted an uncertain space of muddy footwalk and gutter; the long rows of houses, except an occasional lager-bier shop, were closed; now and then she met a band of mill-hands skulking to or from their work.

Not many even of the inhabitants of a manufacturing town know the vast machinery of system by which the bodies of workmen are governed, that goes on unceasingly from year to year. The hands of each mill are divided into watches that relieve each other as regularly as the sentinels of an army. By night and day the work goes on, the unsleeping engines groan and shriek, the fiery pools of metal boil and surge. Only for a day in the week, in half-courtesy to public censure, the fires are partially veiled; but as soon as the clock strikes midnight, the great furnaces break forth with renewed fury, the clamor begins with fresh, breathless vigor, the engines sob and shriek like "gods in pain."

As Deborah hurried down through the heavy rain, the noise of these thousand engines sounded through the sleep and shadow of the city like far-off thunder. The mill to which she was going lay on the river, a mile below the city-limits. It was far, and she was weak, aching from standing twelve hours at the spools. Yet it was her almost nightly walk to take this man his supper, though at every square she sat down to rest, and she knew she should receive small word of thanks.

Perhaps, if she possessed an artist's eye, the picturesque oddity of the scene might have made her step stagger less, and the path seem shorter; but to her the mills were only "summat deilish to look at by night."

The road leading to the mills had been quarried from the solid rock, which rose abrupt and bare on one side of the cinder-covered road, while the river, sluggish and black, crept past on the other. The mills for rolling iron are simply immense tent-like roofs, covering acres of ground open on every side. Beneath these roofs Deborah looked in on a city of fires, that burned hot and fiercely in the night. Fire in every horrible form: pits of flame waving in the wind; liquid metal-flames writhing in tortuous streams through the sand; wide caldrons filled with boiling fire, over which bent ghastly wretches stirring the strange brewing; and through all, crowds of half-clad men, looking like revengeful ghosts in the red light, hurried, throwing masses of glittering fire. It was like a street in Hell. Even Deborah muttered; as she crept through, "'T looks like t' Devil's place!" It did,—in more ways than one.

She found the man she was looking for, at last, heaping coal on a furnace. He had not time to eat his supper; so she went behind the furnace, and waited. Only a few men were with him, and they noticed her only by a "Hyur comes t' hunchback, Wolfe."

Deborah was stupid with sleep; her back pained her sharply; and her teeth chattered with cold, with the rain that soaked her clothes and dripped from her at every step. She stood, however, patiently holding the pail, and waiting.

"Hout, woman! ye look like a drowned cat. Come near to the fire,"—said one of the men, approaching to scrape away the ashes.

She shook her head. Wolfe had forgotten her. He turned, hearing the man, and came closer.

"I did no' think; gi' me my supper, woman."

She watched him eat with a painful eagerness. With a woman's quick instinct, she saw that he was not hungry,—was eating to please her. Her pale, watery eyes began to gather a strange light.

"Is't good, Hugh? T' ale was a bit sour, I feared."

"No, good enough." He hesitated a moment. "Ye're tired, poor lass! Bide here till I go. Lay down there on that heap of ash, and go to sleep."

He threw her an old coat for a pillow, and turned to his work. The heap was the refuse of the burnt iron, and was not a hard bed; the half-smothered warmth, too, penetrated her limbs, dulling their pain and cold shiver.

Miserable enough she looked, lying there on the ashes like a limp, dirty rag,—yet not an unfitting figure to crown the scene of hopeless discomfort and veiled crime: more fitting, if one looked deeper into the heart of things,—at her thwarted woman's form, her colorless life, her waking stupor that smothered pain and hunger,—even more fit to be a type of her class. Deeper yet if one could look, was there nothing worth reading in this wet, faded thing, half-covered with ashes? no story of a soul filled with groping passionate love, heroic unselfishness, fierce jealousy? of years of weary trying to please the one human being whom she loved, to gain one look of real heart-kindness from him? If anything like this were hidden beneath the pale, bleared eyes, and dull, washed-out-looking face, no one had ever taken the trouble to read its faint signs: not the half-clothed furnace-tender, Wolfe, certainly. Yet he was kind to her: it was his nature to be kind, even to the very rats that swarmed in the cellar: kind to her in just the same way. She knew that. And it might be that very knowledge had given to her face its apathy and vacancy more than her low, torpid life. One sees that dead, vacant look steal sometimes over the rarest, finest of women's faces,—in the very most, it may be, of their warmest summer's day; and then one can guess at the secret of intolerable solitude that lies hid beneath the delicate laces and brilliant smile. There was no warmth, no brilliancy, no summer for this woman; so the stupor and vacancy had time to gnaw into her face perpetually. She was young, too, though no one guessed it; so the gnawing was the fiercer.

She lay quiet in the dark corner, listening, through the monotonous din and uncertain glare of the works, to the dull plash of the rain in the far distance,—shrinking back whenever the man Wolfe happened to look towards her. She knew, in spite of all his kindness, that there was that in her face and form which made him loathe the sight of her. She felt by instinct, although she could not comprehend it, the finer nature of the man, which made him among his fellow-workmen something unique, set apart. She knew that, down under all the vileness and coarseness of his life, there was a groping passion for whatever was beautiful and pure,—that his soul sickened with disgust at her deformity, even when his words were kindest. Through this dull consciousness, which never left her, came, like a sting, the recollection of the dark blue eyes and lithe figure of the little Irish girl she had left in the cellar. The recollection struck through even her stupid intellect with a vivid glow of beauty and of grace. Little Janey, timid, helpless, clinging to Hugh as her only friend: that was the sharp thought, the bitter thought, that drove into the glazed eyes a fierce light of pain. You laugh at it? Are pain and jealousy less savage realities down here in this place I am taking you to than in your own house or your own heart,—your heart, which they clutch at sometimes? The note is the same, I fancy, be the octave high or low.

If you could go into this mill where Deborah lay, and drag out from the hearts of these men the terrible tragedy of their lives, taking it as a symptom of the disease of their class, no ghost Horror would terrify you more. A reality of soul-starvation, of living death, that meets you every day under the besotted faces on the street,—I can paint nothing of this, only give you the outside outlines of a night, a crisis in the life of one man: whatever muddy depth of soul-history lies beneath you can read according to the eyes God has given you.

Wolfe, while Deborah watched him as a spaniel its master, bent over the furnace with his iron pole, unconscious of her scrutiny, only stopping to receive orders. Physically, Nature had promised the man but little. He had already lost the strength and instinct vigor of a man, his muscles were thin, his nerves weak, his face (a meek, woman's face) haggard, yellow with consumption. In the mill he was known as one of the girl-men: "Molly Wolfe"[14] was his *sobriquet*.[15] He was never seen in the cockpit,[16] did not own a terrier, drank but seldom; when he did, desperately. He fought sometimes, but was always thrashed, pommeled to a jelly. The man was game enough, when his blood was up: but he was no favorite in the mill; he had the taint of school-learning on him,—not to a dangerous extent, only a quarter or so in the free-school in fact, but enough to ruin him as a good hand in a fight.

For other reasons, too, he was not popular. Not one of themselves, they felt that, though outwardly as filthy and ash-covered; silent, with foreign thoughts and longings breaking out through his quietness in innumerable curious ways: this one, for instance. In the neighboring furnace-buildings lay great heaps of the refuse from the ore after the pig-metal is run. *Korl*[17] we call it here: a light, porous substance, of a delicate, waxen, flesh-colored tinge. Out of the blocks of this korl, Wolfe, in his off-hours from the furnace, had a habit of chipping and molding figures,—hideous, fantastic enough, but sometimes strangely beautiful: even the mill-men saw that, while they jeered at him. It was a curious fancy in the man, almost a passion. The few hours for rest he spent hewing and hacking with his blunt knife, never speaking, until his watch came again,—working at one figure for months, and, when it was finished, breaking it to pieces perhaps, in a fit of disappointment. A morbid, gloomy man, untaught, unled, left to feed his soul in grossness and crime, and hard, grinding labor.

I want you to come down and look at this Wolfe, standing there among the lowest of his kind, and see him just as he is, that you may judge him justly when you hear the story of this night. I want you to look back, as he does every day, at his birth in vice, his starved infancy; to remember the heavy years he has groped through as boy and man,—the slow, heavy years of constant, hot work. So long ago he began, that he thinks sometimes he has worked there for ages. There is no hope that it will ever end. Think that God put into this man's soul a fierce thirst for beauty,—to know it, to create it; to *be*—something, he knows not what,—other than he is. There are moments when a passing cloud, the sun glinting on the purple thistles, a kindly smile, a child's face, will rouse him to a passion of pain,— when his nature starts up with a mad cry of rage against God, man, whoever it is that has forced this vile, slimy life upon him. With all this groping, this mad desire, a great blind intellect stumbling through wrong, a loving poet's heart, the man was by habit only a coarse, vulgar laborer, familiar with sights and words you would blush to name. Be just: when I tell you about this night, see him as he is. Be just,—not like man's law, which seizes on one isolated fact, but like God's judging angel, whose clear, sad eye saw all the countless cankering days of this man's life, all the countless nights, when, sick with starving, his soul fainted in him, before it judged him for this night, the saddest of all.

I called this night the crisis of his life. If it was, it stole on him unawares. These great turning-days of life cast no shadow before, slip by unconsciously. Only a trifle, a little turn of the rudder, and the ship goes to heaven or hell.

Wolfe, while Deborah watched him, dug into the furnace of melting iron with his pole, dully thinking only how many rails the lump would yield. It was late,—nearly Sunday morning; another hour, and the heavy work would be done,—only the furnaces to replenish and cover for the next day. The workmen were growing more noisy, shouting as they had to do, to be heard over the deep clamor of the mills. Suddenly they grew less boisterous,—at the far end, entirely silent. Something unusual had happened. After a moment, the silence came nearer; the men stopped their jeers and drunken choruses. Deborah, stupidly lifting up her head, saw the cause of the quiet. A group of five or six men were slowly approaching, stopping to examine each furnace as they came. Visitors often came to see the mills after night: except by growing less noisy, the men took no notice of them. The furnace where Wolfe worked was near the bounds of the works; they halted there hot and tired: a walk over one of these great foundries is no trifling task. The woman, drawing out of sight, turned over to sleep. Wolfe, seeing them stop, suddenly roused from his indifferent stupor, and watched them keenly. He knew some of them: the overseer; Clarke,—a son of Kirby, one of the mill-owners,—and a Doctor May, one of the town-physicians. The other two were strangers. Wolfe came closer. He seized eagerly every chance that brought him into contact with this mysterious class that shone down on him perpetually with the glamour of another order of being. What made the difference between them? That was the mystery of his life. He had a vague notion that perhaps tonight he could find it out. One of the strangers sat down on a pile of bricks, and beckoned young Kirby to his side.

"This is hot, with a vengeance. A match, please?"—lighting his cigar. "But the walk is worth the trouble. If it were not that you must have heard it so often, Kirby, I would tell you that your works look like Dante's Inferno."

Kirby laughed.

"Yes. Yonder is Farinata[18] himself in the burning tomb,"—pointing to some figure in the shimmering shadows.

"Judging from some of the faces of your men," said the other, "they bid fair to try the reality of Dante's vision, someday."

Young Kirby looked curiously around, as if seeing the faces of his hands for the first time.

"They're bad enough, that's true. A desperate set, I fancy. Eh, Clarke?"

The overseer did not hear him. He was talking of net profits just then,—giving, in fact, a schedule of the annual business of the firm to a sharp peering little Yankee, who jotted down notes on a paper laid on the crown of his hat: a reporter for one of the city-papers, getting up a series of reviews of the leading manufactories. The other gentlemen had accompanied them merely for amusement. They were silent until the notes were finished, drying their feet at the furnaces, and sheltering their faces from the intolerable heat. At last the overseer concluded with—

"I believe that is a pretty fair estimate, Captain."

"Here, some of you men!" said Kirby, "bring up those boards. We may as well sit down, gentlemen, until the rain is over. It cannot last much longer at this rate."

"Pig-metal,"—mumbled the reporter,—"um!—coal facilities,—um!—hands employed, twelve hundred,—bitumen,[19]—um!—all right, I believe, Mr. Clarke;—sinking-fund,—what did you say was your sinking-fund?"[20]

"Twelve hundred hands?" said the stranger, the young man who had first spoken. "Do you control their votes, Kirby?"

"Control? No." The young man smiled complacently. "But my father brought seven hundred votes to the polls for his candidate last November. No force-work, you understand,—only a speech or two, a hint to form themselves into a society, and a bit of red and blue bunting to make them a flag. The Invincible Roughs,—I believe that is their name. I forget the motto: 'Our country's hope,' I think."

There was a laugh. The young man talking to Kirby sat with an amused light in his cool gray eye, surveying critically the half-clothed figures of the puddlers, and the slow swing of their brawny muscles. He was a stranger in the city,—spending a couple of months in the borders of a Slave State, to study the institutions of the South,—a brother-in-law of Kirby's,—Mitchell. He was an amateur gymnast,—hence his anatomical eye; a patron, in a *blasé* way, of the prize-ring; a man who sucked the essence out of a science or philosophy in an indifferent, gentlemanly way; who took Kant, Novalis, Humboldt,[21] for what they were worth in his own scales; accepting all, despising nothing, in heaven, earth, or hell, but one-idead men; with a temper yielding and brilliant as summer water, until his Self was touched, when it was ice, though brilliant still. Such men are not rare in the States.

As he knocked the ashes from his cigar, Wolfe caught with a quick pleasure the contour of the white hand, the blood-glow of a red ring he wore. His voice, too, and that of Kirby's, touched him like music,—low, even, with chording cadences. About this man Mitchell hung the impalpable atmosphere belonging to the thorough-bred gentleman. Wolfe, scraping away the ashes beside him, was conscious of it, did obeisance to it with his artist sense, unconscious that he did so.

The rain did not cease. Clarke and the reporter left the mills; the others, comfortably seated near the furnace, lingered, smoking and talking in a desultory way. Greek would not have been more unintelligible to the furnace-tender whose presence they soon forgot entirely. Kirby drew out a newspaper from his pocket and read aloud some article, which they discussed eagerly. At every sentence, Wolfe listened more and more like a dumb, hopeless animal, with a duller, more stolid look creeping over his face, glancing now and then at Mitchell, marking acutely every smallest sign of refinement, then back to himself, seeing as in a mirror his filthy body, his more stained soul.

Never! He had no words for such a thought, but he knew now, in all the sharpness of the bitter certainty, that between them there was a great gulf never to be passed. Never!

The bell of the mills rang for midnight. Sunday morning had dawned. Whatever hidden message lay in the tolling bells floated past these men unknown. Yet it was there. Veiled in the solemn music ushering the risen Savior was a key-note to solve the darkest secrets of a world gone wrong,—even this social riddle which the brain of the grimy puddler grappled with madly to-night.

The men began to withdraw the metal from the caldrons. The mills were deserted on Sundays, except by the hands who fed the fires, and those who had no lodgings and slept usually on the ash-heaps. The three strangers sat still during the next hour, watching the men cover the furnaces, laughing now and then at some jest of Kirby's.

"Do you know," said Mitchell, "I like this view of the works better than when the glare was fiercest? These heavy shadows and the amphitheater of smothered fires are ghostly, unreal. One could fancy these red smoldering lights to be the half-shut eyes of wild beasts, and the spectral figures their victims in the den."

Kirby laughed. "You are fanciful. Come, let us get out of the den. The spectral figures, as you call them, are a little too real for me to fancy a close proximity in the darkness,—unarmed, too.

The others rose, buttoning their overcoats, and lighting cigars.

"Raining, still," said Doctor May, "and hard. Where did we leave the coach, Mitchell?"

"At the other side of the works.—Kirby, what's that?"

Mitchell started back, half-frightened, as, suddenly turning a corner, the white figure of a woman faced him in the darkness,—a woman, white, of giant proportions, crouching on the ground, her arms flung out in some wild gesture of warning.

"Stop! Make that fire burn there!" cried Kirby, stopping short.

The flame burst out, flashing the gaunt figure into bold relief.

Mitchell drew a long breath.

"I thought it was alive," he said, going up curiously.

The others followed.

"Not marble, eh?" asked Kirby, touching it.

One of the lower overseers stopped.

"Korl, Sir."

"Who did it?"

"Can't say. Some of the hands; chipped it out in off-hours."

"Chipped to some purpose, I should say. What a flesh-tint the stuff has! Do you see, Mitchell?"

"I see."

He had stepped aside where the light fell boldest on the figure, looking at it in silence. There was not one line of beauty or grace in it: a nude woman's form, muscular, grown coarse with labor, the powerful limbs instinct with some one poignant longing. One idea: there it was in the tense, rigid muscles, the clutching hands, the wild, eager face, like that of a

starving wolf's. Kirby and Doctor May walked around it, critical, curious. Mitchell stood aloof, silent. The figure touched
him strangely.

"Not badly done," said Doctor May. "Where did the fellow
learn that sweep of the muscles in the arm and hand? Look at
them! They are groping,—do you see?—clutching: the peculiar action of a man dying of thirst."

"They have ample facilities for studying anatomy," sneered
Kirby, glancing at the half-naked figures.

"Look," continued the Doctor, "at this bony wrist, and the
strained sinews of the instep! A working-woman,—the very
type of her class."

"God forbid!" muttered Mitchell.

"Why?" demanded May. "What does the fellow intend by
the figure? I cannot catch the meaning."

"Ask him," said the other, dryly.

"There he stands,"—pointing to Wolfe, who stood with a
group of men, leaning on his ash-rake.

The Doctor beckoned him with the affable smile which
kind-hearted men put on, when talking to these people.

"Mr. Mitchell has picked you out as the man who did this,—
I'm sure I don't know why. But what did you mean by it?"

"She be hungry."

Wolfe's eyes answered Mitchell, not the Doctor.

"Oh-h! But what a mistake you have made, my fine fellow!
You have given no sign of starvation to the body. It is strong,—
terribly strong. It has the mad, half-despairing gesture of
drowning."

Wolfe stammered, glanced appealingly at Mitchell, who
saw the soul of the thing, he knew. But the cool, probing eyes
were turned on himself now,—mocking, cruel, relentless.

"Not hungry for meat," the furnace-tender said at last.

"What then? Whiskey?" jeered Kirby, with a coarse laugh.

Wolfe was silent a moment, thinking.

"I dunno," he said, with a bewildered look. "It mebbe. Summat to make her live, I think,—like you. Whiskey ull do it, in
a way."

The young man laughed again. Mitchell flashed a look of disgust somewhere,—not at Wolfe.

"May," he broke out impatiently, "are you blind? Look at that woman's face! It asks questions of God, and says, 'I have a right to know.' Good God, how hungry it is!"

They looked a moment; then May turned to the mill-owner:—

"Have you many such hands as this? What are you going to do with them? Keep them at puddling iron?"

Kirby shrugged his shoulders. Mitchell's look had irritated him.

"Ce n'est pas mon affaire.[22] I have no fancy for nursing infant geniuses. I suppose there are some stray gleams of mind and soul among these wretches. The Lord will take care of his own; or else they can work out their own salvation. I have heard you call our American system a ladder which any man can scale. Do you doubt it? Or perhaps you want to banish all social ladders, and put us all on a flat table-land,—eh, May?"

The Doctor looked vexed, puzzled. Some terrible problem lay hid in this woman's face, and troubled these men. Kirby waited for an answer, and, receiving none, went on, warming with his subject.

"I tell you, there's something wrong that no talk of 'Liberté' or 'Égalité' will do away.[23] If I had the making of men, these men who do the lowest part of the world's work should be machines,—nothing more,—hands. It would be kindness. God help them! What are taste, reason, to creatures who must live such lives as that?" He pointed to Deborah, sleeping on the ash-heap. "So many nerves to sting them to pain. What if God had put your brain, with all its agony of touch, into your fingers, and bid you work and strike with that?"[24]

"You think you could govern the world better?" laughed the Doctor.

"I do not think at all."

"That is true philosophy. Drift with the stream, because you cannot dive deep enough to find bottom, eh?"

"Exactly," rejoined Kirby. "I do not think. I wash my hands of all social problems,—slavery, caste, white or black. My duty to my operatives has a narrow limit,—the pay-hour on

Saturday night. Outside of that, if they cut korl, or cut each other's throats, (the more popular amusement of the two,) I am not responsible."

The Doctor sighed,—a good honest sigh, from the depths of his stomach.

"God help us! Who is responsible?"

"Not I, I tell you," said Kirby, testily. "What has the man who pays them money to do with their souls' concerns, more than the grocer or butcher who takes it?"

"And yet," said Mitchell's cynical voice, "look at her! How hungry she is!"

Kirby tapped his boot with his cane. No one spoke. Only the dumb face of the rough image looking into their faces with the awful question, "What shall we do to be saved?" Only Wolfe's face, with its heavy weight of brain, its weak, uncertain mouth, its desperate eyes, out of which looked the soul of his class,—only Wolfe's face turned towards Kirby's. Mitchell laughed,—a cool, musical laugh.

"Money has spoken!" he said, seating himself lightly on a stone with the air of an amused spectator at a play. "Are you answered?"—turning to Wolfe his clear, magnetic face.

Bright and deep and cold as Arctic air, the soul of the man lay tranquil beneath. He looked at the furnace-tender as he had looked at a rare mosaic in the morning; only the man was the more amusing study of the two.

"Are you answered? Why, May, look at him! 'De profundis clamavi.' Or, to quote in English, 'Hungry and thirsty, his soul faints in him.'[25] And so Money sends back its answer into the depths through you, Kirby! Very clear the answer, too!—I think I remember reading the same words somewhere—washing your hands in Eau de Cologne, and saying, 'I am innocent of the blood of this man. See ye to it!'"

Kirby flushed angrily.

"You quote Scripture freely."

"Do I not quote correctly? I think I remember another line, which may amend my meaning: 'Inasmuch as ye did it unto one of the least of these, ye did it unto me.'[26] Deist? Bless you, man, I was raised on the milk of the Word. Now, Doctor, the pocket of the world having uttered its voice, what has the heart to say? You are a philanthropist, in a small way,—*n'est ce pas?*[27] Here, boy, this gentleman can show you how to cut korl better,—or your destiny. Go on, May!"

"I think a mocking devil possesses you to-night," rejoined the Doctor, seriously.

He went to Wolfe and put his hand kindly on his arm. Something of a vague idea possessed the Doctor's brain that much good was to be done here by a friendly word or two: a latent genius to be warmed into life by a waited-for sunbeam. Here it was: he had brought it. So be went on complacently:

"Do you know, boy, you have it in you to be a great sculptor, a great man?—do you understand?" (talking down to the capacity of his hearer: it is a way people have with children, and men like Wolfe,)—"to live a better, stronger life than I, or Mr. Kirby here? A man may make himself anything he chooses. God has given you stronger powers than many men,—me, for instance."

May stopped, heated, glowing with his own magnanimity. And it was magnanimous. The puddler had drunk in every word, looking through the Doctor's flurry, and generous heat, and self-approval, into his will, with those slow, absorbing eyes of his.

"Make yourself what you will. It is your right."

"I know," quietly. "Will you help me?"

Mitchell laughed again. The Doctor turned now, in a passion,—

"You know, Mitchell, I have not the means. You know, if I had, it is in my heart to take this boy and educate him for"—

"The glory of God, and the glory of John May."

May did not speak for a moment; then, controlled, he said,—

"Why should one be raised, when myriads are left?—I have not the money, boy," to Wolfe, shortly.

"Money?" He said it over slowly, as one repeats the guessed answer to a riddle, doubtfully. "That is it? Money?"

"Yes, money,—that is it," said Mitchell, rising, and drawing his furred coat about him. "You've found the cure for all the world's diseases.—Come, May, find your good-humor, and come home. This damp wind chills my very bones. Come and preach your Saint-Simonian[28] doctrines to-morrow to Kirby's hands. Let them have a clear idea of the rights of the soul, and I'll venture next week they'll strike for higher wages. That will be the end of it."

"Will you send the coach-driver to this side of the mills?" asked Kirby, turning to Wolfe.

He spoke kindly: it was his habit to do so. Deborah, seeing the puddler go, crept after him. The three men waited outside. Doctor May walked up and down, chafed. Suddenly he stopped.

"Go back, Mitchell! You say the pocket and the heart of the world speak without meaning to these people. What has its head to say? Taste, culture, refinement? Go!"

Mitchell was leaning against a brick wall. He turned his head indolently, and looked into the mills. There hung about the place a thick, unclean odor. The slightest motion of his hand marked that he perceived it, and his insufferable disgust. That was all. May said nothing, only quickened his angry tramp.

"Besides," added Mitchell, giving a corollary to his answer, "it would be of no use. I am not one of them."

"You do not mean"—said May, facing him.

"Yes, I mean just that. Reform is born of need, not pity. No vital movement of the people's has worked down, for good or evil; fermented, instead, carried up the heaving, cloggy mass. Think back through history, and you will know it. What will this lowest deep—thieves, Magdalens,[29] negroes—do with the light filtered through ponderous Church creeds, Baconian theories, Goethe schemes?[30] Some day, out of their bitter need will be thrown up their own light-bringer,—their Jean Paul, their Cromwell, their Messiah."[31]

"Bah!" was the Doctor's inward criticism. However, in practice, he adopted the theory; for, when, night and morning, afterwards, he prayed that power might be given these degraded souls to rise, he glowed at heart, recognizing an accomplished duty.

Wolfe and the woman had stood in the shadow of the works as the coach drove off. The Doctor had held out his hand in a frank, generous way, telling him to "take care of himself, and to remember it was his right to rise." Mitchell had simply touched his hat, as to an equal, with a quiet look of thorough recognition. Kirby had thrown Deborah some money, which she found, and clutched eagerly enough. They were gone now, all of them. The man sat down on the cinder-road, looking up into the murky sky.

"'T be late, Hugh. Wunnot hur come?"

He shook his head doggedly, and the woman crouched out of his sight against the wall. Do you remember rare moments when a sudden light flashed over yourself, your world, God? when you stood on a mountain-peak, seeing your life as it might have been, as it is? one quick instant, when custom lost its force and every-day usage? when your friend, wife, brother, stood in a new light? your soul was bared, and the grave,—a foretaste of the nakedness of the Judgment-Day? So it came before him, his life, that night. The slow tides of pain he had borne gathered themselves up and surged against his soul. His squalid daily life, the brutal coarseness eating into his brain, as the ashes into his skin: before, these things had been a dull aching into his consciousness; to-night, they were reality. He gripped the filthy red shirt that clung, stiff with soot, about him, and tore it savagely from his arm. The flesh beneath was muddy with grease and ashes—and the heart beneath that! And the soul? God knows.

Then flashed before his vivid poetic sense the man who had left him,—the pure face, the delicate, sinewy limbs, in harmony with all he knew of beauty or truth. In his cloudy fancy he had pictured a Something like this. He had found it in this Mitchell, even when he idly scoffed at his pain: a Man all-knowing, all-seeing, crowned by Nature, reigning,—the keen glance of his eye falling like a scepter on other men. And yet his instinct taught him that he too—He! He looked at himself with sudden loathing, sick, wrung his hands with a cry, and then was silent. With all the phantoms of his heated, ignorant fancy, Wolfe had not been vague in his ambitions. They were practical, slowly built up before him out of his knowledge of what he could do. Through years he had day by day made this

hope a real thing to himself,—a clear, projected figure of himself, as he might become.

Able to speak, to know what was best, to raise these men
and women working at his side up with him: sometimes he
forgot this defined hope in the frantic anguish to escape,—
only to escape,—out of the wet, the pain, the ashes, somewhere, anywhere,—only for one moment of free air on a
hill-side, to lie down and let his sick soul throb itself out in the
sunshine. But to-night he panted for life. The savage strength
of his nature was roused; his cry was fierce to God for justice.

"Look at me!" he said to Deborah, with a low, bitter laugh,
striking his puny chest savagely. "What am I worth, Deb? Is it
my fault that I am no better? My fault? My fault?"

He stopped, stung with a sudden remorse, seeing her hunchback shape writhing with sobs. For Deborah was crying
thankless tears, according to the fashion of women.

"God forgi' me, woman! Things go harder wi' you nor me.
It's a worse share."

He got up and helped her to rise; and they went doggedly
down the muddy street, side by side.

"It's all wrong," he muttered, slowly,—"all wrong! I dunnot
understan'. But it'll end some day."

"Come home, Hugh!" she said, coaxingly; for he had stopped,
looking around bewildered.

"Home,—and back to the mill!" He went on saying this
over to himself, as if he would mutter down every pain in this
dull despair.

She followed him through the fog, her blue lips chattering
with cold. They reached the cellar at last. Old Wolfe had been
drinking since she went out, and had crept nearer the door.
The girl Janey slept heavily in the corner. He went up to her,
touching softly the worn white arm with his fingers. Some bitterer thought stung him, as he stood there. He wiped the drops
from his forehead, and went into the room beyond, livid, trembling. A hope, trifling, perhaps, but very dear, had died just
then out of the poor puddler's life, as he looked at the sleeping,
innocent girl,—some plan for the future, in which she had
borne a part. He gave it up that moment, then and forever.

Only a trifle, perhaps, to us: his face grew a shade paler,—that was all. But, somehow, the man's soul, as God and the angels looked down on it, never was the same afterwards.

Deborah followed him into the inner room. She carried a candle, which she placed on the floor, closing the door after her. She had seen the look on his face, as he turned away: her own grew deadly. Yet, as she came up to him, her eyes glowed. He was seated on an old chest, quiet, holding his face in his hands.

"Hugh!" she said, softly.

He did not speak.

"Hugh, did hur hear what the man said,—him with the clear voice? Did hur hear? Money, money,—that it wud do all?"

He pushed her away,—gently, but he was worn out; her rasping tone fretted him.

"Hugh!"

The candle flared a pale yellow light over the cobwebbed brick walls, and the woman standing there. He looked at her. She was young, in deadly earnest; her faded eyes, and wet, ragged figure caught from their frantic eagerness a power akin to beauty.

"Hugh, it is true! Money ull do it! Oh, Hugh, boy, listen till me! He said it true! It is money!"

"I know. Go back! I do not want you here."

"Hugh, it is t'last time. I'll never worrit hur again."

There were tears in her voice now, but she choked them back.

"Hear till me only to-night! If one of t' witch people wud come, them we heard of t' home, and gif hur all hur wants, what then? Say, Hugh!"

"What do you mean?"

"I mean money."

Her whisper shrilled through his brain.

"If one of t' witch dwarfs wud come from t' lane moors to-night, and gif hur money, to go out,—*out*, I say,—out, lad, where t' sun shines, and t' heath grows, and t' ladies walk in silken gownds, and God stays all t' time,—where t' man lives that talked to us to-night,—Hugh knows,—Hugh could walk there like a king!"

He thought the woman mad, tried to check her, but she went on, fierce in her eager haste.

"If *I* were t' witch dwarf, if I had t' money, wud hur thank me? Wud hur take me out o' this place wid hur and Janey? I wud not come into the gran' house hur wud build, to vex hur wid t' hunch,—only at night, when t' shadows were dark, stand far off to see hur."

Mad? Yes! Are many of us mad in this way?

"Poor Deb! poor Deb!" he said, soothingly.

"It is here," she said, suddenly jerking into his hand a small roll. "*I* took it! *I* did it! Me, me!—not hur! I shall be hanged, I shall be burnt in hell, if anybody knows I took it! Out of his pocket, as he leaned against t' bricks. Hur knows?"

She thrust it into his hand, and then, her errand done, began to gather chips together to make a fire, choking down hysteric sobs.

"Has it come to this?"

That was all he said. The Welsh Wolfe blood was honest. The roll was a small green pocket-book containing one or two gold pieces, and a check for an incredible amount, as it seemed to the poor puddler. He laid it down, biding his face again in his hands.

"Hugh, don't be angry wud me! It's only poor Deb,—hur knows?"

He took the long skinny fingers kindly in his.

"Angry? God help me, no! Let me sleep. I am tired."

He threw himself heavily down on the wooden bench, stunned with pain and weariness. She brought some old rags to cover him.

It was late on Sunday evening before he awoke. I tell God's truth, when I say he had then no thought of keeping this money. Deborah had hid it in his pocket. He found it there. She watched him eagerly, as he took it out.

"I must gif it to him," he said, reading her face.

"Hur knows," she said with a bitter sigh of disappointment. "But it is hur right to keep it."

His right! The word struck him. Doctor May had used the same. He washed himself, and went out to find this man

Mitchell. His right! Why did this chance word cling to him so obstinately? Do you hear the fierce devils whisper in his ear, as he went slowly down the darkening street?

The evening came on, slow and calm. He seated himself at the end of an alley leading into one of the larger streets. His brain was clear to-night, keen, intent, mastering. It would not start back, cowardly, from any hellish temptation, but meet it face to face. Therefore the great temptation of his life came to him veiled by no sophistry, but bold, defiant, owning its own vile name, trusting to one bold blow for victory.

He did not deceive himself. Theft! That was it. At first the word sickened him; then he grappled with it. Sitting there on a broken cart-wheel, the fading day, the noisy groups, the church-bells' tolling passed before him like a panorama, while the sharp struggle went on within. This money! He took it out, and looked at it. If he gave it back, what then? He was going to be cool about it.

People going by to church saw only a sickly mill-boy watching them quietly at the alley's mouth. They did not know that he was mad, or they would not have gone by so quietly: mad with hunger; stretching out his hands to the world, that had given so much to them, for leave to live the life God meant him to live. His soul within him was smothering to death; he wanted so much, thought so much, and *knew*—nothing. There was nothing of which he was certain, except the mill and things there. Of God and heaven he had heard so little, that they were to him what fairy-land is to a child: something real, but not here; very far off. His brain, greedy, dwarfed, full of thwarted energy and unused powers, questioned these men and women going by, coldly, bitterly, that night. Was it not his right to live as they,—a pure life, a good, true-hearted life, full of beauty and kind words? He only wanted to know how to use the strength within him. His heart warmed, as he thought of it. He suffered himself to think of it longer. If he took the money?

Then he saw himself as he might be, strong, helpful, kindly. The night crept on, as this one image slowly evolved itself from the crowd of other thoughts and stood triumphant. He looked at it. As he might be! What wonder, if it blinded him to delirium,—the madness that underlies all revolution, all progress, and all fall?

You laugh at the shallow temptation? You see the error underlying its argument so clearly,—that to him a true life was one of full development rather than self-restraint? that he was deaf to the higher tone in a cry of voluntary suffering for truth's sake than in the fullest flow of spontaneous harmony? I do not plead his cause. I only want to show you the mote in my brother's eye: then you can see clearly to take it out.

The money,—there it lay on his knee, a little blotted slip of paper, nothing in itself; used to raise him out of the pit; something straight from God's hand. A thief! Well, what was it to be a thief? He met the question at last, face to face, wiping the clammy drops of sweat from his forehead. God made this money—the fresh air, too—for his children's use. He never made the difference between poor and rich. The Something who looked down on him that moment through the cool gray sky had a kindly face, he knew,—loved his children alike. Oh, he knew that!

There were times when the soft floods of color in the crimson and purple flames, or the clear depth of amber in the water below the bridge, had somehow given him a glimpse of another world than this,—of an infinite depth of beauty and of quiet somewhere,—somewhere,—a depth of quiet and rest and love. Looking up now, it became strangely real. The sun had sunk quite below the hills, but his last rays struck upward, touching the zenith. The fog had risen, and the town and river were steeped in its thick, gray damp; but overhead, the sun-touched smoke-clouds opened like a cleft ocean,—shifting, rolling seas of crimson mist, waves of billowy silver veined with blood-scarlet, inner depths unfathomable of glancing light. Wolfe's artist-eye grew drunk with color. The gates of that other world! Fading, flashing before him now! What, in that world of Beauty, Content, and Right, were the petty laws, the mine and thine, of mill-owners and mill-hands?

A consciousness of power stirred within him. He stood up. A man,—he thought, stretching out his hands,—free to work, to live, to love! Free! His right! He folded the scrap of paper in his hand. As his nervous fingers took it in, limp and blotted, so his soul took in the mean temptation, lapped it in fancied rights, in dreams of improved existences, drifting and endless as the cloud-seas of color. Clutching it, as if the tightness of his hold would strengthen his sense of possession, he went aimlessly down the street. It was his watch at the mill. He need not go, need never go again, thank God!—shaking off the thought with unspeakable loathing.

Shall I go over the history of the hours of that night? How the man wandered from one to another of his old haunts, with a half-consciousness of bidding them farewell,—lanes and alleys and backyards where the mill-hands lodged,—noting, with a new eagerness, the filth and drunkenness, the pig-pens, the ash-heaps covered with potato-skins, the bloated, pimpled women at the doors,—with a new disgust, a new sense of sudden triumph, and, under all, a new, vague dread, unknown before, smothered down, kept under, but still there? It left him but once during the night, when, for the second time in his life, he entered a church. It was a somber Gothic pile, where the stained light lost itself in far-retreating arches; built to meet the requirements and sympathies of a far other class than Wolfe's. Yet it touched, moved him uncontrollably. The distances, the shadows, the still, marble figures, the mass of silent kneeling worshippers, the mysterious music, thrilled, lifted his soul with a wonderful pain. Wolfe forgot himself, forgot the new life he was going to live, the mean terror gnawing underneath. The voice of the speaker strengthened the charm; it was clear, feeling, full, strong. An old man, who had lived much, suffered much; whose brain was keenly alive, dominant; whose heart was summer-warm with charity. He taught it to-night. He held up Humanity in its grand total; showed the great world-cancer to his people. Who could show it better? He was a Christian reformer; he had studied the age thoroughly; his outlook at man had been free, world-wide, over all time. His faith stood sublime upon the Rock of Ages; his fiery zeal guided vast schemes by which the gospel was to be preached to all nations. How did he preach it to-night? In burning, light-laden words he painted the incarnate Life, Love, the universal Man: words that became reality in the lives of these people,—that lived again in beautiful words and actions, trifling, but heroic. Sin, as he defied it, was a real foe to them; their trials, temptations, were his. His words passed far over the furnace-tender's grasp, toned to suit another class of culture; they sounded in his ears a very pleasant song in an unknown tongue. He meant to cure this world-cancer with a steady eye that had never glared with hunger, and a hand that neither poverty nor strychnine-whiskey had taught to shake. In this morbid, distorted heart of the Welsh puddler he had failed.

Wolfe rose at last, and turned from the church down the street. He looked up; the night had come on foggy, damp; the golden mists had vanished, and the sky lay dull and ash-colored. He wandered again aimlessly down the street, idly wondering what had become of the cloud-sea of crimson and scarlet. The trial-day of this man's life was over, and he had lost the victory. What followed was mere drifting circumstance,—a quicker walking over the path,—that was all. Do you want to hear the end of it? You wish me to make a tragic story out of it? Why, in the police-reports of the morning paper you can find a dozen such tragedies: hints of shipwrecks unlike any that ever befell on the high seas; hints that here a power was lost to heaven,—that there a soul went down where no tide can ebb or flow. Commonplace enough the hints are,—jocose sometimes, done up in rhyme.

Doctor May, a month after the night I have told you of, was reading to his wife at breakfast from this fourth column of the morning-paper: an unusual thing, these police-reports not being, in general, choice reading for ladies; but it was only one item he read.

"Oh, my dear! You remember that man I told you of, that we saw at Kirby's mill?—that was arrested for robbing Mitchell? Here he is; just listen:—'Circuit Court. Judge Day. Hugh Wolfe, operative in Kirby & John's London Mills. Charge, grand larceny. Sentence, nineteen years' hard labor in penitentiary.'—Scoundrel! Serves him right! After all our kindness that night! Picking Mitchell's pocket at the very time!"

His wife said something about the ingratitude of that kind of people, and then they began to talk of something else.

Nineteen years! How easy that was to read! What a simple word for Judge Day to utter! Nineteen years! Half a lifetime!

Hugh Wolfe sat on the window-ledge of his cell, looking out. His ankles were ironed. Not usual in such cases; but he had made two desperate efforts to escape. "Well," as Haley, the jailer, said, "small blame to him! Nineteen years' imprisonment was not a pleasant thing to look forward to." Haley was very good-natured about it, though Wolfe had fought him savagely.

"When he was first caught," the jailer said afterwards, in telling the story, "before the trial, the fellow was cut down at once,—laid there on that pallet like a dead man, with his hands over his eyes. Never saw a man so cut down in my life. Time of the trial, too, came the queerest dodge of any customer I ever had. Would choose no lawyer. Judge gave him one, of course. Gibson it was. He tried to prove the fellow crazy; but it wouldn't go. Thing was plain as daylight: money found on him. 'T was a hard sentence,—all the law allows; but it was for 'xample's sake. These millhands are gettin' onbearable. When the sentence was read, he just looked up, and said the money was his by rights, and that all the world had gone wrong. That night, after the trial, a gentleman came to see him here, name of Mitchell,—him as he stole from. Talked to him for an hour. Thought he came for curiosity, like. After he was gone, thought Wolfe was remarkable quiet, and went into his cell. Found him very low; bed all bloody. Doctor said he had been bleeding at the lungs. He was as weak as a cat; yet, if ye'll b'lieve me, he tried to get a-past me and get out. I just carried him like a baby, and threw him on the pallet. Three days after, he tried it again: that time reached the wall. Lord help you! he fought like a tiger,—giv' some terrible blow. Fightin' for life, you see; for he can't live long, shut up in the stone crib down yonder. Got a death-cough now. 'T took two of us to bring him down that day; so I just put the irons on his feet. There he sits, in there. Goin' to-morrow, with a batch more of 'em. That woman, hunchback, tried with him;—you remember?—she's only got three years. 'Complice. But *she's* a woman, you know. He's been quiet ever since I put on irons: giv' up, I suppose. Looks white, sick-lookin'. It acts different on 'em, bein' sentenced. Most of 'em gets reckless, devilish-like. Some prays awful, and sings them vile songs of the mills, all in a breath. That woman, now, she's desper't'. Been beggin' to see Hugh, as she calls him, for three days. I'm a-goin' to let her in. She don't go with him. Here she is in this next cell. I'm a-goin' now to let her in."

He let her in. Wolfe did not see her. She crept into a corner of the cell, and stood watching him. He was scratching the iron bars of the window with a piece of tin which he had picked up, with an idle, uncertain, vacant stare, just as a child or idiot would do.

"Tryin' to get out, old boy?" laughed Haley. "Them irons will need a crowbar beside your tin, before you can open 'em."

Wolfe laughed, too, in a senseless way.

"I think I'll get out," he said.

"I believe his brain's touched," said Haley, when he came out.

The puddler scraped away with the tin for half an hour. Still Deborah did not speak. At last she ventured nearer, and touched his arm.

"Blood?" she said, looking at some spots on his coat with a shudder.

He looked up at her. "Why, Deb!" he said, smiling,—such a bright, boyish smile, that it went to poor Deborah's heart directly, and she sobbed and cried out loud.

"Oh, Hugh, lad! Hugh! dunnot look at me, when it war my fault! To think I brought hur to it! And I loved hur so! Oh, lad, I dud!"

The confession, even in this wretch, came with the woman's blush through the sharp cry.

He did not seem to hear her,—scraping away diligently at the bars with the bit of tin.

Was he going mad? She peered closely into his face. Something she saw there made her draw suddenly back,—something which Haley had not seen, that lay beneath the pinched, vacant look it had caught since the trial, or the curious gray shadow that rested on it. That gray shadow,—yes, she knew what that meant. She had often seen it creeping over women's faces for months, who died at last of slow hunger or consumption. That meant death, distant, lingering: but this—Whatever it was the woman saw, or thought she saw, used as she was to crime and misery, seemed to make her sick with a new horror. Forgetting her fear of him, she caught his shoulders, and looked keenly, steadily, into his eyes.

"Hugh!" she cried, in a desperate whisper,—"oh, boy, not that! for God's sake, not *that*!"

The vacant laugh went of his face, and he answered her in a muttered word or two that drove her away. Yet the words were kindly enough. Sitting there on his pallet, she cried silently a hopeless sort of tears, but did not speak again. The man looked up furtively at her now and then. Whatever his own trouble was, her distress vexed him with a momentary sting.

It was market-day. The narrow window of the jail looked down directly on the carts and wagons drawn up in a long line, where they had unloaded. He could see, too, and hear distinctly the clink of money as it changed hands, the busy crowd of whites and blacks shoving, pushing one another, and the chaffering and swearing at the stalls. Somehow, the sound, more than anything else had done, wakened him up,—made the whole real to him. He was done with the world and the business of it. He let the tin fall, and looked out, pressing his face close to the rusty bars. How they crowded and pushed! And he,—he should never walk that pavement again! There came Neff Sanders, one of the feeders at the mill, with a basket on his arm. Sure enough, Neff was married the other week. He whistled, hoping he would look up; but he did not. He wondered if Neff remembered he was there,—if any of the boys thought of him up there, and thought that he never was to go down that old cinder-road again. Never again! He had not quite understood it before; but now he did. Not for days or years, but never!—that was it.

How clear the light fell on that stall in front of the market! and how like a picture it was, the dark-green heaps of corn, and the crimson beets, and golden melons! There was another with game: how the light flickered on that pheasant's breast, with the purplish blood dripping over the brown feathers! He could see the red shining of the drops, it was so near. In one minute he could be down there. It was just a step. So easy, as it seemed, so natural to go! Yet it could never be—not in all the thousands of years to come—that he should put his foot on that street again! He thought of himself with a sorrowful pity, as of some one else. There was a dog down in the market, walking after his master with such a stately, grave look!—only a dog, yet he could go backwards and forwards just as he pleased: he had good luck! Why, the very vilest cur, yelping there in the gutter, had not lived his life, had been free to act out whatever thought God had put into his brain; while he— No, he would not think of that! He tried to put the thought away, and to listen to a dispute between a countryman and a woman about some meat; but it would come back. He, what had he done to bear this?

Then came the sudden picture of what might have been, and now. He knew what it was to be in the penitentiary,—how it went with men there. He knew how in these long years he should slowly die, but not until soul and body had become corrupt and rotten,—how, when he came out, if he lived to come, even the lowest of the mill-bands would jeer him,—how his hands would be weak, and his brain senseless and stupid. He believed he was almost that now. He put his hand to his head, with a puzzled, weary look. It ached, his head, with thinking. He tried to quiet himself. It was only right, perhaps; he had done wrong. But was there right or wrong for such as he? What was right? And who had ever taught him? He thrust the whole matter away. A dark, cold quiet crept through his brain. It was all wrong; but let it be! It was nothing to him more than the others. Let it be!

The door grated, as Haley opened it.

"Come, my woman! I must lock up for t' night. Come, stir yerself!"

She went up and took Hugh's hand.

"Good-night, Deb," he said, carelessly.

She had not hoped he would say more; but the tired pain on

her mouth just then was bitterer than death. She took his passive hand and kissed it.

"Hur'll never see Deb again!" she ventured, her lips growing colder and more bloodless.

What did she say that for? Did he not know it? Yet he would not be impatient with poor old Deb. She had trouble of her own, as well as he.

"No, never again," he said, trying to be cheerful.

She stood just a moment, looking at him. Do you laugh at her, standing there, with her hunchback, her rags, her bleared, withered face, and the great despised love tugging at her heart?

"Come, you!" called Haley, impatiently.

She did not move.

"Hugh!" she whispered.

It was to be her last word. What was it?

"Hugh, boy, not THAT!"

He did not answer. She wrung her hands, trying to be silent, looking in his face in an agony of entreaty. He smiled again, kindly.

"It is best, Deb. I cannot bear to be hurted any more."

"Hur knows," she said, humbly.

"Tell my father good-bye; and—and kiss little Janey."

She nodded, saying nothing, looked in his face again, and went out of the door. As she went, she staggered.

"Drinkin' to-day?" broke out Haley, pushing her before him. "Where the Devil did you get it? Here, in with ye!" and he shoved her into her cell, next to Wolfe's, and shut the door.

Along the wall of her cell there was a crack low down by the floor, through which she could see the light from Wolfe's. She had discovered it days before. She hurried in now, and, kneeling down by it, listened, hoping to hear some sound. Nothing but the rasping of the tin on the bars. He was at his old amusement again. Something in the noise jarred on her ear, for she shivered as she heard it. Hugh rasped away at the bars. A dull old bit of tin, not fit to cut korl with.

He looked out of the window again. People were leaving the market now. A tall mulatto girl, following her mistress, her basket on her head, crossed the street just below, and looked up. She was laughing; but, when she caught sight of the haggard face peering out through the bars, suddenly grew grave, and hurried by. A free, firm step, a clear-cut olive face, with a scarlet turban tied on one side, dark, shining eyes, and on the head the basket poised, filled with fruit and flowers, under which the scarlet turban and bright eyes looked out half-shadowed. The picture caught his eye. It was good to see a face like that. He would try to-morrow, and cut one like it. *To-morrow!* He threw down the tin, trembling, and covered his face with his hands. When he looked up again, the daylight was gone.

Deborah, crouching near by on the other side of the wall, heard no noise. He sat on the side of the low pallet, thinking. Whatever was the mystery which the woman had seen on his face, it came out now slowly, in the dark there, and became fixed,—a something never seen on his face before. The evening was darkening fast. The market had been over for an hour; the rumbling of the carts over the pavement grew more infrequent: he listened to each, as it passed, because he thought it was to be for the last time. For the same reason, it was, I suppose, that he strained his eyes to catch a glimpse of each passer-by, wondering who they were, what kind of homes they were going to, if they had children,—listening eagerly to every chance word in the street, as if—(God be merciful to the man! what strange fancy was this?)—as if he never should hear human voices again.

It was quite dark at last. The street was a lonely one. The last passenger, he thought, was gone. No,—there was a quick step: Joe Hill, lighting the lamps. Joe was a good old chap; never passed a fellow without some joke or other. He remembered once seeing the place where he lived with his wife. "Granny Hill" the boys called her. Bedridden she was; but so kind as Joe was to her! kept the room so clean!—and the old woman, when he was there, was laughing at "some of t' lad's foolishness." The step was far down the street; but he could see him place the ladder, run up, and light the gas. A longing seized him to be spoken to once more.

"Joe!" he called, out of the grating. "Good-bye, Joe!"

The old man stopped a moment, listening uncertainly; then hurried on. The prisoner thrust his hand out of the window, and called again, louder; but Joe was too far down the street. It was a little thing; but it hurt him,—this disappointment.

"Good-bye, Joe!" he called, sorrowfully enough.

"Be quiet!" said one of the jailers, passing the door, striking on it with his club.

Oh, that was the last, was it?

There was an inexpressible bitterness on his face as he lay down on the bed, taking the bit of tin, which he had rasped to a tolerable degree of sharpness, in his hand,—to play with, it may be. He bared his arms, looking intently at their corded veins and sinews. Deborah, listening in the next cell, heard a slight clicking sound, often repeated. She shut her lips tightly, that she might not scream; the cold drops of sweat broke over her, in her dumb agony.

"Hur knows best," she muttered at last, fiercely clutching the boards where she lay.

If she could have seen Wolfe, there was nothing about him to frighten her.

He lay quite still, his arms outstretched, looking at the pearly stream of moonlight coming into the window. I think in that one hour that came then he lived back over all the years that had gone before. I think that all the low, vile life, all his wrongs, all his starved hopes, came then, and stung him with a farewell poison that made him sick unto death. He made neither moan nor cry, only turned his worn face now and then to the pure light, that seemed so far off, as one that said, "How long, O Lord? how long?"

The hour was over at last. The moon, passing over her nightly path, slowly came nearer, and threw the light across his bed on his feet. He watched it steadily, as it crept up, inch by inch, slowly. It seemed to him to carry with it a great silence. He had been so hot and tired there always in the mills! The years had been so fierce and cruel! There was coming now quiet and coolness and sleep. His tense limbs relaxed, and settled in a calm languor. The blood ran fainter and slow from his heart. He did not think now with a savage anger of what might be and was not; he was conscious only of deep stillness creeping over him. At first he saw a sea of faces: the mill-men,—women he had known, drunken and bloated,—Janeys timid and pitiful,—poor old Debs: then they floated together like a mist, and faded away, leaving only the clear, pearly moonlight.

Whether, as the pure light crept up the stretched-out figure, it brought with it calm and peace, who shall say? His dumb soul was alone with God in judgment. A Voice may have spoken for it from far-off Calvary, "Father, forgive them, for they know not what they do!"[32] Who dare say? Fainter and fainter the heart rose and fell, slower and slower the moon floated from behind a cloud, until, when at last its full tide of white splendor swept over the cell, it seemed to wrap and fold into a deeper stillness the dead figure that never should move again. Silence deeper than the Night! Nothing that moved, save the black, nauseous stream of blood dripping slowly from the pallet to the floor!

There was outcry and crowd enough in the cell the next day. The coroner and his jury, the local editors, Kirby himself, and boys with their hands thrust knowingly into their pockets and heads on one side, jammed into the corners. Coming and going all day. Only one woman. She came late, and outstayed them all. A Quaker, or Friend, as they call themselves. I think this woman was known by that name in heaven. A homely body, coarsely dressed in gray and white. Deborah (for Haley had let her in) took notice of her. She watched them all—sitting on the end of the pallet, holding his head in her arms—with the ferocity of a watch-dog, if any of them touched the body. There was no meekness, no sorrow, in her face; the stuff out of which murderers are made, instead. All the time Haley and the woman were laying straight the limbs and cleaning the cell, Deborah sat still, keenly watching the Quaker's face. Of all the crowd there that day, this woman alone had not spoken to her,—only once or twice had put some cordial to her lips. After they all were gone, the woman, in the same still, gentle way, brought a vase of wood-leaves and berries, and placed it by the pallet, then opened the narrow window. The fresh air blew in, and swept the woody fragrance over the dead face. Deborah looked up with a quick wonder.

"Did hur know my boy wud like it? Did hur know Hugh?"

"I know Hugh now."

The white fingers passed in a slow, pitiful way over the dead, worn face. There was a heavy shadow in the quiet eyes.

"Did hur know where they'll bury Hugh?" said Deborah in a shrill tone, catching her arm.

This had been the question hanging on her lips all day.

"In t' town-yard? Under t' mud and ash? T' lad 'll smother, woman! He wur born on t' lane moor, where t' air is frick and strong.[33] Take hur out, for God's sake, take hur out where t' air blows!"

The Quaker hesitated, but only for a moment. She put her strong arm around Deborah and led her to the window.

"Thee sees the hills, friend, over the river? Thee sees how the light lies warm there, and the winds of God blow all the day? I live there,—where the blue smoke is, by the trees. Look at me." She turned Deborah's face to her own, clear and earnest. "Thee will believe me? I will take Hugh and bury him there to-morrow."

Deborah did not doubt her. As the evening wore on, she leaned against the iron bars, looking at the hills that rose far off, through the thick sodden clouds, like a bright, unattainable calm. As she looked, a shadow of their solemn repose fell on her face: its fierce discontent faded into a pitiful, humble quiet. Slow, solemn tears gathered in her eyes: the poor weak eyes turned so hopelessly to the place where Hugh was to rest, the grave heights looking higher and brighter and more solemn than ever before. The Quaker watched her keenly. She came to her at last, and touched her arm.

"When thee comes back," she said, in a low, sorrowful tone, like one who speaks from a strong heart deeply moved with remorse or pity, "thee shall begin thy life again,—there on the hills. I came too late; but not for thee,—by God's help, it may be."

Not too late. Three years after, the Quaker began her work.

I end my story here. At evening-time it was light. There is no need to tire you with the long years of sunshine, and fresh air, and slow, patient Christ-love, needed to make healthy and hopeful this impure body and soul. There is a homely pine house, on one of these hills, whose windows overlook broad, wooded slopes and clover-crimsoned meadows,—niched into the very place where the light is warmest, the air freest. It is the Friends' meeting-house. Once a week they sit there, in their grave, earnest way, waiting for the Spirit of Love to speak, opening their simple hearts to receive His words. There is a woman, old, deformed, who takes a humble place among them: waiting like them: in her gray dress, her worn face, pure and meek, turned now and then to the sky. A woman much loved by these silent, restful people; more silent than they, more humble, more loving. Waiting: with her eyes turned to hills higher and purer than these on which she lives,—dim and far off now, but to be reached some day. There may be in her heart some latent hope to meet there the love denied her here,—that she shall find him whom she lost, and that then she will not be all-unworthy. Who blames her? Something is lost in the passage of every soul from one eternity to the other,—something pure and beautiful, which might have been and was not: a hope, a talent, a love, over which the soul mourns, like Esau deprived of his birthright. What blame to the meek Quaker, if she took her lost hope to make the hills of heaven more fair?

Nothing remains to tell that the poor Welsh puddler once lived, but this figure of the mill-woman cut in korl. I have it here in a corner of my library. I keep it hid behind a curtain,— it is such a rough, ungainly thing. Yet there are about it touches, grand sweeps of outline, that show a master's hand. Sometimes,—to-night, for instance,—the curtain is accidentally drawn back, and I see a bare arm stretched out imploringly in the darkness, and an eager, wolfish face watching mine: a wan, woful face, through which the spirit of the dead korl-cutter looks out, with its thwarted life, its mighty hunger, its unfinished work. Its pale, vague lips seem to tremble with a terrible question. "Is this the End?" they say,—"nothing beyond?—no more?" Why, you tell me you have seen that look in the eyes of dumb brutes,—horses dying under the lash. I know.

The deep of the night is passing while I write. The gas-light wakens from the shadows here and there the objects which lie scattered through the room: only faintly, though; for they belong to the open sunlight. As I glance at them, they each recall some task or pleasure of the coming day. A half-molded child's head; Aphrodite; a bough of forest leaves; music; work; homely fragments, in which lie the secrets of all eternal truth and beauty. Prophetic all! Only this dumb, woful face seems to belong to and end with the night. I turn to look at it. Has the power of its desperate need commanded the darkness away? While the room is yet steeped in heavy shadow, a cool, gray light suddenly touches its head like a blessing hand, and its groping arm points through the broken cloud to the far East, where, in the flickering, nebulous crimson, God has set the promise of the Dawn.

"A WHITE HERON"

by Sarah Orne Jewett, 1886

I.

The woods were already filled with shadows one June evening, just before eight o'clock, though a bright sunset still glimmered faintly among the trunks of the trees. A little girl was driving home her cow, a plodding, dilatory, provoking creature in her behavior, but a valued companion for all that. They were going away from the western light, and striking deep into the dark woods, but their feet were familiar with the path, and it was no matter whether their eyes could see it or not.

There was hardly a night the summer through when the old cow could be found waiting at the pasture bars; on the contrary, it was her greatest pleasure to hide herself away among the high huckleberry bushes, and though she wore a loud bell she had made the discovery that if one stood perfectly still it would not ring. So Sylvia had to hunt for her until she found her and call Co'! Co'! with never an answering Moo, until her childish patience was quite spent. If the creature had not given good milk and plenty of it, the case would have seemed very different to her owners. Besides, Sylvia had all the time there was, and very little use to make of it. Sometimes in pleasant weather it was a consolation to look upon the cow's pranks as an intelligent attempt to play hide and seek, and as the child had no playmates she lent herself to this amusement with a good deal of zest. Though this chase had been so long that the wary animal herself had given an unusual signal of her whereabouts, Sylvia had only laughed when she came upon Mistress Moolly at the swampside, and urged her affectionately homeward with a twig of birch leaves. The old cow was not inclined to wander farther, she even turned in the right direction for once as they left the pasture, and stepped along the road at a good pace. She was quite ready to be milked now, and seldom stopped to browse. Sylvia wondered what her grandmother would say because they were so late. It was a great while since she had left home at half-past five o'clock, but everybody knew the difficulty of making this errand a short one. Mrs. Tilley had chased the hornéd torment too many summer evenings herself to blame any one else for lingering, and was only thankful as she waited that she had Sylvia, nowadays, to give such valuable assistance. The good woman suspected that Sylvia loitered occasionally on her own account; there never was such a child for straying about out-of-doors since the world was made! Everybody said that it was a good change for a little maid who had tried to grow for eight years in a crowded manufacturing town, but, as for Sylvia herself, it seemed as if she never had been alive at all before she came to live at the farm. She thought often with wistful compassion of a wretched dry geranium that belonged to a town neighbor.

"'Afraid of folks,'" old Mrs. Tilley said to herself, with a smile, after she had made the unlikely choice of Sylvia from her daughter's houseful of children, and was returning to the farm. "'Afraid of folks,' they said! I guess she won't be troubled no great with 'em up to the old place!" When they reached the door of the lonely house and stopped to unlock it, and the cat came to purr loudly, and rub against them, a deserted pussy, indeed, but fat with young robins, Sylvia whispered that this was a beautiful place to live in, and she never should wish to go home.

The companions followed the shady woodroad, the cow taking slow steps, and the child very fast ones. The cow stopped long at the brook to drink, as if the pasture were not half a swamp, and Sylvia stood still and waited, letting her bare feet cool themselves in the shoal water, while the great twilight moths struck softly against her. She waded on through the brook as the cow moved away, and listened to the thrushes with a heart that beat fast with pleasure. There was a stirring

in the great boughs overhead. They were full of little birds and
beasts that seemed to be wide awake, and going about their
world, or else saying good-night to each other in sleepy twit-
ters. Sylvia herself felt sleepy as she walked along. However, it
was not much farther to the house, and the air was soft and
sweet. She was not often in the woods so late as this, and it
made her feel as if she were a part of the gray shadows and the
moving leaves. She was just thinking how long it seemed since
she first came to the farm a year ago, and wondering if everything went on in the noisy town just the same as when she was
there; the thought of the great red-faced boy who used to chase
and frighten her made her hurry along the path to escape from
the shadow of the trees.

Suddenly this little woods-girl is horror-stricken to hear a
clear whistle not very far away. Not a bird's whistle, which
would have a sort of friendliness, but a boy's whistle, determined, and somewhat aggressive. Sylvia left the cow to whatever sad fate might await her, and stepped discreetly aside into
the bushes, but she was just too late. The enemy had discovered her, and called out in a very cheerful and persuasive tone,
"Halloa, little girl, how far is it to the road?" and trembling
Sylvia answered almost inaudibly, "A good ways."

She did not dare to look boldly at the tall young man, who
carried a gun over his shoulder, but she came out of her bush
and again followed the cow, while he walked alongside.

"I have been hunting for some birds," the stranger said
kindly, "and I have lost my way, and need a friend very much.
Don't be afraid," he added gallantly. "Speak up and tell me
what your name is, and whether you think I can spend the
night at your house, and go out gunning early in the morning."

Sylvia was more alarmed than before. Would not her grandmother consider her much to blame? But who could have foreseen such an accident as this? It did not appear to be her fault,
and she hung her head as if the stem of it were broken, but
managed to answer "Sylvy," with much effort when her companion again asked her name.

Mrs. Tilley was standing in the doorway when the trio came
into view. The cow gave a loud moo by way of explanation.

"Yes, you'd better speak up for yourself, you old trial! Where'd she tucked herself away this time, Sylvy?" Sylvia kept an awed silence; she knew by instinct that her grandmother did not comprehend the gravity of the situation. She must be mistaking the stranger for one of the farmer-lads of the region.

The young man stood his gun beside the door, and dropped a heavy game-bag beside it; then he bade Mrs. Tilley good-evening, and repeated his wayfarer's story, and asked if he could have a night's lodging.

"Put me anywhere you like," he said. "I must be off early in the morning, before day; but I am very hungry, indeed. You can give me some milk at any rate, that's plain."

"Dear sakes, yes," responded the hostess, whose long slumbering hospitality seemed to be easily awakened. "You might fare better if you went out on the main road a mile or so, but you're welcome to what we've got. I'll milk right off, and you make yourself at home. You can sleep on husks or feathers," she proffered graciously. "I raised them all myself. There's good pasturing for geese just below here towards the ma'sh. Now step round and set a plate for the gentleman, Sylvy!" And Sylvia promptly stepped. She was glad to have something to do, and she was hungry herself.

It was a surprise to find so clean and comfortable a little dwelling in this New England wilderness. The young man had known the horrors of its most primitive housekeeping, and the dreary squalor of that level of society which does not rebel at the companionship of hens. This was the best thrift of an old-fashioned farmstead, though on such a small scale that it seemed like a hermitage. He listened eagerly to the old woman's quaint talk, he watched Sylvia's pale face and shining gray eyes with ever growing enthusiasm, and insisted that this was the best supper he had eaten for a month; then, afterward, the new-made friends sat down in the doorway together while the moon came up.

Soon it would be berry-time, and Sylvia was a great help at picking. The cow was a good milker, though a plaguy thing to keep track of, the hostess gossiped frankly, adding presently that she had buried four children, so that Sylvia's mother, and a son (who might be dead) in California were all the children she had left. "Dan, my boy, was a great hand to go gunning," she explained sadly. "I never wanted for pa'tridges or gray squer'ls while he was to home. He's been a great wand'rer, I expect, and he's no hand to write letters. There, I don't blame him, I'd ha' seen the world myself if it had been so I could."

"Sylvia takes after him," the grandmother continued affectionately, after a minute's pause. "There ain't a foot o' ground she don't know her way over, and the wild creatures counts her one o' themselves. Squer'ls she'll tame to come an' feed right out o' her hands, and all sorts o' birds. Last winter she got the jay-birds to bangeing[1] here, and I believe she'd 'a' scanted herself of her own meals to have plenty to throw out amongst 'em, if I hadn't kep' watch. Anything but crows, I tell her, I'm willin' to help support,—though Dan he went an' tamed one o' them that did seem to have reason same as folks. It was round here a good spell after he went away. Dan an' his father they didn't hitch,—but he never held up his head ag'in after Dan had dared him an' gone off."

The guest did not notice this hint of family sorrows in his eager interest in something else.

"So Sylvy knows all about birds, does she?" he exclaimed, as he looked round at the little girl who sat, very demure but increasingly sleepy, in the moonlight. "I am making a collection of birds myself. I have been at it ever since I was a boy." (Mrs. Tilley smiled.) "There are two or three very rare ones I have been hunting for these five years. I mean to get them on my own ground if they can be found."

"Do you cage 'em up?" asked Mrs. Tilley doubtfully, in response to this enthusiastic announcement.

"Oh, no, they're stuffed and preserved, dozens and dozens of them," said the ornithologist, "and I have shot or snared every one myself. I caught a glimpse of a white heron three miles from here on Saturday, and I have followed it in this direction. They have never been found in this district at all. The little white heron, it is," and he turned again to look at Sylvia with the hope of discovering that the rare bird was one of her acquaintances.

But Sylvia was watching a hop-toad in the narrow footpath.

"You would know the heron if you saw it," the stranger continued eagerly. "A queer tall white bird with soft feathers and long thin legs. And it would have a nest perhaps in the top of a high tree, made of sticks, something like a hawk's nest."

Sylvia's heart gave a wild beat; she knew that strange white bird, and had once stolen softly near where it stood in some bright green swamp grass, away over at the other side of the woods. There was an open place where the sunshine always seemed strangely yellow and hot, where tall, nodding rushes grew, and her grandmother had warned her that she might sink in the soft black mud underneath and never be heard of more. Not far beyond were the salt marshes and beyond those was the sea, the sea which Sylvia wondered and dreamed about, but never had looked upon, though its great voice could often be heard above the noise of the woods on stormy nights.

"I can't think of anything I should like so much as to find that heron's nest," the handsome stranger was saying. "I would give ten dollars to anybody who could show it to me," he added desperately, "and I mean to spend my whole vacation hunting for it if need be. Perhaps it was only migrating, or had been chased out of its own region by some bird of prey."

Mrs. Tilley gave amazed attention to all this, but Sylvia still watched the toad, not divining, as she might have done at some calmer time, that the creature wished to get to its hole under the doorstep, and was much hindered by the unusual spectators at that hour of the evening. No amount of thought, that night, could decide how many wished-for treasures the ten dollars, so lightly spoken of, would buy.

The next day the young sportsman hovered about the woods, and Sylvia kept him company, having lost her first fear of the friendly lad, who proved to be most kind and sympathetic. He told her many things about the birds and what they knew and where they lived and what they did with themselves. And he gave her a jack-knife, which she thought as great a treasure as if she were a desert-islander. All day long he did not once make her troubled or afraid except when he brought down some unsuspecting singing creature from its bough. Sylvia would have liked him vastly better without his gun; she could not understand why he killed the very birds he seemed to like so much. But as the day waned, Sylvia still watched the young man with loving admiration. She had never seen anybody so charming and delightful; the woman's heart, asleep in the child, was vaguely thrilled by a dream of love. Some premonition of that great power stirred and swayed these young foresters who traversed the solemn woodlands with soft-footed silent care. They stopped to listen to a bird's song; they pressed forward again eagerly, parting the branches—speaking to each other rarely and in whispers; the young man going first and Sylvia following, fascinated, a few steps behind, with her gray eyes dark with excitement.

She grieved because the longed-for white heron was elusive, but she did not lead the guest, she only followed, and there was no such thing as speaking first. The sound of her own unquestioned voice would have terrified her—it was hard enough to answer yes or no when there was need of that. At last evening began to fall, and they drove the cow home together, and Sylvia smiled with pleasure when they came to the place where she heard the whistle and was afraid only the night before.

II.

Half a mile from home, at the farther edge of the woods, where the land was highest, a great pine-tree stood, the last of its generation. Whether it was left for a boundary mark, or for what reason, no one could say; the woodchoppers who had felled its mates were dead and gone long ago, and a whole forest of sturdy trees, pines and oaks and maples, had grown again. But the stately head of this old pine towered above them all and made a landmark for sea and shore miles and miles away. Sylvia knew it well. She had always believed that whoever climbed to the top of it could see the ocean; and the little girl had often laid her hand on the great rough trunk and looked up wistfully at those dark boughs that the wind always stirred, no matter how hot and still the air might be below. Now she thought of the tree with a new excitement, for why, if one climbed it at break of day, could not one see all the world, and easily discover whence the white heron flew, and mark the place, and find the hidden nest?

What a spirit of adventure, what wild ambition! What fancied triumph and delight and glory for the later morning when she could make known the secret! It was almost too real and too great for the childish heart to bear.

All night the door of the little house stood open, and the whippoorwills came and sang upon the very step. The young sportsman and his old hostess were sound asleep, but Sylvia's great design kept her broad awake and watching. She forgot to think of sleep. The short summer night seemed as long as the winter darkness, and at last when the whippoorwills ceased, and she was afraid the morning would after all come too soon, she stole out of the house and followed the pasture path through the woods, hastening toward the open ground beyond, listening with a sense of comfort and companionship to the drowsy twitter of a half-awakened bird, whose perch she had jarred in passing. Alas, if the great wave of human interest which flooded for the first time this dull little life should sweep away the satisfactions of an existence heart to heart with nature and the dumb life of the forest!

There was the huge tree asleep yet in the paling moonlight, and small and hopeful Sylvia began with utmost bravery to mount to the top of it, with tingling, eager blood coursing the channels of her whole frame, with her bare feet and fingers, that pinched and held like bird's claws to the monstrous ladder reaching up, up, almost to the sky itself. First she must mount the white oak tree that grew alongside, where she was almost lost among the dark branches and the green leaves heavy and wet with dew; a bird fluttered off its nest, and a red squirrel ran to and fro and scolded pettishly at the harmless housebreaker. Sylvia felt her way easily. She had often climbed there, and knew that higher still one of the oak's upper branches chafed against the pine trunk, just where its lower boughs were set close together. There, when she made the dangerous pass from one tree to the other, the great enterprise would really begin.

She crept out along the swaying oak limb at last, and took the daring step across into the old pine-tree. The way was harder than she thought; she must reach far and hold fast, the sharp dry twigs caught and held her and scratched her like angry talons, the pitch made her thin little fingers clumsy and stiff as she went round and round the tree's great stem, higher and higher upward. The sparrows and robins in the woods below were beginning to wake and twitter to the dawn, yet it seemed much lighter there aloft in the pine-tree, and the child knew that she must hurry if her project were to be of any use.

The tree seemed to lengthen itself out as she went up, and to reach farther and farther upward. It was like a great mainmast to the voyaging earth; it must truly have been amazed that morning through all its ponderous frame as it felt this determined spark of human spirit creeping and climbing from higher branch to branch. Who knows how steadily the least twigs held themselves to advantage this light, weak creature on her way! The old pine must have loved his new dependent. More than all the hawks, and bats, and moths, and even the sweet-voiced thrushes, was the brave, beating heart of the solitary gray-eyed child. And the tree stood still and held away the winds that June morning while the dawn grew bright in the east.

Sylvia's face was like a pale star, if one had seen it from the ground, when the last thorny bough was past, and she stood trembling and tired but wholly triumphant, high in the treetop. Yes, there was the sea with the dawning sun making a golden dazzle over it, and toward that glorious east flew two hawks with slow-moving pinions. How low they looked in the air from that height when before one had only seen them far up, and dark against the blue sky. Their gray feathers were as soft as moths; they seemed only a little way from the tree, and Sylvia felt as if she too could go flying away among the clouds. Westward, the woodlands and farms reached miles and miles into the distance; here and there were church steeples, and white villages; truly it was a vast and awesome world!

The birds sang louder and louder. At last the sun came up bewilderingly bright. Sylvia could see the white sails of ships out at sea, and the clouds that were purple and rose-colored and yellow at first began to fade away. Where was the white heron's nest in the sea of green branches, and was this wonderful sight and pageant of the world the only reward for having climbed to such a giddy height? Now look down again, Sylvia, where the green marsh is set among the shining birches and dark hemlocks; there where you saw the white heron once you will see him again; look, look! a white spot of him like a single floating feather comes up from the dead hemlock and grows larger, and rises, and comes close at last, and goes by the landmark pine with steady sweep of wing and outstretched slender neck and crested head. And wait! wait! do not move a foot or a finger, little girl, do not send an arrow of light and consciousness from your two eager eyes, for the heron has perched on a pine bough not far beyond yours, and cries back to his mate on the nest and plumes his feathers for the new day!

The child gives a long sigh a minute later when a company of shouting cat-birds comes also to the tree, and vexed by their fluttering and lawlessness the solemn heron goes away. She knows his secret now, the wild, light, slender bird that floats and wavers, and goes back like an arrow presently to his home in the green world beneath. Then Sylvia, well satisfied, makes her perilous way down again, not daring to look far below the branch she stands on, ready to cry sometimes because her fingers ache and her lamed feet slip. Wondering over and over again what the stranger would say to her, and what he would think when she told him how to find his way straight to the heron's nest.

"Sylvy, Sylvy!" called the busy old grandmother again and again, but nobody answered, and the small husk bed was empty, and Sylvia had disappeared.

The guest waked from a dream, and remembering his day's pleasure hurried to dress himself that it might sooner begin. He was sure from the way the shy little girl looked once or twice yesterday that she had at least seen the white heron, and now she must really be persuaded to tell. Here she comes now, paler than ever, and her worn old frock is torn and tattered, and smeared with pine pitch. The grandmother and the sportsman stand in the door together and question her, and the splendid moment had come to speak of the dead hemlock-tree by the green marsh.

But Sylvia does not speak after all, though the old grandmother fretfully rebukes her, and the young man's kind, appealing eyes are looking straight in her own. He can make them rich with money; he has promised it, and they are poor now. He is so well worth making happy, and he waits to hear the story she can tell.

No, she must keep silence! What is it that suddenly forbids her and makes her dumb? Has she been nine years growing and now, when the great world for the first time puts out a hand to her, must she thrust it aside for a bird's sake? The murmur of the pine's green branches is in her ears, she remembers how the white heron came flying through the golden air and how they watched the sea and the morning together, and Sylvia cannot speak; she cannot tell the heron's secret and give its life away.

Dear loyalty, that suffered a sharp pang as the guest went away disappointed later in the day, that could have served and followed him and loved him as a dog loves! Many a night Sylvia heard the echo of his whistle haunting the pasture path as she came home with the loitering cow. She forgot even her sorrow at the sharp report of his gun and the piteous sight of thrushes and sparrows dropping silent to the ground, their songs hushed and their pretty feathers stained and wet with blood. Were the birds better friends than their hunter might have been,—who can tell? Whatever treasures were lost to her, woodlands and summer-time, remember! Bring your gifts and graces and tell your secrets to this lonely country child!

"THE YELLOW WALL-PAPER"

by Charlotte Perkins Gilman,

1892

It is very seldom that mere ordinary people like John and myself secure ancestral halls for the summer.

A colonial mansion, a hereditary estate, I would say a haunted house, and reach the height of romantic felicity—but that would be asking too much of fate!

Still I will proudly declare that there is something queer about it.

Else, why should it be let so cheaply? And why have stood so long untenanted?

John laughs at me, of course, but one expects that in marriage.

John is practical in the extreme. He has no patience with faith, an intense horror of superstition, and he scoffs openly at any talk of things not to be felt and seen and put down in figures.

John is a physician, and *perhaps*—(I would not say it to a living soul, of course, but this is dead paper and a great relief to my mind—) *perhaps* that is one reason I do not get well faster.

You see, he does not believe I am sick!

And what can one do?

If a physician of high standing, and one's own husband, assures friends and relatives that there is really nothing the matter with one but temporary nervous depression—a slight hysterical tendency—what is one to do?[1]

My brother is also a physician, and also of high standing, and he says the same thing.

So I take phosphates[2] or phosphites—whichever it is, and

tonics, and journeys, and air, and exercise, and am absolutely forbidden to "work" until I am well again.

Personally, I disagree with their ideas.

Personally, I believe that congenial work, with excitement and change, would do me good.

But what is one to do?

I did write for a while in spite of them; but it *does* exhaust me a good deal—having to be so sly about it, or else meet with heavy opposition.

I sometimes fancy that in my condition if I had less opposition and more society and stimulus—but John says the very worst thing I can do is to think about my condition, and I confess it always makes me feel bad.

So I will let it alone and talk about the house.

The most beautiful place! It is quite alone, standing well back from the road, quite three miles from the village. It makes me think of English places that you read about, for there are hedges and walls and gates that lock, and lots of separate little houses for the gardeners and people.

There is a *delicious* garden! I never saw such a garden—large and shady, full of box-bordered paths, and lined with long grape-covered arbors with seats under them.

There were greenhouses, too, but they are all broken now.

There was some legal trouble, I believe, something about the heirs and co-heirs; anyhow, the place has been empty for years.

That spoils my ghostliness, I am afraid, but I don't care—there is something strange about the house—I can feel it.

I even said so to John one moonlight evening, but he said what I felt was a *draught*, and shut the window.

I get unreasonably angry with John sometimes. I'm sure I never used to be so sensitive. I think it is due to this nervous condition.

But John says if I feel so, I shall neglect proper self-control; so I take pains to control myself—before him, at least, and that makes me very tired.

I don't like our room a bit. I wanted one downstairs that opened on the piazza and had roses all over the window, and such pretty old-fashioned chintz hangings! but John would not hear of it.

He said there was only one window and not room for two beds, and no near room for him if he took another.

He is very careful and loving, and hardly lets me stir without special direction.

I have a schedule prescription for each hour in the day; he takes all care from me, and so I feel basely ungrateful not to value it more.

He said we came here solely on my account, that I was to have perfect rest and all the air I could get. "Your exercise depends on your strength, my dear," said he, "and your food somewhat on your appetite; but air you can absorb all the time." So we took the nursery at the top of the house.

It is a big, airy room, the whole floor nearly, with windows that look all ways, and air and sunshine galore. It was nursery first and then playground and gymnasium, I should judge; for the windows are barred for little children, and there are rings and things in the walls.

The paint and paper look as if a boys' school had used it. It is stripped off—the paper—in great patches all around the head of my bed, about as far as I can reach, and in a great place on the other side of the room low down. I never saw a worse paper in my life.

One of those sprawling flamboyant patterns committing every artistic sin.

It is dull enough to confuse the eye in following, pronounced enough to constantly irritate and provoke study, and when you follow the lame uncertain curves for a little distance they suddenly commit suicide—plunge off at outrageous angles, destroy themselves in unheard-of contradictions.

The color is repellant, almost revolting; a smoldering unclean yellow, strangely faded by the slow-turning sunlight.

It is a dull yet lurid orange in some places, a sickly sulphur tint in others.

No wonder the children hated it! I should hate it myself if I had to live in this room long.

There comes John, and I must put this away,—he hates to have me write a word.

* * *

We have been here two weeks, and I haven't felt like writing before, since that first day.

I am sitting by the window now, up in this atrocious nursery, and there is nothing to hinder my writing as much as I please, save lack of strength.

John is away all day, and even some nights when his cases are serious.

I am glad my case is not serious!

But these nervous troubles are dreadfully depressing.

John does not know how much I really suffer. He knows there is no *reason* to suffer, and that satisfies him.

Of course it is only nervousness. It does weigh on me so not to do my duty in any way!

I meant to be such a help to John, such a real rest and comfort, and here I am a comparative burden already!

Nobody would believe what an effort it is to do what little I am able,—to dress and entertain, and order things.

It is fortunate Mary is so good with the baby. Such a dear baby!

And yet I *cannot* be with him, it makes me so nervous.

I suppose John never was nervous in his life. He laughs at me so about this wall-paper!

At first he meant to repaper the room, but afterwards he said that I was letting it get the better of me, and that nothing was worse for a nervous patient than to give way to such fancies.

He said that after the wall-paper was changed it would be the heavy bedstead, and then the barred windows, and then that gate at the head of the stairs, and so on.

"You know the place is doing you good," he said, "and really, dear, I don't care to renovate the house just for a three months' rental."

"Then do let us go downstairs," I said, "there are such pretty rooms there."

Then he took me in his arms and called me a blessed little goose, and said he would go down cellar, if I wished, and have it whitewashed into the bargain.

But he is right enough about the beds and windows and things.

It is an airy and comfortable room as any one need wish, and, of course, I would not be so silly as to make him uncomfortable just for a whim.

I'm really getting quite fond of the big room, all but that horrid paper.

Out of one window I can see the garden, those mysterious deep-shaded arbors, the riotous old-fashioned flowers, and bushes and gnarly trees.

Out of another I get a lovely view of the bay and a little private wharf belonging to the estate. There is a beautiful shaded lane that runs down there from the house. I always fancy I see people walking in these numerous paths and arbors, but John has cautioned me not to give way to fancy in the least. He says that with my imaginative power and habit of story-making, a nervous weakness like mine is sure to lead to all manner of excited fancies, and that I ought to use my will and good sense to check the tendency. So I try.

I think sometimes that if I were only well enough to write a little it would relieve the press of ideas and rest me.

But I find I get pretty tired when I try.

It is so discouraging not to have any advice and companionship about my work. When I get really well John says we will ask Cousin Henry and Julia down for a long visit; but he says he would as soon put fireworks in my pillowcase as to let me have those stimulating people about now.

I wish I could get well faster.

But I must not think about that. This paper looks to me as if it *knew* what a vicious influence it had!

There is a recurrent spot where the pattern lolls like a broken neck and two bulbous eyes stare at you upside down.

I get positively angry with the impertinence of it and the everlastingness. Up and down and sideways they crawl, and those absurd, unblinking eyes are everywhere. There is one place where two breadths didn't match, and the eyes go all up and down the line, one a little higher than the other.

I never saw so much expression in an inanimate thing before, and we all know how much expression they have! I used to lie awake as a child and get more entertainment and terror out of blank walls and plain furniture than most children could find in a toy-store.

I remember what a kindly wink the knobs of our big, old bureau used to have, and there was one chair that always seemed like a strong friend.

I used to feel that if any of the other things looked too fierce I could always hop into that chair and be safe.

The furniture in this room is no worse than inharmonious, however, for we had to bring it all from downstairs. I suppose when this was used as a playroom they had to take the nursery things out, and no wonder! I never saw such ravages as the children have made here.

The wall-paper, as I said before, is torn off in spots, and it sticketh closer than a brother[3]—they must have had perseverance as well as hatred.

Then the floor is scratched and gouged and splintered, the plaster itself is dug out here and there, and this great heavy bed, which is all we found in the room, looks as if it had been through the wars.

But I don't mind it a bit—only the paper.

There comes John's sister. Such a dear girl as she is, and so careful of me! I must not let her find me writing.

She is a perfect and enthusiastic housekeeper, and hopes for no better profession. I verily believe she thinks it is the writing which made me sick!

But I can write when she is out, and see her a long way off from these windows.

There is one that commands the road, a lovely shaded winding road, and one that just looks off over the country. A lovely country, too, full of great elms and velvet meadows.

This wall-paper has a kind of sub-pattern in a different shade, a particularly irritating one, for you can only see it in certain lights, and not clearly then.

But in the places where it isn't faded, and where the sun is just so—I can see a strange, provoking, formless sort of figure, that seems to skulk about behind that silly and conspicuous front design.

There's sister on the stairs!

* * *

Well, the Fourth of July is over! The people are all gone and I am tired out. John thought it might do me good to see a little company, so we just had mother and Nellie and the children down for a week.

Of course I didn't do a thing. Jennie sees to everything now.

But it tired me all the same.

John says if I don't pick up faster he shall send me to Weir Mitchell in the fall.

But I don't want to go there at all. I had a friend who was in his hands once, and she says he is just like John and my brother, only more so!

Besides, it is such an undertaking to go so far.

I don't feel as if it was worth while to turn my hand over for anything, and I'm getting dreadfully fretful and querulous.

I cry at nothing, and cry most of the time.

Of course I don't when John is here, or anybody else, but when I am alone.

And I am alone a good deal just now. John is kept in town very often by serious cases, and Jennie is good and lets me alone when I want her to.

So I walk a little in the garden or down that lovely lane, sit on the porch under the roses, and lie down up here a good deal.

I'm getting really fond of the room in spite of the wall-paper. Perhaps *because* of the wall-paper.

It dwells in my mind so!

I lie here on this great immovable bed—it is nailed down, I

believe—and follow that pattern about by the hour. It is as good as gymnastics, I assure you. I start, we'll say, at the bottom, down in the corner over there where it has not been touched, and I determine for the thousandth time that I *will* follow that pointless pattern to some sort of a conclusion.

I know a little of the principle of design, and I know this thing was not arranged on any laws of radiation, or alternation, or repetition, or symmetry, or anything else that I ever heard of.

It is repeated, of course, by the breadths, but not otherwise.

Looked at in one way each breadth stands alone, the bloated curves and flourishes—a kind of "debased Romanesque" with *delirium tremens*[4]—go waddling up and down in isolated columns of fatuity.

But, on the other hand, they connect diagonally, and the sprawling outlines run off in great slanting waves of optic horror, like a lot of wallowing seaweeds in full chase.

The whole thing goes horizontally, too, at least it seems so, and I exhaust myself in trying to distinguish the order of its going in that direction.

They have used a horizontal breadth for a frieze, and that adds wonderfully to the confusion.

There is one end of the room where it is almost intact, and there, when the crosslights fade and the low sun shines directly upon it, I can almost fancy radiation after all,—the interminable grotesques seem to form around a common center and rush off in headlong plunges of equal distraction.

It makes me tired to follow it. I will take a nap, I guess.

* * *

I don't know why I should write this.

I don't want to.

I don't feel able.

And I know John would think it absurd. But I *must* say what I feel and think in some way—it is such a relief!

But the effort is getting to be greater than the relief.

Half the time now I am awfully lazy, and lie down ever so much.

John says I musn't lose my strength, and has me take cod liver oil and lots of tonics and things, to say nothing of ale and wine and rare meat.

Dear John! He loves me very dearly, and hates to have me sick. I tried to have a real earnest reasonable talk with him the other day, and tell him how I wish he would let me go and make a visit to Cousin Henry and Julia.

But he said I wasn't able to go, nor able to stand it after I got there; and I did not make out a very good case for myself, for I was crying before I had finished.

It is getting to be a great effort for me to think straight. Just this nervous weakness, I suppose.

And dear John gathered me up in his arms, and just carried me upstairs and laid me on the bed, and sat by me and read to me till it tired my head.

He said I was his darling and his comfort and all he had, and that I must take care of myself for his sake, and keep well.

He says no one but myself can help me out of it, that I must use my will and self-control and not let any silly fancies run away with me.

There's one comfort, the baby is well and happy, and does not have to occupy this nursery with the horrid wall-paper.

If we had not used it, that blessed child would have! What a fortunate escape! Why, I wouldn't have a child of mine, an impressionable little thing, live in such a room for worlds.

I never thought of it before, but it is lucky that John kept me here after all. I can stand it so much easier than a baby, you see.

Of course I never mention it to them any more,—I am too wise,—but I keep watch of it all the same.

There are things in that paper that nobody knows but me, or ever will.

Behind that outside pattern the dim shapes get clearer every day.

It is always the same shape, only very numerous.

And it is like a woman stooping down and creeping about

behind that pattern. I don't like it a bit. I wonder—I begin to think—I wish John would take me away from here!

* * *

It is so hard to talk with John about my case, because he is so wise, and because he loves me so.

But I tried it last night.

It was moonlight. The moon shines in all around, just as the sun does.

I hate to see it sometimes, it creeps so slowly, and always comes in by one window or another.

John was asleep and I hated to waken him, so I kept still and watched the moonlight on that undulating wall-paper till I felt creepy.

The faint figure behind seemed to shake the pattern, just as if she wanted to get out.

I got up softly and went to feel and see if the paper *did* move, and when I came back John was awake.

"What is it, little girl?" he said. "Don't go walking about like that—you'll get cold."

I thought it was a good time to talk, so I told him that I really was not gaining here, and that I wished he would take me away.

"Why, darling!" said he, "our lease will be up in three weeks, and I can't see how to leave before.

"The repairs are not done at home, and I cannot possibly leave town just now. Of course if you were in any danger, I could and would, but you really are better, dear, whether you can see it or not. I am a doctor, dear, and I know. You are gaining flesh and color, your appetite is better. I feel really much easier about you."

"I don't weigh a bit more," said I, "nor as much; and my appetite may be better in the evening, when you are here, but it is worse in the morning when you are away."

"Bless her little heart!" said he with a big hug; "she shall be as sick as she pleases! But now let's improve the shining hours by going to sleep, and talk about it in the morning!"

"And you won't go away?" I asked gloomily.

"Why, how can I, dear? It is only three weeks more and then we will take a nice little trip of a few days while Jennie is getting the house ready. Really, dear, you are better!"

"Better in body perhaps—" I began, and stopped short, for he sat up straight and looked at me with such a stern, reproachful look that I could not say another word.

"My darling," said he, "I beg of you, for my sake and for our child's sake, as well as for your own, that you will never for one instant let that idea enter your mind! There is nothing so dangerous, so fascinating, to a temperament like yours. It is a false and foolish fancy. Can you not trust me as a physician when I tell you so?"

So of course I said no more on that score, and we went to sleep before long. He thought I was asleep first, but I wasn't,—I lay there for hours trying to decide whether that front pattern and the back pattern really did move together or separately.

* * *

On a pattern like this, by daylight, there is a lack of sequence, a defiance of law, that is a constant irritant to a normal mind.

The color is hideous enough, and unreliable enough, and infuriating enough, but the pattern is torturing.

You think you have mastered it, but just as you get well underway in following, it turns a back-somersault and there you are. It slaps you in the face, knocks you down, and tramples upon you. It is like a bad dream.

The outside pattern is a florid arabesque, reminding one of a fungus. If you can imagine a toadstool in joints, an interminable string of toadstools, budding and sprouting in endless convolutions—why, that is something like it.

That is, sometimes!

There is one marked peculiarity about this paper, a thing nobody seems to notice but myself, and that is that it changes as the light changes.

When the sun shoots in through the east window—I always watch for that first long, straight ray—it changes so quickly that I never can quite believe it.

That is why I watch it always.

By moonlight—the moon shines in all night when there is a moon—I wouldn't know it was the same paper.

At night in any kind of light, in twilight, candlelight, lamplight, and worst of all by moonlight, it becomes bars! The outside pattern I mean, and the woman behind it is as plain as can be.

I didn't realize for a long time what the thing was that showed behind, that dim sub-pattern, but now I am quite sure it is a woman.

By daylight she is subdued, quiet. I fancy it is the pattern that keeps her so still. It is so puzzling. It keeps me quiet by the hour.

I lie down ever so much now. John says it is good for me, and to sleep all I can.

Indeed, he started the habit by making me lie down for an hour after each meal.

It is a very bad habit, I am convinced, for, you see, I don't sleep.

And that cultivates deceit, for I don't tell them I'm awake—O no!

The fact is I am getting a little afraid of John.

He seems very queer sometimes, and even Jennie has an inexplicable look.

It strikes me occasionally, just as a scientific hypothesis,—that perhaps it is the paper!

I have watched John when he did not know I was looking, and come into the room suddenly on the most innocent excuses, and I've caught him several times *looking at the paper!* And Jennie too. I caught Jennie with her hand on it once.

She didn't know I was in the room, and when I asked her in a quiet, a very quiet voice, with the most restrained manner possible, what she was doing with the paper—she turned around as if she had been caught stealing, and looked quite angry—asked me why I should frighten her so!

Then she said that the paper stained everything it touched, that she had found yellow smooches on all my clothes and John's, and she wished we would be more careful!

Did not that sound innocent? But I know she was studying that pattern, and I am determined that nobody shall find it out but myself!

*   *   *

Life is very much more exciting now than it used to be. You see I have something more to expect, to look forward to, to watch. I really do eat better, and am more quiet than I was.

John is so pleased to see me improve! He laughed a little the other day, and said I seemed to be flourishing in spite of my wall-paper.

I turned it off with a laugh. I had no intention of telling him it was *because* of the wall-paper—he would make fun of me. He might even want to take me away.

I don't want to leave now until I have found it out. There is a week more, and I think that will be enough.

*   *   *

I'm feeling ever so much better! I don't sleep much at night, for it is so interesting to watch developments; but I sleep a good deal in the daytime.

In the daytime it is tiresome and perplexing.

There are always new shoots on the fungus, and new shades of yellow all over it. I cannot keep count of them, though I have tried conscientiously.

It is the strangest yellow, that wall-paper! It makes me think of all the yellow things I ever saw—not beautiful ones like buttercups, but old foul, bad yellow things.

But there is something else about that paper—the smell![5] I noticed it the moment we came into the room, but with so much air and sun it was not bad. Now we have had a week of fog and rain, and whether the windows are open or not, the smell is here.

It creeps all over the house.

I find it hovering in the dining-room, skulking in the parlor, hiding in the hall, lying in wait for me on the stairs.

It gets into my hair.

Even when I go to ride, if I turn my head suddenly and surprise it—there is that smell!

Such a peculiar odor, too! I have spent hours in trying to analyze it, to find what it smelled like.

It is not bad—at first, and very gentle, but quite the subtlest, most enduring odor I ever met.

In this damp weather it is awful. I wake up in the night and find it hanging over me.

It used to disturb me at first. I thought seriously of burning the house—to reach the smell.

But now I am used to it. The only thing I can think of that it is like is the *color* of the paper! A yellow smell.

There is a very funny mark on this wall, low down, near the mopboard. A streak that runs round the room. It goes behind every piece of furniture, except the bed, a long, straight, even *smooch*, as if it had been rubbed over and over.

I wonder how it was done and who did it, and what they did it for. Round and round and round—round and round and round—it makes me dizzy!

* * *

I really have discovered something at last.

Through watching so much at night, when it changes so, I have finally found out.

The front pattern *does* move—and no wonder! The woman behind shakes it!

Sometimes I think there are a great many women behind, and sometimes only one, and she crawls around fast, and her crawling shakes it all over.

Then in the very bright spots she keeps still, and in the very shady spots she just takes hold of the bars and shakes them hard.

And she is all the time trying to climb through. But nobody could climb through that pattern—it strangles so; I think that is why it has so many heads.

They get through, and then the pattern strangles them off and turns them upside down, and makes their eyes white!

If those heads were covered or taken off it would not be half so bad.

* * *

I think that woman gets out in the daytime!

And I'll tell you why—privately—I've seen her!

I can see her out of every one of my windows!

It is the same woman, I know, for she is always creeping, and most women do not creep by daylight.

I see her on that long shaded lane, creeping up and down. I see her in those dark grape arbors, creeping all around the garden.

I see her on that long road under the trees, creeping along, and when a carriage comes she hides under the blackberry vines.

I don't blame her a bit. It must be very humiliating to be caught creeping by daylight!

I always lock the door when I creep by daylight. I can't do it at night, for I know John would suspect something at once.

And John is so queer now, that I don't want to irritate him. I wish he would take another room! Besides, I don't want anybody to get that woman out at night but myself.

I often wonder if I could see her out of all the windows at once.

But, turn as fast as I can, I can only see out of one at one time.

And though I always see her, she *may* be able to creep faster than I can turn!

I have watched her sometimes away off in the open country, creeping as fast as a cloud shadow in a high wind.

* * *

If only that top pattern could be gotten off from the under one! I mean to try it, little by little.

I have found out another funny thing, but I shan't tell it this time! It does not do to trust people too much.

There are only two more days to get this paper off, and I believe John is beginning to notice. I don't like the look in his eyes.

And I heard him ask Jennie a lot of professional questions about me. She had a very good report to give.

She said I slept a good deal in the daytime.

John knows I don't sleep very well at night, for all I'm so quiet!

He asked me all sorts of questions, too, and pretended to be very loving and kind.

As if I couldn't see through him!

Still, I don't wonder he acts so, sleeping under this paper for three months.

It only interests me, but I feel sure John and Jennie are secretly affected by it.

* * *

Hurrah! This is the last day, but it is enough. John is to stay in town over night, and won't be out until this evening.

Jennie wanted to sleep with me—the sly thing! But I told her I should undoubtedly rest better for a night all alone.

That was clever, for really I wasn't alone a bit! As soon as it was moonlight, and that poor thing began to crawl and shake the pattern, I got up and ran to help her.

I pulled and she shook, I shook and she pulled, and before morning we had peeled off yards of that paper.

A strip about as high as my head and half around the room.

And then when the sun came and that awful pattern began to laugh at me I declared I would finish it to-day!

We go away to-morrow, and they are moving all my furniture down again to leave things as they were before.

Jennie looked at the wall in amazement, but I told her merrily that I did it out of pure spite at the vicious thing.

She laughed and said she wouldn't mind doing it herself, but I must not get tired.

How she betrayed herself that time!

But I am here, and no person touches this paper but me—not *alive*!

She tried to get me out of the room—it was too patent! But I said it was so quiet and empty and clean now that I believed I would lie down again and sleep all I could; and not to wake me even for dinner—I would call when I woke.

So now she is gone, and the servants are gone, and the things are gone, and there is nothing left but that great bedstead nailed down, with the canvas mattress we found on it.

We shall sleep downstairs to-night, and take the boat home to-morrow.

I quite enjoy the room, now it is bare again.

How those children did tear about here!

This bedstead is fairly gnawed!

But I must get to work.

I have locked the door and thrown the key down into the front path.

I don't want to go out, and I don't want to have anybody come in, till John comes.

I want to astonish him.

I've got a rope up here that even Jennie did not find. If that woman does get out, and tries to get away, I can tie her!

But I forgot I could not reach far without anything to stand on! This bed will *not* move!

I tried to lift and push it until I was lame, and then I got so angry I bit off a little piece at one corner—but it hurt my teeth.

Then I peeled off all the paper I could reach standing on the floor. It sticks horribly and the pattern just enjoys it! All those strangled heads and bulbous eyes and waddling fungus growths just shriek with derision!

I am getting angry enough to do something desperate. To jump out of the window would be admirable exercise, but the bars are too strong even to try.

Besides I wouldn't do it. Of course not. I know well enough that a step like that is improper and might be misconstrued.

I don't like to *look* out of the windows even—there are so many of those creeping women, and they creep so fast.

I wonder if they all come out of that wall-paper as I did?

But I am securely fastened now by my well-hidden rope—you don't get *me* out in the road there!

I suppose I shall have to get back behind the pattern when it comes night, and that is hard!

It is so pleasant to be out in this great room and creep around as I please!

I don't want to go outside. I won't, even if Jennie asks me to.

For outside you have to creep on the ground, and everything is green instead of yellow.

But here I can creep smoothly on the floor, and my shoulder just fits in that long smooch around the wall, so I cannot lose my way.

Why, there's John at the door!

It is no use, young man, you can't open it!

How he does call and pound!

Now he's crying for an axe.

It would be a shame to break down that beautiful door!

"John dear!" said I in the gentlest voice, "the key is down by the front steps, under a plantain leaf!"

That silenced him for a few moments.

Then he said—very quietly indeed, "Open the door, my darling!"

"I can't," said I. "The key is down by the front door under a plantain leaf!"

And then I said it again, several times, very gently and slowly, and said it so often that he had to go and see, and he got it, of course, and came in. He stopped short by the door.

"What is the matter?" he cried. "For God's sake, what are you doing!"

I kept on creeping just the same, but I looked at him over my shoulder.

"I've got out at last," said I, "in spite of you and Jane?[6] And I've pulled off most of the paper, so you can't put me back!"

Now why should that man have fainted? But he did, and right across my path by the wall, so that I had to creep over him every time!

* * *

WHY I WROTE
THE YELLOW WALLPAPER?

Many and many a reader has asked that. When the story first came out, in the *New England Magazine* about 1891, a Boston physician made protest in *The Transcript*. Such a story ought not to be written, he said; it was enough to drive anyone mad to read it.

Another physician, in Kansas I think, wrote to say that it was the best description of incipient insanity he had ever seen, and—begging my pardon—had I been there?

Now the story of the story is this:

For many years I suffered from a severe and continuous nervous breakdown tending to melancholia—and beyond. During about the third year of this trouble I went, in devout faith and some faint stir of hope, to a noted specialist in nervous diseases, the best known in the country. This wise man put me to bed and applied the rest cure, to which a still-good physique responded so promptly that he concluded there was nothing much the matter with me, and sent me home with solemn advice to "live as domestic a life as far as possible," to "have but two hours' intellectual life a day," and "never to touch pen, brush, or pencil again" as long as I lived. This was in 1887.

I went home and obeyed those directions for some three months, and came so near the borderline of utter mental ruin that I could see over.

Then, using the remnants of intelligence that remained, and helped by a wise friend, I cast the noted specialist's advice to the winds and went to work again—work, the normal life of every human being; work, in which is joy and growth and service, without which one is a pauper and a parasite—ultimately recovering some measure of power.

Being naturally moved to rejoicing by this narrow escape, I wrote *The Yellow Wallpaper*, with its embellishments and additions, to carry out the ideal (I never had hallucinations or objections to my mural decorations) and sent a copy to the physician who so nearly drove me mad. He never acknowledged it.

The little book is valued by alienists and as a good specimen of one kind of literature. It has, to my knowledge, saved one woman from a similar fate—so terrifying her family that they let her out into normal activity and she recovered.

But the best result is this. Many years later I was told that the great specialist had admitted to friends of his that he had altered his treatment of neurasthenia since reading *The Yellow Wallpaper*.

It was not intended to drive people crazy, but to save people from being driven crazy, and it worked.

"THE LITTLE ROOM"

by Madelene Yale Wynne,

1895

"How would it do for a smoking-room?"

"Just the very place; only, you know, Roger, you must not think of smoking in the house. I am almost afraid that having just a plain, common man around, let alone a smoking man, will upset Aunt Hannah. She is New England—Vermont New England boiled down."

"You leave Aunt Hannah to me; I'll find her tender side. I'm going to ask her about the old sea-captain and the yellow calico."

"Not yellow calico—blue chintz."[1]

"Well, yellow *shell*, then."

"No, no! don't mix it up so; you won't know yourself what to expect, and that's half the fun."

"Now you tell me again exactly what to expect; to tell the truth, I didn't half hear about it the other day; I was wool-gathering. It was something queer that happened when you were a child, wasn't it?"

"Something that began to happen long before that, and kept happening, and may happen again; but I hope not."

"What was it?"

"I wonder if the other people in the car can hear us?"

"I fancy not; we don't hear them—not consecutively, at least."

"Well, mother was born in Vermont, you know; she was the only child by a second marriage. Aunt Hannah and Aunt Maria are only half-aunts to me, you know."

"I hope they are half as nice as you are."

"Roger, be still; they certainly will hear us."

"Well, don't you want them to know we are married?"

"Yes, but not just married. There's all the difference in the world."

"You are afraid we look too happy!"

"No; only I want my happiness all to myself."

"Well, the little room?"

"My aunts brought mother up; they were nearly twenty years older than she. I might say Hiram and they brought her up. You see, Hiram was bound out to my grandfather when he was a boy, and when grandfather died Hiram said he 's'posed he went with the farm, 'long o' the critters,' and he has been there ever since. He was my mother's only refuge from the decorum of my aunts. They are simply workers. They make me think of the Maine woman who wanted her epitaph to be: 'She was a *hard* working woman.'"

"They must be almost beyond their working-days. How old are they?"

"Seventy, or thereabouts; but they will die standing; or, at least, on a Saturday night, after all the house-work is done up. They were rather strict with mother, and I think she had a lonely childhood. The house is almost a mile away from any neighbors, and off on top of what they call Stony Hill. It is bleak enough up there, even in summer.

"When mamma was about ten years old they sent her to cousins in Brooklyn, who had children of their own, and knew more about bringing them up. She staid there till she was married; she didn't go to Vermont in all that time, and of course hadn't seen her sisters, for they never would leave home for a day. They couldn't even be induced to go to Brooklyn to her wedding, so she and father took their wedding trip up there."

"And that's why we are going up there on our own?"

"Don't, Roger; you have no idea how loud you speak."

"You never say so except when I am going to say that one little word."

"Well, don't say it, then, or say it very, very quietly."

"Well, what was the queer thing?"

"When they got to the house, mother wanted to take father right off into the little room; she had been telling him about it, just as I am going to tell you, and she had said that of all the rooms, that one was the only one that seemed pleasant to her. She described the furniture and the books and paper and everything, and said it was on the north side, between the front and back room. Well, when they went to look for it, there was no little room there; there was only a shallow china-closet. She asked her sisters when the house had been altered and a closet made of the room that used to be there. They both said the house was exactly as it had been built—that they had never made any changes, except to tear down the old wood-shed and build a smaller one.

"Father and mother laughed a good deal over it, and when anything was lost they would always say it must be in the little room, and any exaggerated statement was called 'little-roomy.' When I was a child I thought that was a regular English phrase, I heard it so often.

"Well, they talked it over, and finally they concluded that my mother had been a very imaginative sort of a child, and had read in some book about such a little room, or perhaps even dreamed it, and then had 'made believe,' as children do, till she herself had really thought the room was there."

"Why, of course, that might easily happen."

"Yes, but you haven't heard the queer part yet; you wait and see if you can explain the rest as easily."

"They staid at the farm two weeks, and then went to New York to live. When I was eight years old my father was killed in the war, and mother was broken-hearted. She never was quite strong afterwards, and that summer we decided to go up to the farm for three months.

"I was a restless sort of a child, and the journey seemed very long to me; and finally, to pass the time, mamma told me the story of the little room, and how it was all in her own imagination, and how there really was only a china-closet there.

"She told it with all the particulars; and even to me, who knew beforehand that the room wasn't there, it seemed just as real as could be. She said it was on the north side, between the front and back rooms; that it was very small, and they some times called it an entry. There was a door also that opened out-of-doors, and that one was painted green, and was cut in the middle like the old Dutch doors, so that it could be used for a window by opening the top part only. Directly opposite the door was a lounge or couch; it was covered with blue chintz— India chintz—some that had been brought over by an old Salem sea-captain as a 'venture.' He had given it to Hannah when she was a young girl. She was sent to Salem for two years to school. Grandfather originally came from Salem."

"I thought there wasn't any room or chintz.

"*That is just it.* They had decided that mother had imagined it all, and yet you see how exactly everything was painted in her mind, for she had even remembered that Hiram had told her that Hannah could have married the sea-captain if she had wanted to!

"The India cotton was the regular blue stamped chintz, with the peacock figure on it.[2] The head and body of the bird were in profile, while the tail was full front view behind it. It had seemed to take mamma's fancy, and she drew it for me on a piece of paper as she talked. Doesn't it seem strange to you that she could have made all that up, or even dreamed it?

"At the foot of the lounge were some hanging shelves with some old books on them. All the books were leather-colored except one; that was bright red, and was called the *Ladies' Album.*[3] It made a bright break between the other thicker books.

"On the lower shelf was a beautiful pink sea-shell, lying on a mat made of balls of red shaded worsted. This shell was greatly coveted by mother, but she was only allowed to play with it when she had been particularly good. Hiram had showed her how to hold it close to her ear and hear the roar of the sea in it.

"I know you will like Hiram, Roger; he is quite a character in his way.

"Mamma said she remembered, or *thought* she remembered, having been sick once, and she had to lie quietly for some days on the lounge; then was the time she had become so familiar with everything in the room, and she had been allowed to have the shell to play with all the time. She had had her toast brought to her in there, with make-believe tea. It was one of her pleasant memories of her childhood; it was the first time she had been of any importance to anybody, even herself.

"Right at the head of the lounge was a light-stand, as they called it, and on it was a very brightly polished brass candle stick and a brass tray, with snuffers.[4] That is all I remember of her describing, except that there was a braided rag rug on the floor, and on the wall was a beautiful flowered paper—roses and morning-glories in a wreath on a light blue ground. The same paper was in the front room."

"And all this never existed except in her imagination?"

"She said that when she and father went up there, there wasn't any little room at all like it anywhere in the house; there was a china-closet where she had believed the room to be."

"And your aunts said there had never been any such room."

"That is what they said."

"Wasn't there any blue chintz in the house with a peacock figure?"

"Not a scrap, and Aunt Hannah said there had never been any that she could remember; and Aunt Maria just echoed her—she always does that. You see, Aunt Hannah is an up-and-down New England woman. She looks just like herself; I mean, just like her character. Her joints move up and down or backward and forward in a plain square fashion. I don't believe she ever leaned on anything in her life, or sat in an easy-chair. But Maria is different; she is rounder and softer; she hasn't any ideas of her own; she never had any. I don't believe she would think it right or becoming to have one that differed from Aunt Hannah's, so what would be the use of having any? She is an echo, that's all.

"When mamma and I got there, of course I was all excite-ment to see the china-closet, and I had a sort of feeling that it would be the little room after all. So I ran ahead and threw open the door, crying, 'Come and see the little room.'"

"And, Roger," said Mrs. Grant, laying her hand in his, "there really was a little room there, exactly as mother had remem-bered it. There was the lounge, the peacock chintz, the green door, the shell, the morning-glory, and rose paper, *everything exactly as she had described it to me.*"

"What in the world did the sisters say about it?"

"Wait a minute and I will tell you. My mother was in the front hall still talking with Aunt Hannah. She didn't hear me at first, but I ran out there and dragged her through the front room, saying, 'The room *is* here—it is all right.'

"It seemed for a minute as if my mother would faint. She clung to me in terror. I can remember now how strained her eyes looked and how pale she was.

"I called out to Aunt Hannah and asked her when they had had the closet taken away and the little room built; for in my excitement I thought that that was what had been done.

"'That little room has always been there,' said Aunt Hannah, 'ever since the house was built.'

"'But mamma said there wasn't any little room here, only a china-closet, when she was here with papa,' said I.

"'No, there has never been any china-closet there; it has always been just as it is now,' said Aunt Hannah.

"Then mother spoke; her voice sounded weak and far off. She said, slowly, and with an effort, 'Maria, don't you remember that you told me that there had *never been any little room here?* and Hannah said so too, and then I said I must have dreamed it?'

"'No, I don't remember anything of the kind,' said Maria, without the slightest emotion. 'I don't remember you ever said anything about any china-closet. The house has never been altered; you used to play in this room when you were a child, don't you remember?'

"'I know it,' said mother, in that queer slow voice that made me feel frightened. 'Hannah, don't you remember my finding the china-closet here, with the gilt-edged china[5] on the shelves, and then *you* said that the *china-closet* had always been here?'

"'No,' said Hannah, pleasantly but unemotionally—'no, I don't think you ever asked me about any china-closet, and we haven't any gilt-edged china that I know of.'

"And that was the strangest thing about it. We never could make them remember that there had ever been any question about it. You would think they could remember how surprised mother had been before, unless she had imagined the whole thing. Oh, it was so queer! They were always pleasant about it, but they didn't seem to feel any interest or curiosity. It was always this answer: 'The house is just as it was built; there have never been any changes, so far as we know.'

"And my mother was in an agony of perplexity. How cold their gray eyes looked to me! There was no reading anything in them. It just seemed to break my mother down, this queer thing. Many times that summer, in the middle of the night, I have seen her get up and take a candle and creep softly down stairs. I could hear the steps creak under her weight. Then she would go through the front room and peer into the darkness, holding her thin hand between the candle and her eyes. She seemed to think the little room might vanish. Then she would come back to bed and toss about all night, or lie still and shiver; it used to frighten me.

"She grew pale and thin, and she had a little cough; then she did not like to be left alone. Sometimes she would make errands in order to send me to the little room for something—a book, or her fan, or her handkerchief; but she would never sit there or let me stay in there long, and sometimes she wouldn't let me go in there for days together. Oh, it was pitiful!"

"Well, don't talk any more about it, Margaret, if it makes you feel so," said Mr. Grant.

"Oh yes, I want you to know all about it, and there isn't much more—no more about the room.

"Mother never got well, and she died that autumn. She used often to sigh, and say, with a wan little laugh, 'There is one thing I am glad of, Margaret: your father knows now all about the little room.' I think she was afraid I distrusted her. Of course, in a child's way, I thought there was something queer about it, but I did not brood over it. I was too young then, and took it as a part of her illness. But, Roger, do you know, it really did affect me. I almost hate to go there after talking about it; I somehow feel as if it might, you know, be a china-closet again."

"That's an absurd idea."

"I know it; of course it can't be. I saw the room, and there isn't any china-closet there, and no gilt-edged china in the house, either."

And then she whispered: "But, Roger, you may hold my hand as you do now, if you will, when we go to look for the little room."

"And you won't mind Aunt Hannah's gray eyes?"

"I won't mind *anything*."

It was dusk when Mr. and Mrs. Grant went into the gate under the two old Lombardy poplars and walked up the narrow path to the door, where they were met by the two aunts.

Hannah gave Mrs. Grant a frigid but not unfriendly kiss; and Maria seemed for a moment to tremble on the verge of an emotion, but she glanced at Hannah, and then gave her greeting in exactly the same repressed and non-committal way.

Supper was waiting for them. On the table was the *gilt-edged china*. Mrs. Grant didn't notice it immediately, till she saw her husband smiling at her over his teacup; then she felt fidgety, and couldn't eat. She was nervous, and kept wondering what was behind her, whether it would be a little room or a closet.

After supper she offered to help about the dishes, but, mercy! she might as well have offered to help bring the seasons round; Maria and Hannah couldn't be helped.

So she and her husband went to find the little room, or closet, or whatever was to be there.

Aunt Maria followed them, carrying the lamp, which she set down, and then went back to the dish-washing.

Margaret looked at her husband. He kissed her, for she seemed troubled; and then, hand in hand, they opened the door. It opened into a *china-closet*. The shelves were neatly draped with scalloped paper; on them was the gilt-edged china, with the dishes missing that had been used at the supper, and which at that moment were being carefully washed and wiped by the two aunts.

Margaret's husband dropped her hand and looked at her. She was trembling a little, and turned to him for help, for some explanation, but in an instant she knew that something was wrong. A cloud had come between them; he was hurt; he was antagonized.

He paused for an appreciable instant, and then said, kindly enough, but in a voice that cut her deeply:

"I am glad this ridiculous thing is ended; don't let us speak of it again."

"Ended!" said she. "How ended?"

And somehow her voice sounded to her as her mother's voice had when she stood there and questioned her sisters about the little room. She seemed to have to drag her words out. She spoke slowly: "It seems to me to have only just begun in my case. It was just so with mother when she—"

"I really wish, Margaret, you would let it drop. I don't like to hear you speak of your mother in connection with it. It—" He hesitated, for was not this their wedding-day? "It doesn't seem quite the thing, quite delicate, you know, to use her name in the matter."

She saw it all now: *he didn't believe her.* She felt a chill sense of withering under his glance.

"Come," he added, "let us go out, or into the dining-room, somewhere, anywhere, only drop this nonsense."

He went out; he did not take her hand now—he was vexed, baffled, hurt. Had he not given her his sympathy, his attention, his belief—and his hand?—and she was fooling him. What did it mean?—she so truthful, so free from morbidness—a thing he hated. He walked up and down under the poplars, trying to get into the mood to go and join her in the house.

Margaret heard him go out; then she turned and shook the shelves; she reached her hand behind them and tried to push the boards away; she ran out of the house on to the north side and tried to find in the darkness, with her hands, a door, or some steps leading to one. She tore her dress on the old rose-trees, she fell and rose and stumbled, then she sat down on the ground and tried to think. What could she think—was she dreaming?

She went into the house and out into the kitchen, and begged Aunt Maria to tell her about the little room—what had become of it, when had they built the closet, when had they bought the gilt-edged china?

They went on washing dishes and drying them on the spotless towels with methodical exactness; and as they worked they said that there had never been any little room, so far as they knew; the china-closet had always been there, and the gilt-edged china had belonged to their mother, it had always been in the house.

"No, I don't remember that your mother ever asked about any little room," said Hannah. "She didn't seem very well that summer, but she never asked about any changes in the house; there hadn't ever been any changes."

There it was again: not a sign of interest, curiosity, or annoyance, not a spark of memory.

She went out to Hiram. He was telling Mr. Grant about the farm. She had meant to ask him about the room, but her lips were sealed before her husband.

Months afterwards, when time had lessened the sharpness of their feelings, they learned to speculate reasonably about the phenomenon, which Mr. Grant had accepted as something not to be scoffed away, not to be treated as a poor joke, but to be put aside as something inexplicable on any ordinary theory.

Margaret alone in her heart knew that her mother's words carried a deeper significance than she had dreamed of at the time. "One thing I am glad of, your father knows now," and she wondered if Roger or she would ever know.

Five years later they were going to Europe. The packing was done; the children were lying asleep, with their traveling things ready to be slipped on for an early start.

Roger had a foreign appointment. They were not to be back in America for some years. She had meant to go up to say good-by to her aunts; but a mother of three children intends to do a great many things that never get done. One thing she had done that very day, and as she paused for a moment between the writing of two notes that must be posted before she went to bed, she said:

"Roger, you remember Rita Lash? Well, she and Cousin Nan go up to the Adirondacks every autumn. They are clever girls, and I have intrusted to them something I want done very much."

"They are the girls to do it, then, every inch of them."

"I know it, and they are going to."

"Well?"

"Why, you see, Roger, that little room—"

"Oh—"

"Yes, I was a coward not to go myself, but I didn't find time, because I hadn't the courage."

"Oh! *that* was it, was it?"

"Yes, just that. They are going, and they will write us about it."

"Want to bet?"

"No; I only want to know."

Rita Lash and Cousin Nan planned to go to Vermont on their way to the Adirondacks. They found they would have three hours between trains, which would give them time to drive up to the Keys farm, and they could still get to the camp that night. But, at the last minute, Rita was prevented from going. Nan had to go to meet the Adirondack party, and she promised to telegraph her when she arrived at the camp. Imagine Rita's amusement when she received this message: "Safely arrived; went to the Keys farm; it is a little room."

Rita was amused, because she did not in the least think Nan had been there. She thought it was a hoax; but it put it into her mind to carry the joke further by really stopping herself when she went up, as she meant to do the next week.

She did stop over. She introduced herself to the two maiden ladies, who seemed familiar, as they had been described by Mrs. Grant.

They were, if not cordial, at least not disconcerted at her visit, and willingly showed her over the house. As they did not speak of any other stranger's having been to see them lately, she became confirmed in her belief that Nan had not been there.

In the north room she saw the roses and morning-glory paper on the wall, and also the door that should open into—what?

She asked if she might open it.

"Certainly," said Hannah; and Maria echoed, "Certainly."

She opened it, and found the china-closet. She experienced a certain relief; she at least was not under any spell. Mrs. Grant left it a china-closet; she found it the same. Good.

But she tried to induce the old sisters to remember that there had at various times been certain questions relating to a confusion as to whether the closet had always been a closet. It was no use; their stony eyes gave no sign.

Then she thought of the story of the sea-captain, and said, "Miss Keys, did you ever have a lounge covered with India chintz, with a figure of a peacock on it, given to you in Salem by a sea-captain, who brought it from India?"

"I dun'no' as I ever did," said Hannah. That was all. She thought Maria's cheeks were a little flushed, but her eyes were like a stone wall.

She went on that night to the Adirondacks. When Nan and she were alone in their room she said, "By-the-way, Nan, what did you see at the farm-house? and how did you like Maria and Hannah?"

Nan didn't mistrust that Rita had been there, and she began excitedly to tell her all about her visit. Rita could almost have believed Nan had been there if she hadn't known it was not so. She let her go on for some time, enjoying her enthusiasm, and the impressive way in which she described her opening the door and finding the "little room." Then Rita said: "Now, Nan, that is enough fibbing. I went to the farm myself on my way up yesterday, and there is *no* little room, and there *never* has been any; it is a china-closet, just as Mrs. Grant saw it last."

She was pretending to be busy unpacking her trunk, and did not look up for a moment; but as Nan did not say anything, she glanced at her over her shoulder. Nan was actually pale, and it was hard to say whether she was most angry or frightened. There was something of both in her look. And then Rita began to explain how her telegram had put her in the spirit of going up there alone. She hadn't meant to cut Nan out. She only thought—Then Nan broke in: "It isn't that; I am sure you can't think it is that. But I went myself, and you did not go; you can't have been there, for *it is a little room*."

Oh, what a night they had! They couldn't sleep. They talked and argued, and then kept still for a while, only to break out again, it was so absurd. They both maintained that they had been there, but both felt sure the other one was either crazy or obstinate beyond reason. They were wretched; it was perfectly ridiculous, two friends at odds over such a thing; but there it was—"little room," "china-closet,"—"china-closet," "little room."

The next morning Nan was tacking up some tarlatan[6] at a window to keep the midges out. Rita offered to help her, as she had done for the past ten years. Nan's "No, thanks," cut her to the heart.

"Nan," said she, "come right down from that stepladder and pack your satchel. The stage leaves in just twenty minutes. We can catch the afternoon express train, and we will go together to the farm. I am either going there or going home. You better go with me."

Nan didn't say a word. She gathered up the hammer and tacks, and was ready to start when the stage came round.

It meant for them thirty miles of staging and six hours of train, besides crossing the lake; but what of that, compared with having a lie lying round loose between them! Europe would have seemed easy to accomplish, if it would settle the question.

At the little junction in Vermont they found a farmer with a wagon full of meal-bags. They asked him if he could not take them up to the old Keys farm and bring them back in time for the return train, due in two hours.

They had planned to call it a sketching trip, so they said, "We have been there before, we are artists, and we might find some views worth taking; and we want also to make a short call upon the Misses Keys."

"Did ye calculate to paint the old *house* in the picture?"

They said it was possible they might do so. They wanted to see it, anyway.

"Waal, I guess you are too late. The *house* burnt down last night, and everything in it."

"THE NEW WOMAN"

by Barbara E. Pope,

1896

Margaret Hartwell was beautiful. Everybody admitted that. She was intelligent, industrious, and amiable. Her husband loved her and was proud of her; but he found, rather to his dismay, that the little peculiarities which had amused him in the days of his short courtship, and which had occasionally called forth a hearty laugh while on the wedding tour, were not mere girlish whims and fancies. They were the straws which indicate the true direction of the wind.

Margaret was refined and gentle. She had virtues enough for two or three women; but she was a daughter of Wyoming, and Frank Hartwell was forced to acknowledge that his lovely wife had deeply imbibed the social and political heresy of her native State. She not only believed in the emancipation of women, but she had evidently been accustomed to a full measure of freedom, which she intended still to enjoy.

It was not Frank Hartwell's desire to become the lord and master of his wife; but he did expect her to lean on him somewhat. Woman in his opinion was a very high order of being; but she was too delicately constructed, morally and physically, for general usefulness. Her fields were the home and church; and even in those sacred enclosures she needed the support and protection of him for whose happiness she was created.

Housekeeping had been started on a scale suitable to a couple in moderate circumstances, and Margaret had shown excellent judgment in the selection of their one servant, who, after furnishing the usual references, had been carefully examined as to her knowledge of housework.

"Lucinda does not belong to the ignorant class of women

who hire out before they have fitted themselves for any employment," said the young mistress to her husband, as they arose from the dinner table. "She understands cooking, washing and ironing—has learned them as a carpenter masters his trade."

"Speaking of the carpenter reminds me of the kitchen window shutters," said Frank; "has Jenkins been here?"

"He sent word that he wouldn't come before next week, so I bought the screws and hinges and hung the shutters myself."

Margaret was leaning against the sideboard. In stature she was barely medium, but her form was exquisitely molded, and she was remarkably graceful. A European might have been puzzled as to her nationality; not because of the tiny mouth with its dainty curves, nor the nose, whose contours deviated from the purely Grecian only enough to impart brightness of expression. Her complexion was brownish yellow, with skin soft and clear; she had large black eyes shaded by the longest and silkiest lashes; her hair was black and glossy as the raven tresses of the Mongolian, but finer in texture, and possessed of that much coveted quality, a slight waviness; she wore a pale cream house gown of soft material, the bodice tastefully trimmed with dark red velvet and chiffon.

"Did you say that you hung the shutters, Margaret?" asked Frank.

"Yes, I thought it unsafe to be longer without them."

"Who instructed you in carpentry?" he asked, when he had returned from an inspection of the work.

"There is a manual training department in our schools,[1] and Albert and I took a course in the various branches. We both intended to study professions, but every civilized person should know how to be handy about a house."

"Did you and Albert learn the same branches, may I ask?"

"We went through the entire department. Albert won first prize for cake-making, but I beat him in the metal shop."

"Would it not have been proper for you to confine yourselves within certain limits—the one to the feminine and the other to the masculine portion?"

"I beg your pardon, Frank. We did not regard labor as masculine and feminine. Albert is larger and stronger than I, but we both have human facilities."

"Hereafter, my dear," said Mr. Hartwell, taking one of her pretty dimpled hands in his, "you must leave the men's part to me. I don't want you to injure your health and make yourself coarse."

"The bargain was that you would practice law and I take charge of the home; but neither of us must be selfish, and each will call on the other for assistance when needed," replied Margaret, smiling sweetly.

From the dining-room the husband and wife went to the parlor, where an hour or more was spent at the piano playing and singing; then they passed into the library, and Frank read aloud while Margaret sat by his side and knitted a lace centerpiece for the table.

"How easily your fingers go through those intricate movements," said Frank, closing his book. "What is the art? Crocheting?"

"Knitting. It is very easy. Wouldn't you like to learn?" asked Margaret.

"Have you forgotten the penwiper?"[2]

He had admired a penwiper which she was making, and expressed a wish to have one like it. She gave him some of the cloth and explained the pattern, but finding that he could not even cut the parts, and failing in the attempt to teach him, she took the scissors out of his hand with a look of commiseration that caused him to be nearly convulsed with laughter.

"Never mind the penwiper. I will begin with something easy. Now look. Can't you see how I put this loop on the needle?"

"The manipulation of the needles is the stumbling block. My fingers were not fashioned for such work, my dear. They are too clumsy," said Frank, his handsome face turning red in his struggle to maintain his gravity.

"Your fingers were made for all good uses to which you may choose to put them. They lack training, that is all. Take the needles. I will show you how to use them."

To humor her he took them, but the laugh would come, and

he put the slender pieces of steel down with a shake of the head.

"Very well. You prefer, I see, to go through life with your powers of body and mind partially developed," was the gently administered rebuke.

"Come, Margaret, be reasonable," he pleaded, becoming grave. "Don't you know, my little woman, that such occupations would make me weak and effeminate?"

"Is my brother weak and effeminate?"

"Who? Albert Manning? Oh, no!"

"I can do nothing that he cannot do as well."

"It must be some magic effect of climate, then, that preserves his manhood. You can't try this sort of thing in this section of the country."

The next morning conversation turned to business for the day.

"I fear I shall grow lazy," said Margaret. "I have too much leisure."

"Don't you know how to kill time?" replied Frank. "Visit your friends. Go shopping, read, take naps. You are not to work all day long. It would wear you out."

"No danger. I shall always have my hours for rest and recreation. But I will go shopping only when I want to purchase, and will visit only when you can enjoy the pleasure with me. I have been thinking of perfecting myself in music for the purpose of giving lessons."

"There is no necessity for your teaching, but I would like to have you cultivate your talent for music."

"The professor is out of town at present. What do you intend to do at the office to-day?"

"I have a case in court at one o'clock," answered Frank, reaching for his hat.

"Don't you want a clerk?"

"The young man who is reading law with us will assist me."

"Wouldn't you rather have me come down and clerk for you?"

"What! Go into court with me?"

"Why not, Frank? Didn't I tell you that law was to be my profession, and that I worked in father's office for a year? I had been keeping house about ten months when you met me, because mother was obliged to take Jennie traveling for her health. Albert had begun the practice of medicine, and, being younger, I consented to stay at home."

"Did your father allow you to go into court?"

"I accompanied him to every trial."

"Did he confine himself that year to select cases?"

"No; he simply observed his rule not to claim innocence for those whom he believed guilty."

"The court room is seldom a fit place for a woman, Margaret," said Frank, smoothing back the hair from her broad brow.

"The details of crime and vice shock and disgust all good people, especially the young; but one cannot afford to run away from everything distasteful. Your practice is similar to father's. Don't you attend the trials?"

"You must remember that I am a man."

"But you are as pure-minded as I am, are you not?" she inquired, looking up earnestly into his face.

"I have endeavored to keep my thoughts as pure as those of my kind can be. There is a difference, you know, Margaret, in our spiritual natures."

"What caused the difference? Is it a matter of schooling?"

"Good-by, dearest."

He kissed her, as he always did when they parted.

Although, as directress of domestic affairs, Margaret had assumed control of everything pertaining to their establishment, from the orderly keeping of house and grounds to the buying of provisions and the preparation of food, Frank's taste was consulted and his comfort duly considered. If he took upon himself the performance of any of her duties she graciously accepted the aid rendered, and never failed to thank him for it.

His darning and mending—well, she repaired his garments out of compassion for his ignorance of needlework; and her tender regard for him was further manifested by the trouble she took to have his easy-chair and slippers in a convenient place when he came home tired from office or court. The money

which he earned she looked upon as joint property; and, strange
to relate, while bent upon changing many of her absurd views,
Frank could not find it in his heart to deny her free access to the
family purse. It was fortunate that she understood the value and
the proper use of dollars and cents.

There was another departure from established custom with
which Frank's chivalry prompted him to comply. When, on a
holiday, the hired girl was excused from her duties, Margaret,
in her artless way, would divide the house-work remaining to
be done, offering to her husband, because of his superior
strength, that portion which required the greater exertion.

The two members of the firm of Hartwell and Wilcox were
on the point of leaving for their respective homes one afternoon in November, when Mrs. Hartwell came in. She had
called for Frank, and was very attractive in her costume of seal
brown, with a stock collar of bright colored Dresden ribbon,
and scarlet poppies clustered against her black hair under the
brim of the stylish felt hat.[3] Her advanced ideas did not in-
clude bloomers; and she rejected the prevailing fashions only
when they interfered with health or comfort.

"Good afternoon, Mrs. Hartwell. I had the pleasure of seeing you in court this morning," said Mr. Wilcox.

"Yes. I wanted to observe your Eastern methods."

"Did you come down on your wheel, Margaret?"[4] Frank
broke in, in a rather hard tone.

"No; I remembered that yours is in the shop, so I rode on
the cars."

"I am glad you take interest in our profession, Mrs. Hartwell," said Mr. Wilcox, politely, as he mounted his bicycle at
the office door. "I hope on some future occasion to learn what
you think of law as practiced in this part of the country."

Margaret made some suitable answer, and glanced at Frank,
as if surprised by his cold manner. As he did not appear to be
inclined to talk, she too kept silence. They went home in the
street car. It was crowded, and when a feeble old man came in,
and no one offered him a seat, Margaret promptly arose and
gave him hers. Then Frank rose also, and requested her to sit

down. She was not in the least fatigued, while he appeared tired and worried; so in a charming manner she thanked him, and made known her determination to stand. Some one tittered, and Frank bit his lip and went out on the platform.

While walking from the car to their house, the Hartwells were overtaken by Mrs. Wells, a neighbor.

"I saw you painting this morning, Mrs. Hartwell, and I wanted to come over; but baby was so fretful that I couldn't get away from him," said Mrs. Wells.

"I was finishing your work," was Margaret's explanation to Frank.

He had been painting the iron railing of the front stoop; and her words meant that she had exposed herself to public gaze while engaged in unfeminine employment.

"I have an old-fashioned rocking-chair which would be lovely painted white. Would you mind showing me how to do it?" asked Mrs. Wells.

"Certainly not," answered Margaret. "Aren't you my pupil?"

"Mrs. Hartwell has taught me to harness our horse, and now I can drive without troubling anybody. You don't know how independent I feel," said Mrs. Wells to Frank.

"Is Mr. Wells pleased with your new accomplishments?" was his query.

"He used to be a dreadful fogy; but Mrs. Hartwell does things so gracefully that she has overcome his prejudices. He says imitating her will do me no harm; and what do you think he has promised us for Christmas gifts? Picks and shovels!"

The easy-chair and slippers looked very tempting in the library, where a wood fire was blazing on the tiled hearth. It was a cozy room, with rugs and cushions and shaded lamps. Books of various kinds filled the bookcases, and engravings of noted places and of historical scenes were here and there on the walls. A table, supporting a small vase of cut flowers, a lamp, and the latest periodicals, had been drawn up close to the big arm-chair; and on this table Frank Hartwell placed his evening paper, walked slowly up-stairs to the room in which his wife was removing her wraps, entered, and closed the door.

He had patiently borne with her foibles, waiting for the improvement which he hoped would be produced by change of environment. Familiarity with her surroundings, however, had only served to remove restraint; her visit to the courtroom was the last straw, and he felt it incumbent upon him to exercise a husband's authority.

He began by explaining to the young wife the difference between true and false theories; he pointed out the errors in which she had been reared; and, when he had said what should have been enough to convince her that her judgment was defective, he told her, kindly but plainly, that she must submit to his guidance.

"I regret that there is a disagreement between us," said Margaret. "Were you and I the only persons concerned, my affection for you, and my desire for peace and harmony, would cause me to yield. But even in our love for each other, we must be careful to do nothing that will retard the progress of civilization. We should not forget that the future happiness of the human race depends largely upon the physical and intellectual development of women—"

"I will make a list, after dinner, of the public places which you may visit and of those to which I cannot permit you to go. I will set down, too, what you must henceforth consider your legitimate occupations," said Frank, his face pale and determined.

"You forget, dear, that although you are four years my senior, I am twenty-three. If you have no objection, we will go to dinner. May I pin this rosebud on your coat?"

It was useless to oppose her. She clung to her tenets with a tenacity that no argument could weaken. Firm in her convictions, she went steadily on, and of course Frank could not resort to harsh measures. Despite her foibles she was a charming woman, and an affectionate one. If coldness came between them both were unhappy. So Frank eventually ceased to contend, and settled down to the enjoyment of all that was agreeable in the companionship.

In the end, this proved to be a wise course. Margaret, appreciating his forbearance, began to yield to him in small ways, and no longer made herself conspicuous in public. Little by little each left the disputed ground to advance toward a common platform on which they may one day stand in perfect harmony. Meanwhile, Frank declares he has a most accomplished wife, and Margaret declares that he is fast becoming as delightful a comrade as her brother Albert.

"SOULS BELATED"

by Edith Wharton,
1899

I

Their railway carriage had been full when the train left Bologna; but at the first station beyond Milan their only remaining companion—a courtly person who ate garlic out of a carpetbag—had left his crumb-strewn seat with a bow.

Lydia's eye regretfully followed the shiny broadcloth of his retreating back till it lost itself in the cloud of touts and cab drivers hanging about the station; then she glanced across at Gannett and caught the same regret in his look. They were both sorry to be alone.

"*Par-ten-za!*" shouted the guard.[1] The train vibrated to a sudden slamming of doors; a waiter ran along the platform with a tray of fossilized sandwiches; a belated porter flung a bundle of shawls and band-boxes into a third-class carriage; the guard snapped out a brief *Partenza!* which indicated the purely ornamental nature of his first shout; and the train swung out of the station.

The direction of the road had changed, and a shaft of sunlight struck across the dusty red velvet seats into Lydia's corner. Gannett did not notice it. He had returned to his *Revue de Paris*, and she had to rise and lower the shade of the farther window. Against the vast horizon of their leisure such incidents stood out sharply.

Having lowered the shade, Lydia sat down, leaving the length of the carriage between herself and Gannett. At length he missed her and looked up.

"I moved out of the sun," she hastily explained.

He looked at her curiously: the sun was beating on her through the shade.

"Very well," he said pleasantly; adding, "You don't mind?" as he drew a cigarette case from his pocket.

It was a refreshing touch, relieving the tension of her spirit with the suggestion that, after all, if he could *smoke*—! The relief was only momentary. Her experience of smokers was limited (her husband had disapproved of the use of tobacco) but she knew from hearsay that men sometimes smoked to get away from things; that a cigar might be the masculine equivalent of darkened windows and a headache. Gannett, after a puff or two, returned to his review.

It was just as she had foreseen; he feared to speak as much as she did. It was one of the misfortunes of their situation that they were never busy enough to necessitate, or even to justify, the postponement of unpleasant discussions. If they avoided a question it was disagreeable. They had unlimited leisure and an accumulation of mental energy to devote to any subject that presented itself; new topics were in fact at a premium. Lydia sometimes had premonitions of a famine-stricken period when there would be nothing left to talk about, and she had already caught herself doling out piecemeal what, in the first prodigality of their confidences, she would have flung to him in a breath. Their silence therefore might simply mean that they had nothing to say; but it was another disadvantage of their position that it allowed infinite opportunity for the classification of minute differences. Lydia had learned to distinguish between real and factitious silences; and under Gannett's she now detected a hum of speech to which her own thoughts made breathless answer.

How could it be otherwise, with that thing between them? She glanced up at the rack overhead. The *thing* was there, in her dressing bag, symbolically suspended over her head and his. He was thinking of it now, just as she was; they had been thinking of it in unison ever since they had entered the train. While the carriage had held other travelers they had screened her from his thoughts; but now that he and she were alone she knew exactly what was passing through his mind; she could almost hear him asking himself what he should say to her.

The thing had come that morning, brought up to her in an innocent-looking envelope with the rest of their letters, as they were leaving the hotel at Bologna. As she tore it open, she and Gannett were laughing over some ineptitude of the local guide-book—they had been driven, of late, to make the most of such incidental humors of travel. Even when she had unfolded the document she took it for some unimportant business paper sent abroad for her signature, and her eye traveled inattentively over the curly *Whereases* of the preamble until a word arrested her:—Divorce. There it stood, an impassable barrier, between her husband's name and hers.

She had been prepared for it, of course, as healthy people are said to be prepared for death, in the sense of knowing it must come without in the least expecting that it will. She had known from the first that Tillotson meant to divorce her—but what did it matter? Nothing mattered, in those first days of supreme deliverance, but the fact that she was free; and not so much (she had begun to be aware) that freedom had released her from Tillotson as that it had given her to Gannett. This discovery had not been agreeable to her self-esteem. She had preferred to think that Tillotson had himself embodied all her reasons for leaving him; and those he represented had seemed cogent enough to stand in no need of reinforcement. Yet she had not left him till she met Gannett. It was her love for Gannett that had made life with Tillotson so poor and incomplete a business. If she had never, from the first, regarded her marriage as a full canceling of her claims upon life, she had at least, for a number of years, accepted it as a provisional compensation,—she had made it "do." Existence in the commodious Tillotson mansion in Fifth Avenue—with Mrs. Tillotson senior commanding the approaches from the second-story front windows—had been reduced to a series of purely automatic acts. The moral atmosphere of the Tillotson interior was as carefully screened and curtained as the house itself:

Mrs. Tillotson senior dreaded ideas as much as a draft in her back. Prudent people liked an even temperature; and to do anything unexpected was as foolish as going out in the rain. One of the chief advantages of being rich was that one need not be exposed to unforeseen contingencies: by the use of ordinary firmness and common sense one could make sure of doing exactly the same thing every day at the same hour. These doctrines, reverentially imbibed with his mother's milk, Tillotson (a model son who had never given his parents an hour's anxiety) complacently expounded to his wife, testifying to his sense of their importance by the regularity with which he wore galoshes on damp days, his punctuality at meals, and his elaborate precautions against burglars and contagious diseases.[2] Lydia, coming from a smaller town, and entering New York life through the portals of the Tillotson mansion, had mechanically accepted this point of view as inseparable from having a front pew in church and a parterre box at the opera.[3] All the people who came to the house revolved in the same small circle of prejudices. It was the kind of society in which, after dinner, the ladies compared the exorbitant charges of their children's teachers, and agreed that, even with the new duties on French clothes, it was cheaper in the end to get everything from Worth;[4] while the husbands, over their cigars, lamented municipal corruption, and decided that the men to start a reform were those who had no private interests at stake.

To Lydia this view of life had become a matter of course, just as lumbering about in her mother-in-law's locomotion, and listening every Sunday to a fashionable Presbyterian divine the inevitable atonement for having thought oneself bored on the other six days of the week. Before she met Gannett her life had seemed merely dull; his coming made it appear like one of those dismal Cruikshank prints in which the people are all ugly and all engaged in occupations that are either vulgar or stupid.[5]

It was natural that Tillotson should be the chief sufferer from this readjustment of focus. Gannett's nearness had made her husband ridiculous, and a part of the ridicule had been reflected on herself. Her tolerance laid her open to a suspicion of obtuseness from which she must, at all costs, clear herself in Gannett's eyes.

She did not understand this until afterwards. At the time she fancied that she had merely reached the limits of endurance. In so large a charter of liberties as the mere act of leaving Tillotson seemed to confer, the small question of divorce or no divorce did not count. It was when she saw that she had left her husband only to be with Gannett that she perceived the significance of anything affecting their relations. Her husband, in casting her off, had virtually flung her at Gannett: it was thus that the world viewed it. The measure of alacrity with which Gannett would receive her would be the subject of curious speculation over afternoon tea tables and in club corners. She knew what would be said—she had heard it so often of others! The recollection bathed her in misery. The men would probably back Gannett to "do the decent thing"; but the ladies' eyebrows would emphasize the worthlessness of such enforced fidelity; and after all, they would be right. She had put herself in a position where Gannett "owed" her something; where, as a gentleman, he was bound to "stand the damage." The idea of accepting such compensation had never crossed her mind; the so-called rehabilitation of such a marriage had always seemed to her the only real disgrace. What she dreaded was the necessity of having to explain herself; of having to combat his arguments; of calculating, in spite of herself, the exact measure of insistence with which he pressed them. She knew not whether she most shrank from his insisting too much or too little. In such a case the nicest sense of proportion might be at fault; and how easily to fall into the error of taking her resistance for a test of his sincerity! Whichever way she turned, an ironical implication confronted her: she had the exasperated sense of having walked into the trap of some stupid practical joke.

Beneath all these preoccupations lurked the dread of what he was thinking. Sooner or later, of course, he would have to speak; but that, in the meantime, he should think, even for a moment, that there was any use in speaking, seemed to her simply unendurable. Her sensitiveness on this point was aggravated by another fear, as yet barely on the level of consciousness; the fear of unwillingly involving Gannett in the trammels of her dependence. To look upon him as the instrument of her liberation; to resist in herself the least tendency to a wifely taking possession of his future; had seemed to Lydia the one way of maintaining the dignity of their relation. Her view had not changed, but she was aware of a growing inability to keep her thoughts fixed on the essential point—the point of parting with Gannett. It was easy to face as long as she kept it sufficiently far off: but what was this act of mental postponement but a gradual encroachment on his future? What was needful was the courage to recognize the moment when, by some word or look, their voluntary fellowship should be transformed into a bondage the more wearing that it was based on none of those common obligations which make the most imperfect marriage in some sort a center of gravity.

When the porter, at the next station, threw the door open, Lydia drew back, making way for the hoped-for intruder; but none came, and the train took up its leisurely progress through the spring wheat fields and budding copses.[6] She now began to hope that Gannett would speak before the next station. She watched him furtively, half-disposed to return to the seat opposite his, but there was an artificiality about his absorption that restrained her. She had never before seen him read with so conspicuous an air of warding off interruption. What could he be thinking of? Why should he be afraid to speak? Or was it her answer that he dreaded?

The train paused for the passing of an express, and he put down his book and leaned out of the window. Presently he turned to her with a smile.

"There's a jolly old villa out here," he said.

His easy tone relieved her, and she smiled back at him as she crossed over to his corner.

Beyond the embankment, through the opening in a mossy wall, she caught sight of the villa, with its broken balustrades, its stagnant fountains, and the stone satyr closing the perspective of a dusky grass walk.

"How should you like to live there?" he asked as the train moved on.

"There?"

"In some such place, I mean. One might do worse, don't you think so? There must be at least two centuries of solitude under those yew trees. Shouldn't you like it?"

"I don't know," she faltered. She knew now that he meant to speak.

He lit another cigarette. "We shall have to live somewhere, you know," he said as he bent above the match.

Lydia tried to speak carelessly. "*Je n'en vois pas la nécessité!*[7] Why not live everywhere, as we have been doing?"

"But we can't travel forever, can we?"

"Oh, forever's a long word," she objected, picking up the review he had thrown aside.

"For the rest of our lives then," he said, moving nearer.

She made a slight gesture which caused his hand to slip from hers.

"Why should we make plans? I thought you agreed with me that it's pleasanter to drift."

He looked at her hesitatingly. "It's been pleasant, certainly; but I suppose I shall have to get at my work again some day. You know I haven't written a line since—all this time," he hastily amended.

She flamed with sympathy and self-reproach. "Oh, if you mean *that*—if you want to write—of course we must settle down. How stupid of me not to have thought of it sooner! Where shall we go? Where do you think you could work best? We oughtn't to lose any more time."

He hesitated again. "I had thought of a villa in these parts. It's quiet; we shouldn't be bothered. Should you like it?"

"Of course I should like it." She paused and looked away. "But I thought—I remember your telling me once that your best work had been done in a crowd—in big cities. Why should you shut yourself up in a desert?"

Gannett, for a moment, made no reply. At length he said, avoiding her eye as carefully as she avoided his: "It might be different now; I can't tell, of course, till I try. A writer ought not be dependent on his *milieu*;[8] it's a mistake to humor oneself in that way; and I thought that just at first you might prefer to be—"

She faced him. "To be what?"

"Well—quiet. I mean—"

"What do you mean by 'at first'?" she interrupted.

He paused again. "I mean after we are married."

She thrust up her chin and turned toward the window. "Thank you!" she tossed back at him.

"Lydia!" he exclaimed blankly; and she felt in every fiber of her averted person that he had made the inconceivable, the unpardonable mistake of anticipating her acquiescence.

The train rattled on and he groped for a third cigarette. Lydia remained silent.

"I haven't offended you?" he ventured at length, in the tone of a man who feels his way.

She shook her head with a sigh. "I thought you understood," she moaned. Their eyes met and she moved back to his side.

"Do you want to know how not to offend me? By taking it for granted, once for all, that you've said your say on the odious question and that I've said mine, and that we stand just where we did this morning before that—that hateful paper came to spoil everything between us!"

"To spoil everything between us? What on earth do you mean? Aren't you glad to be free?"

"I was free before."

"Not to marry me," he suggested.

"But I don't *want* to marry you!" she cried.

She saw that he turned pale. "I'm obtuse, I suppose," he said slowly. "I confess I don't see what you're driving at. Are you tired of the whole business? Or was I simply a—an excuse for getting away? Perhaps you didn't care to travel alone? Was that it? And now you want to chuck me?" His voice had grown harsh. "You owe me a straight answer, you know; don't be tender-hearted!"

Her eyes swam as she leaned to him. "Don't you see it's because I care—because I care so much? Oh, Ralph! Can't you see how it would humiliate me? Try to feel it as a woman would! Don't you see the misery of being made your wife in this way? If I'd known you as a girl—that would have been a real marriage! But now—this vulgar fraud upon society— and upon a society we despised and laughed at—this sneaking back into a position that we've voluntarily forfeited: don't you see what a cheap compromise it is? We neither of us believe in the abstract 'sacredness' of marriage; we both know that no ceremony is needed to consecrate our love for each other; what object can we have in marrying, except the secret fear of each that the other may escape, or the secret longing to work our way back gradually—oh, very gradually—into the esteem of the people whose conventional morality we have always ridi-culed and hated? And the very fact that, after a decent inter-val, these same people would come and dine with us—the women who would let me die in a gutter today because I am 'leading a life of sin'—doesn't that disgust you more than their turning their backs on us now? I can stand being cut by them, but I couldn't stand their coming to call and asking what I meant to do about visiting that unfortunate Mrs. So-and-so!"

She paused, and Gannett maintained a perplexed silence.

"You judge things too theoretically," he said at length, slowly. "Life is made up of compromises."

"The life we ran away from—yes! If we had been willing to accept them"—she flushed—"we might have gone on meeting each other at Mrs. Tillotson's dinners."

He smiled slightly. "I didn't know that we ran away to found a new system of ethics. I supposed it was because we loved each other."

"Life is complex, of course; isn't it the very recognition of that fact that separates us from the people who see it *tout d'une pièce*?[9] If *they* are right—if marriage is sacred in itself and the individual must always be sacrificed to the family— then there can be no real marriage between us, since our—our being together is a protest against the sacrifice of the individ-ual to the family." She interrupted herself with a laugh. "You'll say now that I'm giving you a lecture on sociology! Of course one acts as one can—as one must, perhaps—pulled by all sorts of invisible threads; but at least one needn't pretend, for social advantages, to subscribe to a creed that ignores the complexity of human motives—that classifies people by arbitrary signs, and puts it in everybody's reach to be on Mrs. Tillotson's visiting list. It may be necessary that the world should be ruled by conventions—but if we believed in them, why did we break through them? And if we don't believe in them, is it honest to take advantage of the protection they afford?"

Gannett hesitated. "One may believe in them or not; but as long as they do rule the world it is only by taking advantage of their protection that one can find a *modus vivendi*."[10]

"Do outlaws need a *modus vivendi*?"

He looked at her hopelessly. Nothing is more perplexing to man than the mental process of a woman who reasons her emotions.

She thought she had scored a point and followed it up passionately. "You do understand, don't you? You see how the very thought of the thing humiliates me! We are together today because we choose to be—don't let us look any farther than that!" She caught his hands. "*Promise* me you'll never speak of it again; promise me you'll never *think* of it even," she implored, with a tearful prodigality of italics.

Through what followed—his protests, his arguments, his final unconvinced submission to her wishes—she had a sense of his but half-discerning all that, for her, had made the moment so tumultuous. They had reached that memorable point in every heart-history when, for the first time, the man seems obtuse and the woman irrational. It was the abundance of his intentions that consoled her, on reflection, for what they lacked in quality. After all, it would have been worse, incalculably worse, to have detected any overreadiness to understand her.

II

When the train at nightfall brought them to their journey's end at the edge of one of the lakes, Lydia was glad that they were not, as usual, to pass from one solitude to another. Their wanderings during the year had indeed been like the flight of the outlaws: through Sicily, Dalmatia, Transylvania, and Southern Italy they had persisted in their tacit avoidance of their kind. Isolation, at first, had deepened the flavor of their happiness, as night intensifies the scent of certain flowers; but in the new phase on which they were entering, Lydia's chief wish was that they should be less abnormally exposed to the action of each other's thoughts.

She shrank, nevertheless, as the brightly-looming bulk of the fashionable Anglo-American hotel on the water's brink began to radiate toward their advancing boat its vivid suggestion of social order, visitors' lists, Church services, and the bland inquisition of the *table-d'hote*.[11] The mere fact that in a moment or two she must take her place on the hotel register as Mrs. Gannett seemed to weaken the springs of her resistance.

They had meant to stay for a night only, on their way to a lofty village among the glaciers of Monte Rosa; but after the first plunge into publicity, when they entered the dining room, Lydia felt the relief of being lost in a crowd, of ceasing for a moment to be the center of Gannett's scrutiny; and in his face she caught the reflection of her feeling. After dinner, when she went upstairs, he strolled into the smoking room, and an hour or two later, sitting in the darkness of her window, she heard his voice below and saw him walking up and down the terrace with a companion cigar at his side. When he came he told her he had been talking to the hotel chaplain—a very good sort of fellow.

"Queer little microcosms, these hotels! Most of these people live here all summer and then migrate to Italy or the Riviera. The English are the only people who can lead that kind of life with dignity—those soft-voiced old ladies in Shetland shawls somehow carry the British Empire under their caps. *Civis Romanus sum.*[12] It's a curious study—there might be some good things to work up here."

He stood before her with the vivid preoccupied stare of the novelist on the trail of a "subject." With a relief that was half painful she noticed that, for the first time since they had been together, he was hardly aware of her presence.

"Do you think you could write here?"

"Here? I don't know." His stare dropped. "After being out of things so long one's first impressions are bound to be tremendously vivid, you know. I see a dozen threads already that one might follow—"

He broke off with a touch of embarrassment.

"Then follow them. We'll stay," she said with sudden decision.

"Stay here?" He glanced at her in surprise, and then, walking to the window, looked out upon the dusky slumber of the garden.

"Why not?" she said at length, in a tone of veiled irritation.

"The place is full of old cats in caps who gossip with the chaplain. Shall you like—I mean, it would be different if—"

She flamed up.

"Do you suppose I care? It's none of their business."

"Of course not; but you won't get them to think so."

"They may think what they please."

He looked at her doubtfully.

"It's for you to decide."

"We'll stay," she repeated.

Gannett, before they met, had made himself known as a successful writer of short stories and of a novel which had achieved the distinction of being widely discussed. The reviewers called him "promising," and Lydia now accused herself of having too long interfered with the fulfillment of his promise. There was a special irony in the fact, since his passionate assurance that only the stimulus of her companionship could bring out his latent faculty had almost given the dignity of a "vocation" to her course: there had been moments when she had felt unable to assume, before posterity, the responsibility of thwarting his career. And, after all, he had not written a line since they had been together: his first desire to write had come from renewed contact with the world! Was it all a mistake then? Must the most intelligent choice work more disastrously than the blundering combinations of chance? Or was there a still more humiliating answer to her perplexities? His sudden impulse of activity so exactly coincided with her own wish to withdraw, for a time, from the range of his observation, that she wondered if he too were not seeking sanctuary from intolerable problems.

"You must begin tomorrow!" she cried, hiding a tremor under the laugh with which she added, "I wonder if there's any ink in the inkstand?"

Whatever else they had at the Hotel Bellosguardo, they had, as Miss Pinsent said, "a certain tone." It was to Lady Susan Condit that they owed this inestimable benefit; an advantage ranking in Miss Pinsent's opinion above even the lawn tennis courts and the resident chaplain. It was the fact of Lady Susan's annual visit that made the hotel what it was. Miss Pinsent was certainly the last to underrate such a privilege:—"It's so important, my dear, forming as we do a little family, that there should be some one to give *the tone*; and no one could do it better than Lady Susan—an earl's daughter and a person of such determination. Dear Mrs. Ainger now—who really *ought*, you know, when Lady Susan's away—absolutely refuses to assert herself." Miss Pinsent sniffed derisively. "A bishop's niece!—my dear, I saw her once actually give in to some South American—and before us all. She gave up her seat at table to oblige them—such a lack of dignity! Lady Susan spoke to her very plainly about it afterwards."

Miss Pinsent glanced across the lake and adjusted her auburn front.[13]

"But of course I don't deny that the stand Lady Susan takes is not always easy to live up to—for the rest of us, I mean. Monsieur Grossart, our good proprietor, finds it trying at times, I know—he has said as much, privately, to Mrs. Ainger and me. After all, the poor man is not to blame for wanting to fill his hotel, is he? And Lady Susan is so difficult—so very difficult—about new people. One might almost say that she disapproves of them beforehand, on principle. And yet she's had warnings—she very nearly made a dreadful mistake once with the Duchess of Levens, who dyed her hair and—well, swore and smoked. One would have thought that might have been a lesson to Lady Susan." Miss Pinsent resumed her knitting with a sigh. "There are exceptions, of course. She took at once to you and Mr. Gannett—it was quite remarkable, really. Oh, I don't mean that either—of course not! It was perfectly natural—we *all* thought you so charming and interesting from the first day—we knew at once that Mr. Gannett was intellectual, by the magazines you took in; but you know what I mean. Lady Susan is so very—well, I won't say prejudiced, as Mrs. Ainger does—but so prepared *not* to like new people, that her taking to you in that way was a surprise to us all, I confess."

Miss Pinsent sent a significant glance down the long laurustinus alley from the other end of which two people—a lady and a gentleman—were strolling toward them through the smiling neglect of the garden.

"In this case, of course, it's very different; that I'm willing to admit. Their looks are against them; but, as Mrs. Ainger says, one can't exactly tell them so."

"She's very handsome," Lydia ventured, with her eyes on the lady, who showed, under the dome of a vivid sunshade, the hourglass figure and superlative coloring of a Christmas chromo.[14]

"That's the worst of it. She's too handsome."

"Well, after all, she can't help that."

"Other people manage to," said Miss Pinsent skeptically.

"But isn't it rather unfair of Lady Susan—considering that nothing is known about them?"

"But, my dear, that's the very thing that's against them. It's infinitely worse than any actual knowledge."

Lydia mentally agreed that, in the case of Mrs. Linton, it possibly might be.

"I wonder why they came here?" she mused.

"That's against them too. It's always a bad sign when loud people come to a quiet place. And they've brought van-loads of boxes—her maid told Mrs. Ainger's that they meant to stop indefinitely."

"And Lady Susan actually turned her back on her in the *salon*?"

"My dear, she said it was for our sakes; that makes it so unanswerable! But poor Grossart is in a way! The Lintons have taken his most expressive *suite*, you know—the yellow damask drawing room above the portico—and they have champagne with every meal!"

They were silent as Mr. and Mrs. Linton sauntered by; the lady with tempestuous brows and challenging chin; the gentleman, a blond stripling, trailing after her, head downward, like a reluctant child dragged by his nurse.

"What does your husband think of them, my dear?" Miss Pinsent whispered as they passed out of earshot.

Lydia stooped to pick a violet in the border.

"He hasn't told me."

"Of your speaking to them, I mean. Would he approve of that? I know how very particular nice Americans are. I think your action might make a difference; it would certainly carry weight with Lady Susan."

"Dear Miss Pinsent, you flatter me!"

Lydia rose and gathered up her book and sunshade.

"Well, if you're asked for an opinion—if Lady Susan asks you for one—I think you ought to be prepared," Miss Pinsent admonished her as she moved away.

III

Lady Susan held her own. She ignored the Lintons, and her little family, as Miss Pinsent phrased it, followed suit. Even Mrs. Ainger agreed that it was obligatory. If Lady Susan owed it to the others not to speak to the Lintons, the others clearly owed it to Lady Susan to back her up. It was generally found expedient, at the Hotel Bellosguardo, to adopt this form of reasoning.

Whatever effect this combined action may have had upon the Lintons, it did not at least have that of driving them away. Monsieur Grossart, after a few days of suspense, had the satisfaction of seeing them settle down in his yellow damask *premier*[15] with what looked like a permanent installation of palm-trees and silk sofa-cushions, and a gratifying continuance in the consumption of champagne. Mrs. Linton trailed her Doucet[16] draperies up and down the garden with the same challenging air, while her husband, smoking innumerable cigarettes, dragged himself dejectedly in her wake; but neither of them, after the first encounter with Lady Susan, made any attempt to extend their acquaintance. They simply ignored their ignorers. As Miss Pinsent resentfully observed, they behaved exactly as though the hotel were empty.

It was therefore a matter of surprise, as well as of displeasure, to Lydia, to find, on glancing up one day from her seat in the garden, that the shadow which had fallen across her book was that of the enigmatic Mrs. Linton.

"I want to speak to you," that lady said, in a rich hard voice that seemed the audible expression of her gown and her complexion.

Lydia started. She certainly did not want to speak to Mrs. Linton.

"Shall I sit down here?" the latter continued, fixing her intensely-shaded eyes on Lydia's face, "or are you afraid of being seen with me?"

"Afraid?" Lydia colored. "Sit down, please. What is it that you wish to say?"

Mrs. Linton, with a smile, drew up a garden-chair and crossed one open-work ankle above the other.

"I want you to tell me what my husband said to your husband last night."

Lydia turned pale.

"My husband—to yours?" she faltered, staring at the other.

"Didn't you know they were closeted together for hours in the smoking-room after you went upstairs? My man didn't get to bed until nearly two o'clock and when he did I couldn't get a word out of him. When he wants to be aggravating I'll back him against anybody living!" Her teeth and eyes flashed persuasively upon Lydia. "But you'll tell me what they were talking about, won't you? I know I can trust you—you look so awfully kind. And it's for his own good. He's such a precious donkey and I'm so afraid he's got into some beastly scrape or other. If he'd only trust his own old woman! But they're always writing to him and setting him against me. And I've got nobody to turn to." She laid her hand on Lydia's with a rattle of bracelets. "You'll help me, won't you?"

Lydia drew back from the smiling fierceness of her brows.

"I'm sorry—but I don't think I understand. My husband has said nothing to me of—of yours."

The great black crescents above Mrs. Linton's eyes met angrily.

"I say—is that true?" she demanded.

Lydia rose from her seat.

"Oh, look here, I didn't mean that, you know—you mustn't take one up so! Can't you see how rattled I am?"

Lydia saw that, in fact, her beautiful mouth was quivering beneath softened eyes.

"I'm beside myself!" the splendid creature wailed, dropping into her seat.

"I'm so sorry," Lydia repeated, forcing herself to speak kindly; "but how can I help you?"

Mrs. Linton raised her head sharply.

"By finding out—there's a darling!"

"Finding what out?"

"What Trevenna told him."

"Trevenna—?" Lydia echoed in bewilderment.

Mrs. Linton clapped her hand to her mouth.

"Oh, Lord—there, it's out! What a fool I am! But I supposed of course you knew; I supposed everybody knew." She dried her eyes and bridled. "Didn't you know that he's Lord Trevenna? I'm Mrs. Cope."

Lydia recognized the names. They had figured in a flamboyant elopement which had thrilled fashionable London some six months earlier.

"Now you see how it is—you understand, don't you?" Mrs. Cope continued on a note of appeal. "I knew you would—that's the reason I came to you. I suppose *he* felt the same thing about your husband; he's not spoken to another soul in the place." Her face grew anxious again. "He's awfully sensitive, generally—he feels our position, he says—as if it wasn't *my* place to feel that! But when he does get talking there's no knowing what he'll say. I know he's been brooding over something lately, and I *must* find out what it is—it's to his interest that I should. I always tell him that I think only of his interest; if he'd only trust me! But he's been so odd lately—I can't think what he's plotting. You will help me, dear?"

Lydia, who had remained standing, looked away uncomfortably.

"If you mean by finding out what Lord Trevenna has told my husband, I'm afraid it's impossible."

"Why impossible?"

"Because I infer that it was told in confidence."

Mrs. Cope stared incredulously.

"Well, what of that? Your husband looks such a dear—any one can see he's awfully gone on you. What's to prevent your getting it out of him?"

Lydia flushed.

"I'm not a spy!" she exclaimed.

"A spy—a spy? How dare you?" Mrs. Cope flamed out. "Oh, I don't mean that either! Don't be angry with me—I'm so miserable." She essayed a softer note. "Do you call that spying—for one woman to help out another? I do need help so dreadfully! I'm at my wits' end with Trevenna, I am indeed. He's such a boy—a mere baby, you know; he's only two-and-twenty." She dropped her orbed lids. "He's younger than me—only fancy, a few months younger. I tell him he ought to listen to me as if I was his mother, oughtn't he now? But he won't, he won't! All his people are at him, you see—oh, I know *their* little game! Trying to get him away from me before I can get my divorce—that's what they're up to. At first he wouldn't listen to them; he used to toss their letters over to me to read; but now he reads them himself, and answers 'em too, I fancy; he's always shut up in his room, writing. If I only knew what his plan is I could stop him fast enough—he's such a simpleton. But he's dreadfully deep too—at times I can't make him out. But I know he's told your husband everything—I knew that last night the minute I laid eyes on him. And I *must* find out—you must help me—I've got no one else to turn to!"

She caught Lydia's fingers in a stormy pressure.

"Say you'll help me—you and your husband."

Lydia tried to free herself.

"What you ask is impossible; you must see that it is. No one could interfere in—in the way you ask."

Mrs. Cope's clutch tightened.

"You won't, then? You won't?"

"Certainly not. Let me go, please."

Mrs. Cope released her with a laugh.

"Oh, go by all means—pray don't let me detain you! Shall you go and tell Lady Susan Condit that there's a pair of us—or shall I save you the trouble of enlightening her?"

Lydia stood still in the middle of the path, seeing her antagonist through a mist of terror. Mrs. Cope was still laughing.

"Oh, I'm not spiteful by nature, my dear; but you're a little more than flesh and blood can stand! It's impossible, is it? Let you go, indeed! You're too good to be mixed up in my affairs, are you? Why, you little fool, the first day I laid eyes on you I saw that you and I were both in the same box—that's the reason I spoke to you."

She stepped nearer, her smile dilating on Lydia like a lamp through a fog.

"You can take your choice, you know; I always play fair. If you'll tell I'll promise not to. Now then, which is it to be?"

Lydia, involuntarily, had begun to move away from the pelting storm of words; but at this she turned and sat down again.

"You may go," she said simply. "I shall stay here."

IV

She stayed there for a long time, in the hypnotized contemplation, not of Mrs. Cope's present, but of her own past. Gannett, early that morning, had gone off on a long walk—he had fallen into the habit of taking these mountain-tramps with various fellow lodgers; but even had he been within reach she could not have gone to him just then. She had to deal with herself first. She was surprised to find how, in the last months, she had lost the habit of introspection. Since their coming to the Hotel Bellosguardo she and Gannett had tacitly avoided themselves and each other.

She was aroused by the whistle of the three o'clock steamboat as it neared the landing just beyond the hotel gates. Three o'clock! Then Gannett would soon be back—he had told her to expect him before four. She rose hurriedly, her face averted from the inquisitorial façade of the hotel. She could not see him just yet; she could not go indoors. She slipped through one of the overgrown garden-alleys and climbed a steep path to the hills.

It was dark when she opened their sitting-room door. Gannett was sitting on the window-ledge smoking a cigarette. Cigarettes were now his chief resource: he had not written a line during the two months they had spent at the Hotel Bellosguardo. In that respect, it had turned out not to be the right *milieu* after all.

He started up at Lydia's entrance.

"Where have you been? I was getting anxious."

She sat down in a chair near the door.

"Up the mountain," she said wearily.

"Alone?"

"Yes."

Gannett threw away his cigarette: the sound of her voice made him want to see her face.

"Shall we have a little light?" he suggested.

She made no answer and he lifted the globe from the lamp and put a match to the wick. Then he looked at her.

"Anything wrong? You look done up."

She sat glancing vaguely about the little sitting room, dimly lit by the pallid-globed lamp, which left in twilight the outlines of the furniture, of his writing-table heaped with books and papers, of the tea roses and jasmine drooping on the mantel-piece. How like home it had all grown—how like home!

"Lydia, what is wrong?" he repeated.

She moved away from him, feeling for her hatpins and turning to lay her hat and sunshade on the table.

Suddenly she said: "That woman has been talking to me."
Gannett stared.

"That woman? What woman?"

"Mrs. Linton—Mrs. Cope."

He gave a start of annoyance, still, as she perceived, not grasping the full import of her words.

"The deuce! She told you—?"

"She told me everything."

Gannett looked at her anxiously.

"What impudence! I'm so sorry that you should have been exposed to this, dear."

"Exposed!" Lydia laughed.

Gannett's brow clouded and they looked away from each other.

"Do you know *why* she told me? She had the best of reasons. The first time she laid eyes on me she saw that we were both in the same box."

"Lydia!"

"So it was natural, of course, that she should turn to me in a difficulty."

"What difficulty?"

"It seems she has reason to think that Lord Trevenna's people are trying to get him away from her before she gets her divorce—"

"Well?"

"And she fancied he had been consulting with you last night as to—as to the best way of escaping from her."

Gannett stood up with an angry forehead.

"Well—what concern of yours was all this dirty business? Why should she go to you?"

"Don't you see? It's so simple. I was to wheedle his secret out of you."

"To oblige that woman?"

"Yes; or, if I was unwilling to oblige her, then to protect myself."

"To protect yourself? Against whom?"

"Against her telling everyone in the hotel that she and I are in the same box."

"She threatened that?"

"She left me the choice of telling it myself or of doing it for me."

"The beast!"

There was a long silence. Lydia had seated herself on the sofa, beyond the radius of the lamp, and he leaned against the window. His next question surprised her.

"When did this happen? At what time, I mean?"

She looked at him vaguely.

"I don't know—after luncheon, I think. Yes, I remember; it must have been at about three o'clock."

He stepped into the middle of the room and as he approached the light she saw that his brow had cleared.

"Why do you ask?" she said.

"Because when I came in, at about half-past three, the mail was just being distributed, and Mrs. Cope was waiting as usual to pounce on her letters; you know she was always watching for the postman. She was standing so close to me that I couldn't help seeing a big official-looking envelope that was handed to her. She tore it open, gave one look at the inside, and rushed off upstairs like a whirlwind, with the director shouting after her that she had left all her other letters behind. I don't believe she ever thought of you again after that paper was put into her hand."

"Why?"

"Because she was too busy. I was sitting in the window, watching for you, when the five o'clock boat left, and who should go on board, bag and baggage, valet and maid, dressing bags and poodle, but Mrs. Cope and Trevenna. Just an hour and a half to pack up in! And you should have seen her when they started. She was radiant—shaking hands with everybody— waving her handkerchief from the deck—distributing bows and smiles like an empress. If ever a woman got what she wanted just in the nick of time that woman did. She'll be Lady Trevenna within a week, I'll wager."

"You think she has her divorce?"

"I'm sure of it. And she must have got it just after her talk with you."

Lydia was silent.

At length she said, with a kind of reluctance, "She was horribly angry when she left me. It wouldn't have taken long to tell Lady Susan Condit."

"Lady Susan Condit has not been told."

"How do you know?"

"Because when I went downstairs half an hour ago I met Lady Susan on the way—"

He stopped, half smiling.

"Well?"

"And she stopped to ask if I thought you would act as patroness to a charity concert she is getting up."

In spite of themselves they both broke into a laugh. Lydia's ended in sobs and she sank down with her face hidden. Gannett bent over her, seeking her hands.

"That vile woman—I ought to have warned you to keep away from her; I can't forgive myself! But he spoke to me in confidence; and I never dreamed—well, it's all over now."

Lydia lifted her head.

"Not for me. It's only just beginning."

"What do you mean?"

She put him gently aside and moved in her turn to the window. Then she went on, with her face turned toward the shimmering blackness of the lake, "You see of course that it might happen again at any moment."

"What?"

"This—this risk of being found out. And we could hardly count again on such a lucky combination of chances, could we?"

He sat down with a groan.

Still keeping her face toward the darkness, she said, "I want you to go and tell Lady Susan—and the others."

Gannett, who had moved towards her, paused a few feet off.

"Why do you wish me to do this?" he said at length, with less surprise in his voice than she had been prepared for.

"Because I've behaved basely, abominably, since we came here: letting these people believe we were married—lying with every breath I drew—"

"Yes, I've felt that too," Gannett exclaimed with sudden energy.

The words shook her like a tempest: all her thoughts seemed to fall about her in ruins.

"You—you've felt so?"

"Of course I have." He spoke with low-voiced vehemence. "Do you suppose I like playing the sneak any better than you do? It's damnable."

He had dropped on the arm of a chair, and they stared at each other like blind people who suddenly see.

"But you have liked it here," she faltered.

"Oh, I've liked it—I've liked it." He moved impatiently. "Haven't you?"

"Yes," she burst out; "that's the worst of it—that's what I can't bear. I fancied it was for your sake that I insisted on staying—because you thought you could write here; and perhaps just at first that really was the reason. But afterwards I wanted to stay myself—I loved it." She broke into a laugh. "Oh, do you see the full derision of it? These people—the very prototypes of the bores you took me away from, with the same fenced-in view of life, the same keep-off-the-grass morality, the same little cautious virtues and the same little frightened vices—well, I've clung to them, I've delighted in them, I've done my best to please them. I've toadied Lady Susan, I've gossiped with Miss Pinsent, I've pretended to be shocked with Mrs. Ainger. Respectability! It was the one thing in life that I was sure I didn't care about, and it's grown so precious to me that I've stolen it because I couldn't get it any other way."

She moved across the room and returned to his side with another laugh.

"I who used to fancy myself unconventional! I must have been born with a card-case in my hand.[17] You should have seen me with that poor woman in the garden. She came to me for help, poor creature, because she fancied that, having 'sinned,' as they call it, I might feel some pity for others who had been tempted in the same way. Not I! She didn't know me. Lady Susan would have been kinder, because Lady Susan wouldn't have been afraid. I hated the woman—my one thought was not to be seen with her—I could have killed her for guessing my secret. The one thing that mattered to me at that moment was my standing with Lady Susan!"

Gannett did not speak.

"And you—you've felt it too!" she broke out accusingly. "You've enjoyed being with these people as much as I have; you've let the chaplain talk to you by the hour about 'The Reign of Law' and Professor Drummond.[18] When they asked you to hand the plate in church I was watching you—*you wanted to accept.*"

She stepped close, laying her hand on his arm.

"Do you know, I begin to see what marriage is for. It's to keep people away from each other. Sometimes I think that two people who love each other can be saved from madness only by the things that come between them—children, duties, visits, bores, relations—the things that protect married people from each other. We've been too close together—that has been our sin. We've seen the nakedness of each other's souls."

She sank again on the sofa, hiding her face in her hands.

Gannett stood above her perplexedly: he felt as though she were being swept away by some implacable current while he stood helpless on its bank.

At length he said, "Lydia, don't think me a brute—but don't you see yourself that it won't do?"

"Yes, I see it won't do," she said without raising her head.

His face cleared.

"Then we'll go tomorrow."

"Go—where?"

"To Paris; to be married."

For a long time she made no answer; then she asked slowly, "Would they have us here if we were married?"

"Have us here?"

"I mean Lady Susan—and the others."

"Have us here? Of course they would."

"Not if they knew—at least, not unless they could pretend not to know."

He made an impatient gesture.

"We shouldn't come back here, of course; and other people needn't know—no one need know."

She sighed. "Then it's only another form of deception and a meaner one. Don't you see that?"

"I see that we're not accountable to any Lady Susans on earth!"

"Then why are you ashamed of what we are doing here?"

"Because I'm sick of pretending that you're my wife when you're not—when you won't be."

She looked at him sadly.

"If I were your wife you'd have to go on pretending. You'd have to pretend that I'd never been—anything else. And our friends would have to pretend that they believed what you pretended."

Gannett pulled off the sofa-tassel and flung it away.

"You're impossible," he groaned.

"It's not I—it's our being together that's impossible. I only want you to see that marriage won't help it."

"What will help it then?"

She raised her head.

"My leaving you."

"Your leaving me?" He sat motionless, staring at the tassel which lay at the other end of the room. At length some impulse of retaliation for the pain she was inflicting made him say deliberately:

"And where would you go if you left me?"

"Oh!" she cried.

He was at her side in an instant.

"Lydia—Lydia—you know I didn't mean it; I couldn't mean it! But you've driven me out of my senses; I don't know what I'm saying. Can't you get out of this labyrinth of self-torture? It's destroying us both."

"That's why I must leave you."

"How easily you say it!" He drew her hands down and made her face him. "You're very scrupulous about yourself—and others. But have you thought of me? You have no right to leave me unless you've ceased to care—"

"It's because I care—"

"Then I have a right to be heard. If you love me you can't leave me."

Her eyes defied him.

"Why not?"

He dropped her hands and rose from her side.

"Can you?" he said sadly.

The hour was late and the lamp flickered and sank. She stood up with a shiver and turned toward the door of her room.

V

At daylight a sound in Lydia's room woke Gannett from a troubled sleep. He sat up and listened. She was moving about softly, as though fearful of disturbing him. He heard her push back one of the creaking shutters; then there was a moment's silence, which seemed to indicate that she was waiting to see if the noise had roused him.

Presently she began to move again. She had spent a sleepless night, probably, and was dressing to go down to the garden for a breath of air. Gannett rose also; but some undefinable instinct made his movements as cautious as hers. He stole to his window and looked out through the slats of the shutter.

It had rained in the night and the dawn was gray and lifeless. The cloud-muffled hills across the lake were reflected in its surface as in a tarnished mirror. In the garden, the birds were beginning to shake the drops from the motionless laurustinus-boughs.

An immense pity for Lydia filled Gannett's soul. Her seeming intellectual independence had blinded him for a time to the feminine cast of her mind. He had never thought of her as a woman who wept and clung: there was a lucidity in her intuitions that made them appear to be the result of reasoning. Now he saw the cruelty he had committed in detaching her from the normal conditions of life; he felt, too, the insight with which she had hit upon the real cause of their suffering. Their life was "impossible," as she had said—and its worst penalty was that it had made any other life impossible for them. Even had his love lessened, he was bound to her now by a hundred

ties of pity and self-reproach; and she, poor child, must turn
back to him as Latude returned to his cell . . .[19]

A new sound startled him: it was the stealthy closing of Lydia's door. He crept to his own and heard her footsteps passing
down the corridor. Then he went back to the window and
looked out.

A minute or two later he saw her go down the steps of the
porch and enter the garden. From his post of observation her
face was invisible, but something about her appearance struck
him. She wore a long traveling cloak and under its folds he detected the outline of a bag or bundle. He drew a deep breath
and stood watching her.

She walked quickly down the laurustinus alley toward the
gate; there she paused a moment, glancing about the little shady
square. The stone benches under the trees were empty, and she
seemed to gather resolution from the solitude about her, for
she crossed the square to the steam-boat landing, and he saw
her pause before the ticket office at the head of the wharf. Now
she was buying her ticket. Gannett turned his head a moment
to look at the clock: the boat was due in five minutes. He had
time to jump into his clothes and overtake her—

He made no attempt to move; an obscure reluctance restrained him. If any thought emerged from the tumult of his
sensations, it was that he must let her go if she wished it. He
had spoken last night of his rights: what were they? At the last
issue, he and she were two separate beings, not made one by
the miracle of common forbearances, duties, abnegations, but
bound together in a *noyade* of passion that left them resisting
yet clinging as they went down.[20]

After buying her ticket, Lydia had stood for a moment looking out across the lake; then he saw her seat herself on one of
the benches near the landing. He and she, at that moment,
were both listening for the same sound: the whistle of the boat
as it rounded the nearest promontory. Gannett turned again to
glance at the clock: the boat was due now.

Where would she go? What would her life be when she had
left him? She had no near relations and few friends. There was
money enough . . . but she asked so much of life, in ways so

complex and immaterial. He thought of her as walking bare-footed through a stony waste. No one would understand her—no one would pity her—and he, who did both, was powerless to come to her aid . . .

He saw that she had risen from the bench and walked toward the edge of the lake. She stood looking in the direction from which the steamboat was to come; then she turned to the ticket office, doubtless to ask the cause of the delay. After that she went back to the bench and sat down with bent head. What was she thinking of?

The whistle sounded; she started up, and Gannett involuntarily made a movement toward the door. But he turned back and continued to watch her. She stood motionless, her eyes on the trail of smoke that preceded the appearance of the boat. Then the little craft rounded the point, a dead-white object on the leaden water: a minute later it was puffing and backing at the wharf.

The few passengers who were waiting—two or three peasants and a snuffy priest—were clustered near the ticket-office. Lydia stood apart under the trees.

The boat lay alongside now; the gang-plank was run out and the peasants went on board with their baskets of vegetables, followed by the priest. Still Lydia did not move. A bell began to ring querulously; there was a shriek of steam, and someone must have called to her that she would be late, for she started forward, as though in answer to a summons. She moved waveringly, and at the edge of the wharf she paused. Gannett saw a sailor beckon to her; the bell rang again and she stepped upon the gang-plank.

Halfway down the short incline to the deck she stopped again; then she turned and ran back to the land. The gang-plank was drawn in, the bell ceased to ring, and the boat backed out into the lake. Lydia, with slow steps, was walking toward the garden . . .

As she approached the hotel she looked up furtively and Gannett drew back into the room. He sat down beside a table; a Bradshaw lay at his elbow, and mechanically, without knowing what he did, he began looking out the trains to Paris . . . [21]

"MRS. SPRING FRAGRANCE"

by Sui Sin Far,

1912

I

When Mrs. Spring Fragrance first arrived in Seattle, she was unacquainted with even one word of the American language. Five years later her husband, speaking of her, said: "There are no more American words for her learning." And everyone who knew Mrs. Spring Fragrance agreed with Mr. Spring Fragrance.

Mr. Spring Fragrance, whose business name was Sing Yook, was a young curio merchant.[1] Though conservatively Chinese in many respects, he was at the same time what is called by the Westerners, "Americanized." Mrs. Spring Fragrance was even more "Americanized."

Next door to the Spring Fragrances lived the Chin Yuens. Mrs. Chin Yuen was much older than Mrs. Spring Fragrance; but she had a daughter of eighteen with whom Mrs. Spring Fragrance was on terms of great friendship. The daughter was a pretty girl whose Chinese name was Mai Gwi Far (a rose) and whose American name was Laura. Nearly everybody called her Laura, even her parents and Chinese friends. Laura had a sweetheart, a youth named Kai Tzu. Kai Tzu, who was American-born, and as ruddy and stalwart as any young Westerner, was noted amongst baseball players as one of the finest pitchers on the Coast. He could also sing, "Drink to me only with thine eyes," to Laura's piano accompaniment.

Now the only person who knew that Kai Tzu loved Laura and that Laura loved Kai Tzu, was Mrs. Spring Fragrance. The reason for this was that, although the Chin Yuen parents lived in a house furnished in American style, and wore American clothes, yet they religiously observed many Chinese customs, and their ideals of life were the ideals of their Chinese forefathers. Therefore, they had betrothed their daughter, Laura, at the age of fifteen, to the eldest son of the Chinese Government school-teacher in San Francisco. The time for the consummation of the betrothal was approaching.

Laura was with Mrs. Spring Fragrance and Mrs. Spring Fragrance was trying to cheer her.

"I had such a pretty walk today," said she. "I crossed the banks above the beach and came back by the long road. In the green grass the daffodils were blowing, in the cottage gardens the currant bushes were flowering, and in the air was the perfume of the wallflower. I wished, Laura, that you were with me."

Laura burst into tears. "That is the walk," she sobbed, "Kai Tzu and I so love; but never, ah, never, can we take it together again."

"Now, Little Sister," comforted Mrs. Spring Fragrance, "you really must not grieve like that. Is there not a beautiful American poem written by a noble American named Tennyson, which says:

> "'Tis better to have loved and lost,
>   Than never to have loved at all?"[2]

Mrs. Spring Fragrance was unaware that Mr. Spring Fragrance, having returned from the city, tired with the day's business, had thrown himself down on the bamboo settee on the veranda, and that although his eyes were engaged in scanning the pages of the *Chinese World*, his ears could not help receiving the words which were borne to him through the open window.[3]

> "'Tis better to have loved and lost,
>   Than never to have loved at all,"

repeated Mr. Spring Fragrance. Not wishing to hear more of the secret talk of women, he arose and sauntered around the veranda to the other side of the house. Two pigeons circled around his head. He felt in his pocket for a li-chi which he usually carried for their pecking.[4] His fingers touched a little box. It contained a jadestone pendant, which Mrs. Spring Fragrance had particularly admired the last time she was down town. It was the fifth anniversary of Mr. and Mrs. Spring Fragrance's wedding day.

Mr. Spring Fragrance pressed the little box down into the depths of his pocket.

A young man came out of the back door of the house at Mr. Spring Fragrance's left. The Chin Yuen house was at his right.

"Good evening," said the young man. "Good evening," returned Mr. Spring Fragrance. He stepped down from his porch and went and leaned over the railing which separated this yard from the yard in which stood the young man.

"Will you please tell me," said Mr. Spring Fragrance, "the meaning of two lines of an American verse which I have heard?"

"Certainly," returned the young man with a genial smile. He was a star student at the University of Washington, and had not the slightest doubt that he could explain the meaning of all things in the universe.

"Well," said Mr. Spring Fragrance, "it is this:

> "'Tis better to have loved and lost,
> Than never to have loved at all."

"Ah!" responded the young man with an air of profound wisdom. "That, Mr. Spring Fragrance, means that it is a good thing to love anyway—even if we can't get what we love, or, as the poet tells us, lose what we love. Of course, one needs experience to feel the truth of this teaching."

The young man smiled pensively and reminiscently. More than a dozen young maidens "loved and lost" were passing before his mind's eye.

"The truth of the teaching!" echoed Mr. Spring Fragrance, a little testily. "There is no truth in it whatever. It is disobedient to reason. Is it not better to have what you do not love than to love what you do not have?"

"That depends," answered the young man, "upon temperament."

"I thank you. Good evening," said Mr. Spring Fragrance. He turned away to muse upon the unwisdom of the American way of looking at things.

Meanwhile, inside the house, Laura was refusing to be comforted.

"Ah, no! no!" cried she. "If I had not gone to school with Kai Tzu, nor talked nor walked with him, nor played the accompaniments to his songs, then I might consider with complacency, or at least without horror, my approaching marriage with the son of Man You. But as it is—oh, as it is—!"

The girl rocked herself to and fro in heartfelt grief.

Mrs. Spring Fragrance knelt down beside her, and clasping her arms around her neck, cried in sympathy:

"Little Sister, oh, Little Sister! Dry your tears—do not despair. A moon has yet to pass before the marriage can take place. Who knows what the stars may have to say to one another during its passing? A little bird has whispered to me—"

For a long time Mrs. Spring Fragrance talked. For a long time Laura listened. When the girl arose to go, there was a bright light in her eyes.

II

Mrs. Spring Fragrance, in San Francisco on a visit to her cousin, the wife of the herb doctor of Clay Street, was having a good time. She was invited everywhere that the wife of an honorable Chinese merchant could go. There was much to see and hear, including more than a dozen babies who had been born in the families of her friends since she last visited the city of the Golden Gate. Mrs. Spring Fragrance loved babies. She had had two herself, but both had been transplanted into the spirit land before the completion of even one moon. There were also many dinners and theater-parties given in her honor. It was at one of the theater-parties that Mrs. Spring Fragrance met Ah Oi, a young girl who had the reputation of being the prettiest Chinese girl in San Francisco, and the naughtiest. In spite of gossip, however, Mrs. Spring Fragrance took a great fancy to Ah Oi and invited her to a tête-à-tête picnic on the following day. This invitation Ah Oi joyfully accepted. She was a sort of bird girl and never felt so happy as when out in the park or woods.

On the day after the picnic Mrs. Spring Fragrance wrote to Laura Chin Yuen thus:

MY PRECIOUS LAURA,—May the bamboo ever wave. Next week I accompany Ah Oi to the beauteous town of San José. There will we be met by the son of the Illustrious Teacher, and in a little Mission, presided over by a benevolent American priest, the little Ah Oi and the son of the Illustrious Teacher will be joined together in love and harmony—two pieces of music made to complete one another.

The Son of the Illustrious Teacher, having been through an American Hall of Learning, is well able to provide for his orphan bride and fears not the displeasure of his parents, now that he is assured that your grief at his loss will not be inconsolable. He wishes me to waft to you and to Kai Tzu— and the little Ah Oi joins with him—ten thousand rainbow wishes for your happiness.

My respects to your honorable parents, and to yourself, the heart of your loving friend,

JADE SPRING FRAGRANCE

To Mr. Spring Fragrance, Mrs. Spring Fragrance also indited a letter:

GREAT AND HONORED MAN,—Greeting from your plum blossom,[5] who is desirous of hiding herself from the sun of your presence for a week of seven days more. My honorable cousin is preparing for the Fifth Moon Festival, and wishes me to compound for the occasion some American "fudge," for which delectable sweet, made by my clumsy hands, you have sometimes shown a slight prejudice.[6] I am enjoying a most agreeable visit, and American friends, as also our own, strive benevolently for the accomplishment of my pleasure. Mrs. Samuel Smith, an American lady, known to my cousin, asked for my accompaniment to a magniloquent lecture the other evening. The subject was "America, the Protector of China!" It was most exhilarating, and the effect of so much expression of benevolence leads me to beg of you to forget to remember that the barber charges you one dollar for a shave while he humbly submits to the American man a bill of fifteen cents. And murmur no more because your honored elder brother, on a visit to this country, is detained under the roof-tree of this great Government instead of under your own humble roof. Console him with the reflection that he is protected under the wing of the Eagle, the Emblem of Liberty. What is the loss of ten hundred years or ten thousand times ten dollars compared with the happiness of knowing oneself so securely sheltered? All of this I have learned from Mrs. Samuel Smith, who is as brilliant and great of mind as one of your own superior sex.

For me it is sufficient to know that the Golden Gate Park is most enchanting, and the seals on the rock at the Cliff House extremely entertaining and amiable. There is much feasting and merry-making under the lanterns in honor of your Stupid Thorn.

I have purchased for your smoking a pipe with an amber mouth. It is said to be very sweet to the lips and to emit a cloud of smoke fit for the gods to inhale.

Awaiting, by the wonderful wire of the telegram message, your gracious permission to remain for the celebration of the Fifth Moon Festival and the making of American "fudge," I continue for ten thousand times ten thousand years,

Your ever loving and obedient woman,
JADE

P.S. Forget not to care for the cat, the birds, and the flowers. Do not eat too quickly nor fan too vigorously now that the weather is warming.

Mrs. Spring Fragrance smiled as she folded this last epistle. Even if he were old-fashioned, there was never a husband so good and kind as hers. Only on one occasion since their marriage had he slighted her wishes. That was when, on the last anniversary of their wedding, she had signified a desire for a certain jadestone pendant, and he had failed to satisfy that desire.

But Mrs. Spring Fragrance, being of a happy nature, and disposed to look upon the bright side of things, did not allow her mind to dwell upon the jadestone pendant. Instead, she gazed complacently down upon her bejeweled fingers and folded in with her letter to Mr. Spring Fragrance a bright little sheaf of condensed love.

III

Mr. Spring Fragrance sat on his doorstep. He had been reading two letters, one from Mrs. Spring Fragrance, and the other from an elderly bachelor cousin in San Francisco. The one from the elderly bachelor cousin was a business letter, but contained the following postscript:

> Tsen Hing, the son of the Government school-master, seems to be much in the company of your young wife. He is a good-looking youth, and pardon me, my dear cousin; but if women are allowed to stray at will from under their husbands' mulberry roofs, what is to prevent them from becoming butterflies?

"Sing Foon is old and cynical," said Mr. Spring Fragrance to himself. "Why should I pay any attention to him? This is America, where a man may speak to a woman, and a woman listen, without any thought of evil."

He destroyed his cousin's letter and re-read his wife's. Then he became very thoughtful. Was the making of American fudge sufficient reason for a wife to wish to remain a week longer in a city where her husband was not?

The young man who lived in the next house came out to water the lawn.

"Good evening," said he. "Any news from Mrs. Spring Fragrance?"

"She is having a very good time," returned Mr. Spring Fragrance.

"Glad to hear it. I think you told me she was to return the end of this week."

"I have changed my mind about her," said Mr. Spring Fragrance. "I am bidding her remain a week longer, as I wish to give a smoking party during her absence. I hope I may have the pleasure of your company."

"I shall be delighted," returned the young fellow. "But, Mr. Spring Fragrance, don't invite any other white fellows. If you do not I shall be able to get in a scoop. You know, I'm a sort of honorary reporter for the *Gleaner*."[7]

"Very well," absently answered Mr. Spring Fragrance.

"Of course, your friend the Consul will be present. I shall call it 'A high-class Chinese stag party!'"

In spite of his melancholy mood, Mr. Spring Fragrance smiled.

"Everything is 'high-class' in America," he observed.

"Sure!" cheerfully assented the young man. "Haven't you ever heard that all Americans are princes and princesses, and just as soon as a foreigner puts his foot upon our shores, he also becomes of the nobility—I mean, the royal family."

"What about my brother in the Detention Pen?" dryly inquired Mr. Spring Fragrance.

"Now, you've got me," said the young man, rubbing his head. "Well, that is a shame—'a beastly shame,' as the Englishman says. But understand, old fellow, we that are real Americans are up against that—even more than you. It is against our principles."

"I offer the real Americans my consolations that they should be compelled to do that which is against their principles."

"Oh, well, it will all come right some day. We're not a bad sort, you know. Think of the indemnity money returned to the Dragon by Uncle Sam."[8]

Mr. Spring Fragrance puffed his pipe in silence for some moments. More than politics was troubling his mind.

At last he spoke. "Love," said he, slowly and distinctly, "comes before the wedding in this country, does it not?"

"Yes, certainly."

Young Carman knew Mr. Spring Fragrance well enough to receive with calmness his most astounding queries.

"Presuming," continued Mr. Spring Fragrance—"presuming that some friend of your father's, living—presuming—in England—has a daughter that he arranges with your father to be your wife. Presuming that you have never seen that daughter, but that you marry her, knowing her not. Presuming that she marries you, knowing you not.—After she marries you and knows you, will that woman love you?"

"Emphatically, no," answered the young man.

"That is the way it would be in America—that the woman who marries the man like that—would not love him?"

"Yes, that is the way it would be in America. Love, in this country, must be free, or it is not love at all."

"In China, it is different!" mused Mr. Spring Fragrance.

"Oh, yes, I have no doubt that in China it is different."

"But the love is in the heart all the same," went on Mr. Spring Fragrance.

"Yes, all the same. Everybody falls in love some time or another. Some"—pensively—"many times."

Mr. Spring Fragrance arose.

"I must go down town," said he.

As he walked down the street he recalled the remark of a business acquaintance who had met his wife and had had some conversation with her: "She is just like an American woman."

He had felt somewhat flattered when this remark had been made. He looked upon it as a compliment to his wife's cleverness; but it rankled in his mind as he entered the telegraph office. If his wife was becoming as an American woman, would it not be possible for her to love as an American woman—a man to whom she was not married? There also floated in his memory the verse which his wife had quoted to the daughter of Chin Yuen. When the telegraph clerk handed him a blank, he wrote this message:

"Remain as you wish, but remember that 'Tis better to have loved and lost, than never to have loved at all.'"

When Mrs. Spring Fragrance received this message, her laughter tinkled like falling water. How droll! How delightful! Here was her husband quoting American poetry in a telegram. Perhaps he had been reading her American poetry books since she had left him! She hoped so. They would lead him to understand her sympathy for her dear Laura and Kai Tzu. She need no longer keep from him their secret. How joyful! It had been such a hardship to refrain from confiding in him before. But discreetness had been most necessary, seeing that Mr. Spring Fragrance entertained as old-fashioned notions concerning marriage as did the Chin Yuen parents. Strange that that should be so, since he had fallen in love with her picture before *ever* he had seen her, just as she had fallen in love with his![9] And when the marriage veil was lifted and each beheld the other for the first time in the flesh, there had been no disillusion—no lessening of the respect and affection, which those who had brought about the marriage had inspired in each young heart.

Mrs. Spring Fragrance began to wish she could fall asleep and wake to find the week flown, and she in her own little home pouring tea for Mr. Spring Fragrance.

IV

Mr. Spring Fragrance was walking to business with Mr. Chin Yuen. As they walked they talked.

"Yes," said Mr. Chin Yuen, "the old order is passing away, and the new order is taking its place, even with us who are Chinese. I have finally consented to give my daughter in marriage to young Kai Tzu."

Mr. Spring Fragrance expressed surprise. He had understood that the marriage between his neighbor's daughter and the San Francisco school-teacher's son was all arranged.

"So 'twas," answered Mr. Chin Yuen; "but, it seems the young renegade, without consultation or advice, has placed his affections upon some untrustworthy female, and is so under her influence that he refuses to fulfill his parents' promise to me for him."

"So!" said Mr. Spring Fragrance. The shadow on his brow deepened.

"But," said Mr. Chin Yuen, with affable resignation, "it is all ordained by Heaven. Our daughter, as the wife of Kai Tzu, for whom she has long had a loving feeling, will not now be compelled to dwell with a mother-in-law and where her own mother is not. For that, we are thankful, as she is our only one and the conditions of life in this Western country are not as in China. Moreover, Kai Tzu, though not so much of a scholar as the teacher's son, has a keen eye for business and that, in America, is certainly much more desirable than scholarship. What do you think?"

"Eh! What!" exclaimed Mr. Spring Fragrance. The latter part of his companion's remarks had been lost upon him.

That day the shadow which had been following Mr. Spring Fragrance ever since he had heard his wife quote, "'Tis better to have loved," etc., became so heavy and deep that he quite lost himself within it.

At home in the evening he fed the cat, the bird, and the flowers. Then, seating himself in a carved black chair—a present from his wife on his last birthday—he took out his pipe and smoked. The cat jumped into his lap. He stroked it softly and tenderly. It had been much fondled by Mrs. Spring Fragrance, and Mr. Spring Fragrance was under the impression that it missed her. "Poor thing!" said he. "I suppose you want her back!" When he arose to go to bed he placed the animal carefully on the floor, and thus apostrophized it:

"O Wise and Silent One, your mistress returns to you, but her heart she leaves behind her, with the Tommies[10] in San Francisco."

The Wise and Silent One made no reply. He was not a jealous cat.

Mr. Spring Fragrance slept not that night; the next morning he ate not. Three days and three nights without sleep and food went by.

There was a springlike freshness in the air on the day that Mrs. Spring Fragrance came home. The skies overhead were as blue as Puget Sound stretching its gleaming length toward the mighty Pacific, and all the beautiful green world seemed to be throbbing with springing life.

Mrs. Spring Fragrance was never so radiant.

"Oh," she cried light-heartedly, "is it not lovely to see the sun shining so clear, and everything so bright to welcome me?"

Mr. Spring Fragrance made no response. It was the morning after the fourth sleepless night.

Mrs. Spring Fragrance noticed his silence, also his grave face.

"Everything—everyone is glad to see me but you," she declared, half seriously, half jestingly.

Mr. Spring Fragrance set down her valise. They had just entered the house.

"If my wife is glad to see me," he quietly replied, "I also am glad to see her!"

Summoning their servant boy, he bade him look after Mrs. Spring Fragrance's comfort.

"I must be at the store in half an hour," said he, looking at his watch. "There is some very important business requiring attention."

"What is the business?" inquired Mrs. Spring Fragrance, her lip quivering with disappointment.

"I cannot just explain to you," answered her husband.

Mrs. Spring Fragrance looked up into his face with honest and earnest eyes. There was something in his manner, in the tone of her husband's voice, which touched her.

"Yen," said she, "you do not look well. You are not well. What is it?"

Something arose in Mr. Spring Fragrance's throat which prevented him from replying.

"O darling one! O sweetest one!" cried a girl's joyous voice. Laura Chin Yuen ran into the room and threw her arms around Mrs. Spring Fragrance's neck.

"I spied you from the window," said Laura, "and I couldn't rest until I told you. We are to be married next week, Kai Tzu and I. And all through you, all through you—the sweetest jade jewel in the world!"

Mr. Spring Fragrance passed out of the room.

"So the son of the Government teacher and little Happy Love are already married," Laura went on, relieving Mrs. Spring Fragrance of her cloak, her hat, and her folding fan. Mr. Spring Fragrance paused upon the doorstep.

"Sit down, Little Sister, and I will tell you all about it," said Mrs. Spring Fragrance, forgetting her husband for a moment.

When Laura Chin Yuen had danced away, Mr. Spring Fragrance came in and hung up his hat.

"You got back very soon," said Mrs. Spring Fragrance, covertly wiping away the tears which had begun to fall as soon as she thought herself alone.

"I did not go," answered Mr. Spring Fragrance. "I have been listening to you and Laura."

"But if the business is very important, do not you think you should attend to it?" anxiously queried Mrs. Spring Fragrance.

"It is not important to me now," returned Mr. Spring Fragrance. "I would prefer to hear again about Ah Oi and Man You and Laura and Kai Tzu."

"How lovely of you to say that!" exclaimed Mrs. Spring Fragrance, who was easily made happy. And she began to chat away to her husband in the friendliest and wifeliest fashion possible. When she had finished she asked him if he were not glad to hear that those who loved as did the young lovers whose secrets she had been keeping, were to be united; and he replied that indeed he was; that he would like every man to be as happy with a wife as he himself had ever been and ever would be.

"You did not always talk like that," said Mrs. Spring Fragrance slyly. "You must have been reading my American poetry books!"

"American poetry!" ejaculated Mr. Spring Fragrance almost fiercely, "American poetry is detestable, *abhorrable*!"

"Why! why!" exclaimed Mrs. Spring Fragrance, more and more surprised.

But the only explanation which Mr. Spring Fragrance vouchsafed was a jadestone pendant.

"THE VINE-LEAF"

by María Cristina Mena,

1914

It is a saying in the capital of Mexico that Dr. Malsufrido[1] carries more family secrets under his hat than any archbishop, which applies, of course, to family secrets of the rich. The poor have no family secrets, or none that Dr. Malsufrido would trouble to carry under his hat.

The doctor's hat is, appropriately enough, uncommonly capacious, rising very high, and sinking so low that it seems to be supported by his ears and eyebrows, and it has a furry look, as if it had been brushed the wrong way, which is perhaps what happens to it if it is ever brushed at all. When the doctor takes it off, the family secrets do not fly out like a flock of parrots, but remain nicely bottled up beneath a dome of old and highly polished ivory, which, with its unbroken fringe of dyed black hair, has the effect of a tonsure; and then Dr. Malsufrido looks like one of the early saints.[2] I've forgotten which one.

So edifying is his personality that, when he marches into a sick-room, the forces of disease and infirmity march out of it, and do not dare to return until he has taken his leave. In fact, it is well known that none of his patients has ever had the bad manners to die in his presence.

If you will believe him, he is almost ninety years old, and everybody knows that he has been dosing good Mexicans for half a century. He is forgiven for being a Spaniard on account of a legend that he physicked royalty in his time, and that a certain princess—but that has nothing to do with this story.[3]

It is sure he has a courtly way with him that captivates his female patients, of whom he speaks as his *penitentes*,[4] insisting on confession as a prerequisite of diagnosis, and declaring

that the physician who undertakes to cure a woman's body
without reference to her soul is a more abominable kill-healthy
than the famous *Dr. Sangrado*, who taught medicine to *Gil
Blas*.[5]

"Describe me the symptoms of your conscience, Señora," he
will say. "Fix yourself that I shall forget one tenth of what you
tell me."

"But what of the other nine tenths, Doctor?" the troubled
lady will exclaim.

"The other nine tenths I shall take care not to believe," Dr.
Malsufrido will reply, with a roar of laughter. And sometimes
he will add:

"Do not confess your neighbor's sins; the doctor will have
enough with your own."

When an inexperienced one fears to become a *penitente* lest
that terrible old doctor betray her confidence, he reassures her
as to his discretion, and at the same time takes her mind off
her anxieties by telling her the story of his first patient.

"Figure you my prudence, Señora," he begins, "that, although she was my patient, I did not so much as see her face."

And then, having enjoyed the startled curiosity of his hearer,
he continues:

"On that day of two crosses when I first undertook the
mending of mortals, she arrived to me beneath a veil as impen-
etrable as that of a nun, saying:

"'To you I come, Señor Doctor, because no one knows you.'

"'Who would care for fame, Señorita,' said I, 'when obscurity brings such excellent fortune?'

"And the lady, in a voice which trembled slightly, returned:

"'If your knife is as apt as your tongue, and your discretion
equal to both, I shall not regret my choice of a surgeon.'

"With suitable gravity I reassured her, and inquired how I
might be privileged to serve her. She replied:

"'By ridding me of a blemish, if you are skillful enough to
leave no trace on the skin.'

"'Of that I will judge, with the help of God, when the señorita shall have removed her veil.'

"'No, no; you shall not see my face. Praise the saints the blemish is not there!'

"'Wherever it be,' said I, resolutely, 'my science tells me that it must be seen before it can be well removed.'

"The lady answered with great simplicity that she had no anxiety on that account, but that, as she had neither duenna nor servant with her, I must help her.[6] I had no objection, for a surgeon must needs be something of a lady's maid. I judged from the quality of her garments that she was of an excellent family, and I was ashamed of my clumsy fingers; but she was a patient as marble, caring only to keep her face closely covered. When at last I saw the blemish she had complained of, I was astonished, and said:

"'But it seems to me a blessed stigma, Señorita, this delicate, wine-red vine-leaf, staining a surface as pure as the petal of any magnolia. With permission, I should say that the god Bacchus himself painted it here in the arch of this chaste back, where only the eyes of Cupid could find it; for it is safely below the line of the most fashionable gown.'[7]

"But she replied:

"'I have my reasons. Fix yourself that I am superstitious.'

"I tried to reason with her on that, but she lost her patience and cried:

"'For favor, good surgeon, your knife!'

"Even in those days I had much sensibility, Señora, and I swear that my heart received more pain from the knife than did she. Neither the cutting nor the stitching brought a murmur from her. Only some strong ulterior thought could have armed a delicate woman with such valor. I beat my brains to construe the case, but without success. A caprice took me to refuse the fee she offered me.

"'No, Señorita,' I said, 'I have not seen your face, and if I were to take your money, it might pass that I should not see the face of a second patient, which would be a great misfortune. You are my first, and I am as superstitious as you."

"I would have added that I had fallen in love with her, but I feared to appear ridiculous, having seen no more than her back.

"'You would place me under an obligation,' she said. I felt that her eyes studied me attentively through her veil. 'Very well, I can trust you the better for that. *Adiós*, Señor Surgeon.'

"She came once more to have me remove the stitches, as I had told her, and again her face was concealed, and again I refused payment; but I think she knew that the secret of the vine-leaf was buried in my heart."

"But that secret, what was it, Doctor? Did you ever see the mysterious lady again?"

"*Chist!*[8] Little by little one arrives to the *rancho*, Señora. Five years passed, and many patients arrived to me, but, although all showed me their faces, I loved none of them better than the first one. Partly through family influence, partly through well-chosen friendships, and perhaps a little through that diligence in the art of Hippocrates for which in my old age I am favored by the most charming of Mexicans, I had prospered, and was no longer unknown.

"At a meeting of a learned society I became known to a certain *marqués* who had been a great traveler in his younger days.[9] We had a discussion on a point of anthropology, and he invited me to his house, to see the curiosities he had collected in various countries. Most of them recalled scenes of horrors, for he had a morbid fancy.

"Having taken from my hand the sword with which he had seen five Chinese pirates sliced into small pieces, he led me toward a little door, saying:

"'Now you shall see the most mysterious and beautiful of my mementos, one which recalls a singular event in our own peaceful Madrid.'

"We entered a room lighted by a skylight, and containing little but an easel on which rested a large canvas. The *marqués* led me where the most auspicious light fell upon it. It was a nude, beautifully painted. The model stood poised divinely, with her back to the beholder, twisting flowers in her hair before a mirror. And there, in the arch of that chaste back, staining a surface as pure as the petal of any magnolia, what did my eyes see? Can you possibly imagine, Señora?"

"*Válgame Dios!*[10] The vine-leaf, Doctor!"

"What penetration of yours, Señora! It was veritably the vine-leaf, wine-red, as it had appeared to me before my knife barbarously extirpated it from the living flesh; but in the picture it seemed unduly conspicuous, as if Bacchus had been angry when he kissed. You may imagine how the sight startled me. But those who know Dr. Malsufrido need no assurance that even in those early days he never permitted himself one imprudent word. No, Señora; I only remarked, after praising the picture in proper terms:

"'What an interesting moon is that upon the divine creature's back!'

"'Does it not resemble a young vine-leaf in early spring?' said the *marqués*, who contemplated the picture with the ardor of a connoisseur. I agreed politely, saying:

"'Now that you suggest it, *Marqués*, it has some of the form and color of a tender vine-leaf. But I could dispense me a better vine-leaf, with many bunches of grapes, to satisfy the curiosity I have to see such a well-formed lady's face. What a misfortune that it does not appear in that mirror, as the artist doubtless intended! The picture was never finished, then?'

"'I have reason to believe that it was finished,' he replied, 'but that the face painted in the mirror was obliterated. Observe that its surface is an opaque and disordered smudge of many pigments, showing no brushwork, but only marks of a rude rubbing that in some places has overlapped the justly painted frame of the mirror.'

"'This promises an excellent mystery,' I commented lightly. 'Was it the artist or his model who was dissatisfied with the likeness, *Marqués*?'"

"'I suspect that the likeness was more probably too good than not good enough,' returned the *marqués*. 'Unfortunately poor Andrade is not here to tell us.'

"'Andrade! The picture was his work?'

"'The last his hand touched. Do you remember when he was found murdered in his studio?'

"'With a knife sticking between his shoulders. I remember it very well.'

"The *marqués* continued:

"'I had asked him to let me have this picture. He was then working on that rich but subdued background. The figure was finished, but there was no vine-leaf, and the mirror was empty of all but a groundwork of paint, with a mere luminous suggestion of a face.

"'Andrade, however, refused to name me a price, and tried to put me off with excuses. His friends were jesting about the unknown model, whom no one had managed to see, and all suspected that he designed to keep the picture for himself. That made me the more determined to possess it. I wished to make it a betrothal gift to the beautiful Señorita Lisarda Monte Alegre, who, had then accepted the offer of my hand, and who is now the *marquesa*. When I have a desire, Doctor, it bites me, and I make it bite others. That poor Andrade, I gave him no peace.

"'He fell into one of his solitary fits, shutting himself in his studio, and seeing no one; but that did not prevent him from knocking at his door whenever I had nothing else to do. Well, one morning the door was open.'

"'Yes, yes!' I exclaimed. 'I remember now, *Marqués*, that it was you who found the body.'

"'You have said it. He was lying in front of this picture, having dragged himself across the studio. After assuring myself that he was beyond help, and while awaiting the police, I made certain observations. The first thing to strike my attention was this vine-leaf. The paint was fresh, whereas the rest of the figure was comparatively dry. Moreover, its color had not been mixed with Andrade's usual skill. Observe you, Doctor, that the blemish is not of the texture of the skin, or bathed in its admirable atmosphere. It presents itself as an excrescence. And why? Because that color had been mixed and applied with feverish haste by the hand of a dying man, whose one thought was to denounce his assassin—she who undoubtedly bore such a mark on her body, and who had left him for dead, after carefully obliterating the portrait of herself which he had painted in the mirror.'

"'*Ay Dios!* But the police, *Marqués*—they never reported these details so significant?'

"'Our admirable police are not connoisseurs of the painter's art, my friend. Moreover, I had taken the precaution to remove from the dead man's fingers the empurpled brush with which he had traced that accusing symbol.'

"'You wished to be the accomplice of an unknown assassin?'

"'Inevitably, Señor, rather than deliver that lovely body to the hands of the public executioner.'

"The *marqués* raised his lorgnette and gazed at the picture.[11] And I—I was recovering from my agitation, Señora. I said:

"'It seems to me, *Marqués*, that if I were a woman and loved you, I should be jealous of that picture.'

"He smiled and replied:

"'It is true that the *marquesa* affects some jealousy on that account, and will not look at the picture. However, she is one who errs on the side of modesty, and prefers more austere objects of contemplation. She is excessively religious.'

"'I have been called superstitious,' pronounced a voice behind me.

"It was a voice that I had heard before. I turned, Señora, and I ask you to try to conceive whose face I now beheld."

"*Válgame la Virgen*, Dr. Malsufrido, was it not the face of the good *marquesa*, and did she not happen to have been also your first patient?"[12]

"Again such penetration, Señora, confounds me. It was she. The *marqués* did me the honor to present me to her.

"'I have heard of your talents, Señor Surgeon,' she said.

"'And I of your beauty, *Marquesa*,' I hastened to reply; 'but that tale was not so well told.' And I added, 'If you are superstitious, I will be, too.'

"With one look from her beautiful and devout eyes she thanked me for that prudence which to this day, Señora, is at the service of my *penitentes*, little daughters of my affections and my prayers; and then she signed and said:

"'Can you blame me for not loving this questionable lady of the vine-leaf, of whom my husband is such a gallant accomplice?'

"'Not for a moment,' I replied, 'for I am persuaded, *Marquesa*, that a lady of rare qualities may have power to bewitch an unfortunate man without showing him the light of her face.'"

"THE WIDESPREAD ENIGMA CONCERNING BLUE-STAR WOMAN"

by Zitkála-Šá,

1921

It was summer on the western plains. Fields of golden sunflowers facing eastward, greeted the rising sun. Blue-Star Woman, with windshorn braids of white hair over each ear, sat in the shade of her log hut before an open fire. Lonely but unmolested she dwelt here like the ground squirrel that took its abode nearby,—both through the easy tolerance of the land owner. The Indian woman held a skillet over the burning embers. A large round cake, with long slashes in its center, was baking and crowding the capacity of the frying pan.

In deep abstraction Blue-Star Woman prepared her morning meal. "Who am I?" had become the obsessing riddle of her life. She was no longer a young woman, being in her fifty-third year. In the eyes of the white man's law, it was required of her to give proof of her membership in the Sioux tribe. The unwritten law of heart prompted her naturally to say, "I am a being. I am Blue-Star Woman. A piece of earth is my birthright."

It was taught for reasons now forgot that an Indian should never pronounce his or her name in answer to any inquiry. It was probably a means of protection in the days of black magic. Be this as it may, Blue-Star Woman lived in times when this teaching was disregarded. It gained her nothing, however, to pronounce her name to the government official to whom she applied for her share of tribal land. His persistent question was always, "Who were your parents?"

Blue-Star Woman was left an orphan at a tender age. She did not remember them. They were long gone to the spirit-land,—and she could not understand why they should be recalled to earth on her account. It was another one of the old, old teachings of her race that the names of the dead should not be idly spoken. It had become a sacrilege to mention carelessly the name of any departed one, especially in matters of disputes over worldly possessions. The unfortunate circumstances of her early childhood, together with the lack of written records of a roving people, placed a formidable barrier between her and her heritage. The fact was events of far greater importance to the tribe than her reincarnation had passed unrecorded in books. The verbal reports of the old-time men and women of the tribe were varied,—some were actually contradictory. Blue-Star Woman was unable to find even a twig of her family tree.

She sharpened one end of a long stick and with it speared the fried bread when it was browned. Heedless of the hot bread's "Tsing!" in a high treble as it was lifted from the fire, she added it to the six others which had preceded it. It had been many a moon since she had had a meal of fried bread, for she was too poor to buy at any one time all the necessary ingredients, particularly the fat in which to fry it. During the breadmaking, the smoke-blackened coffeepot boiled over. The aroma of freshly made coffee smote her nostrils and roused her from the tantalizing memories.

The day before, friendly spirits, the unseen ones, had guided her aimless footsteps to her Indian neighbor's house. No sooner had she entered than she saw on the table some grocery bundles. "Iye-que, fortunate one!" she exclaimed as she took the straight-backed chair offered her.[1] At once the Indian hostess untied the bundles and measured out a cupful of green coffee beans and a pound of lard. She gave them to Blue-Star Woman, saying, "I want to share my good fortune. Take these home with you." Thus it was that Blue-Star Woman had come into the unexpected possession of the materials which now contributed richly to her breakfast.

The generosity of her friend had often saved her from starvation. Generosity is said to be a fault of Indian people, but neither the Pilgrim Fathers nor Blue-Star Woman ever held it seriously against them. Blue-Star Woman was even grateful for this gift of food. She was fond of coffee,—that black drink brought hither by those daring voyagers of long ago. The coffee habit was one of the signs of her progress in the white man's civilization, also had she emerged from the tepee into a log hut, another achievement. She had learned to read the primer and to write her name. Little Blue-Star attended school unhindered by a fond mother's fears that a foreign teacher might not spare the rod with her darling.

Blue-Star Woman was her individual name. For untold ages the Indian race had not used family names. A newborn child was given a brand-new name. Blue-Star Woman was proud to write her name for which she would not be required to substitute another's upon her marriage, as is the custom of civilized peoples.

"The times are changed now," she muttered under her breath. "My individual name seems to mean nothing." Looking out into space, she saw the nodding sunflowers, and they acquiesced with her. Their drying leaves reminded her of the near approach of autumn. Then soon, very soon, the ice would freeze along the banks of the muddy river. The day of the first ice was her birthday. She would be fifty-four winters old. How futile had been all these winters to secure her a share in tribal lands. A weary smile flickered across her face as she sat there on the ground like a bronze figure of patience and long-suffering.

The breadmaking was finished. The skillet was set aside to cool. She poured the appetizing coffee into her tin cup. With fried bread and black coffee she regaled herself. Again her mind reverted to her riddle. "The missionary preacher said he could not explain the white man's law to me. He who reads daily from the Holy Bible, which he tells me is God's book, cannot understand mere man's laws. This also puzzles me," thought she to herself. "Once a wise leader of our people, addressing a president of this country, said: 'I am a man. You

are another. The Great Spirit is our witness!' This is simple
and easy to understand, but the times are changed. The white
man's laws are strange."

Blue-Star Woman broke off a piece of fried bread between a
thumb and forefinger. She ate it hungrily, and sipped from her
cup of fragrant coffee. "I do not understand the white man's
law. It's like walking in the dark. In this darkness, I am growing fearful of everything."

Oblivious to the world, she had not heard the footfall of two
Indian men who now stood before her.

Their short-cropped hair looked blue-black in contrast to
the faded civilian clothes they wore. Their white man's shoes
were rusty and unpolished. To the unconventional eyes of the
old Indian woman, their celluloid collars appeared like shining marks of civilization. Blue-Star Woman looked up from
the lap of mother earth without rising. "Hinnu, hinnu!" she ejaculated in undisguised surprise.[2] "Pray, who are these would-be
white men?" she inquired.

In one voice and by an assumed relationship the two Indian
men addressed her. "Aunt, I shake hands with you." Again
Blue-Star Woman remarked, "Oh, indeed! these near white
men speak my native tongue and shake hands according to our
custom." Did she guess the truth, she would have known they
were simply deluded mortals, deceiving others and themselves
most of all. Boisterously laughing and making conversation,
they each in turn gripped her withered hand.

Like a sudden flurry of wind, tossing loose ends of things,
they broke into her quiet morning hour and threw her groping
thoughts into greater chaos. Masking their real errand with
long-drawn faces, they feigned a concern for her welfare only.
"We come to ask how you are living. We heard you were
slowly starving to death. We heard you are one of those Indians who have been cheated out of their share in tribal lands by
the government officials."

Blue-Star Woman became intensely interested.

"You see we are educated in the white man's ways," they
said with protruding chests. One unconsciously thrust his

thumbs into the armholes of his ill-fitting coat and strutted about in his pride. "We can help you get your land. We want to help our aunt. All old people like you ought to be helped before the younger ones. The old will die soon, and they may never get the benefit of their land unless some one like us helps them to get their rights, without further delay."

Blue-Star Woman listened attentively.

Motioning to the mats she spread upon the ground, she said: "Be seated, my nephews." She accepted the relationship assumed for the occasion. "I will give you some breakfast." Quickly she set before them a generous helping of fried bread and cups of coffee. Resuming her own meal, she continued, "You are wonderfully kind. It is true, my nephews, that I have grown old trying to secure my share of land. It may not be long till I shall pass under the sod."

The two men responded with "How, how," which meant, "Go on with your story. We are all ears." Blue-Star Woman had not yet detected any particular sharpness about their ears, but by an impulse she looked up into their faces and scrutinized them. They were busily engaged in eating. Their eyes were fast upon the food in front of their crossed shins. Inwardly she made a passing observation how, like ravenous wolves, her nephews devoured their food. Coyotes in midwinter could not have been more starved. Without comment she offered them the remaining fried cakes, and between them they took it all. She offered the second helping of coffee, which they accepted without hesitancy. Filling their cups, she placed her empty coffeepot on the dead ashes.

To them she rehearsed her many hardships. It had become a habit now to tell her long story of disappointments with all its petty details. It was only another instance of good intentions gone awry. It was a paradox upon a land of prophecy that its path to future glory be stained with the blood of its aborigines. Incongruous as it is, the two nephews, with their white associates, were glad of a condition so profitable to them. Their solicitation for Blue-Star Woman was not at all altruistic. They thrived in their grafting business. They and their occupation were the by-product of an unwieldy bureaucracy over the nation's wards.

"Dear aunt, you failed to establish the facts of your identity," they told her. Hereupon Blue-Star Woman's countenance fell. It was ever the same old words. It was the old song of the government official she loathed to hear. The next remark restored her courage. "If any one can discover evidence, it's us! I tell you, aunt, we'll fix it all up for you." It was a great relief to the old Indian woman to be thus unburdened of her riddle, with a prospect of possessing land. "There is one thing you will have to do,—that is, to pay us one half of your land and money when you get them." Here was a pause, and Blue-Star Woman answered slowly, "Y-e-s," in an uncertain frame of mind.

The shrewd schemers noted her behavior. "Wouldn't you rather have a half of a crust of bread than none at all?" they asked. She was duly impressed with the force of their argument. In her heart she agreed, "A little something to eat is better than nothing!" The two men talked in regular relays. The flow of smooth words was continuous and so much like purring that all the woman's suspicions were put soundly to sleep. "Look here, aunt, you know very well that prairie fire is met with a back-fire." Blue-Star Woman, recalling her experiences in fire-fighting, quickly responded, "Yes, oh, yes."

"In just the same way, we fight crooks with crooks. We have clever white lawyers working with us. They are the back-fire." Then, as if remembering some particular incident, they both laughed aloud and said, "Yes, and sometimes they use us as the back-fire! We trade fifty-fifty."

Blue-Star Woman sat with her chin in the palm of one hand with elbow resting in the other. She rocked herself slightly forward and backward. At length she answered, "Yes, I will pay you half of my share in tribal land and money when I get them. In bygone days, brave young men of the order of the White-Horse-Riders sought out the aged, the poor, the widows and orphans to aid them, but they did their good work without pay.[3] The White-Horse-Riders are gone. The times are changed. I am a poor old Indian woman. I need warm clothing before winter begins to blow its icicles through us. I need fire wood. I need food. As you have said, a little help is better than none."

Hereupon the two pretenders scored another success.

They rose to their feet. They had eaten up all the fried bread and drained the coffeepot. They shook hands with Blue-Star Woman and departed. In the quiet that followed their departure, she sat munching her small piece of bread, which, by a lucky chance, she had taken on her plate before the hungry wolves had come. Very slowly she ate the fragment of fried bread as if to increase it by diligent mastication. A self-condemning sense of guilt disturbed her. In her dire need she had become involved with tricksters. Her nephews laughingly told her, "We use crooks, and crooks use us in the skirmish over Indian lands."

The friendly shade of the house shrank away from her and hid itself under the narrow eaves of the dirt covered roof. She shrugged her shoulders. The sun high in the sky had witnessed the affair and now glared down upon her white head. Gathering upon her arm the mats and cooking utensils, she hobbled into her log hut.

Under the brooding wilderness silence, on the Sioux Indian Reservation, the superintendent summoned together the leading Indian men of the tribe. He read a letter which he had received from headquarters in Washington, D.C. It announced the enrollment of Blue-Star Woman on their tribal roll of members and the approval of allotting land to her.

It came as a great shock to the tribesmen. Without their knowledge and consent their property was given to a strange woman. They protested in vain. The superintendent said, "I received this letter from Washington. I have read it to you for your information. I have fulfilled my duty. I can do no more." With these hateful words he dismissed the assembly.

Heavy hearted, Chief High Flier returned to his dwelling. Smoking his long-stemmed pipe he pondered over the case of Blue-Star Woman. The Indian's guardian had got into a way of usurping autocratic power in disposing of the wards' property. It was growing intolerable. "No doubt this Indian woman is entitled to allotment, but where? Certainly not here," he thought to himself.

Laying down his pipe, he called his little granddaughter from her play. "You are my interpreter and scribe," he said. "Bring your paper and pencil." A letter was written in the child's sprawling hand, and signed by the old chieftain. It read:

"My Friend:

"I make letter to you. My heart is sad. Washington give my tribe's land to a woman called Blue-Star. We do not know her. We were not asked to give land, but our land is taken from us to give to another Indian. This is not right. Lots of little children of my tribe have no land. Why this strange woman get our land which belongs to our children? Go to Washington and ask if our treaties tell him to give our property away without asking us. Tell him I thought we made good treaties on paper, but now our children cry for food. We are too poor. We cannot give even to our own little children. Washington is very rich. Washington now owns our country. If he wants to help this poor Indian woman, Blue-Star, let him give her some of his land and his money. This is all I will say until you answer me. I shake hands with you with my heart. The Great Spirit hears my words. They are true.

"Your friend,
"CHIEF HIGH FLIER.
"X (his mark.)"

The letter was addressed to a prominent American woman. A stamp was carefully placed on the envelope.

Early the next morning, before the dew was off the grass, the chieftain's riding pony was caught from the pasture and brought to his log house. It was saddled and bridled by a younger man, his son with whom he made his home. The old chieftain came out, carrying in one hand his long-stemmed pipe and tobacco pouch. His blanket was loosely girdled about his waist. Tightly holding the saddle horn, he placed a moccasined foot carefully into the stirrup and pulled himself up awkwardly into the saddle, muttering to himself, "Alas, I can no more leap into my saddle. I now must crawl about in my helplessness." He was past eighty years of age, and no longer agile.

He set upon his ten-mile trip to the only post office for hundreds of miles around. In his shirt pocket, he carried the letter destined, in due season, to reach the heart of American people. His pony, grown old in service, jogged along the dusty road. Memories of other days thronged the wayside, and for the lonely rider transformed all the country. Those days were gone when the Indian youths were taught to be truthful,—to be merciful to the poor. Those days were gone when moral cleanliness was a chief virtue; when public feasts were given in honor of the virtuous girls and young men of the tribe. Untold mischief is now possible through these broken ancient laws. The younger generation were not being trained in the high virtues. A slowly starving race was growing mad, and the pitifully weak sold their lands for a pot of porridge.

"He, he, he! He, he, he!" he lamented. "Small Voice Woman, my own relative is being represented as the mother of this strange Blue-Star—the papers were made by two young Indian men who have learned the white man's ways. Why must I be forced to accept the mischief of children? My memory is clear. My reputation for veracity is well known.

Small Voice Woman lived in my house until her death. She had only one child and it was a *boy*!" He held his hand over this thumping heart, and was reminded of the letter in his pocket. "This letter,—what will happen when it reaches my good friend?" he asked himself. The chieftain rubbed his dim eyes and groaned, "If only my good friend knew the folly of turning my letter into the hands of bureaucrats! In face of repeated defeat, I am daring once more to send this one letter." An inner voice said in his ear, "And this one letter will share the same fate of the other letters."

Startled by the unexpected voice, he jerked upon the bridle reins and brought the drowsy pony to a sudden halt. There was no one near. He found himself a mile from the post office, for the cluster of government buildings, where lived the super-intendent, were now in plain sight. His thin frame shook with emotion. He could not go there with his letter.

He dismounted from his pony. His quavering voice chanted a bravery song as he gathered dry grasses and the dead stalks of last year's sunflowers. He built a fire, and crying aloud, for his sorrow was greater than he could bear, he cast the letter into the flames. The fire consumed it. He sent his message on the wings of fire and he believed she would get it. He yet trusted that help would come to his people before it was too late. The pony tossed his head in readiness to go. He knew he was on the return trip and he was glad to travel.

The wind which blew so gently at dawn was now increased into a gale as the sun approached the zenith. The chieftain, on his way home, sensed a coming storm. He looked upward to the sky and around in every direction. Behind him, in the distance, he saw a cloud of dust. He saw several horsemen whipping their ponies and riding at great speed. Occasionally he heard their shouts, as if calling after some one. He slackened his pony's pace and frequently looked over his shoulder to see who the riders were advancing in hot haste upon him. He was growing curious. In a short time the riders surrounded him. On their coats shone brass buttons, and on their hats were gold cords and tassels. They were Indian police.

"Wan!" he exclaimed, finding himself the object of their chase. It was their foolish ilk who had murdered the great leader, Sitting Bull.[4] "Pray, what is the joke? Why do young men surround an old man quietly riding home?"

"Uncle," said the spokesman, "we are hirelings, as you know. We are sent by the government superintendent to arrest you and take you back with us. The superintendent says you are one of the bad Indians, singing war songs and opposing the government all the time; this morning you were seen trying to set fire to the government agency."

"Hunhunhe!" replied the old chief, placing the palm of his hand over his mouth agape in astonishment. "All this is unbelievable!"

The policeman took hold of the pony's bridle and turned the

reluctant little beast around. They led it back with them and the old chieftain set unresisting in the saddle. High Flier was taken before the superintendent, who charged him with setting fires to destroy government buildings and found him guilty. Thus Chief High Flier was sent to jail. He had already suffered much during his life. He was the voiceless man of America. And now in his old age he was cast into prison. The chagrin of it all, together with his utter helplessness to defend his own or his people's human rights, weighed heavily upon his spirit.

The foul air of the dingy cell nauseated him who loved the open. He sat wearily down upon the tattered mattress, which lay on the rough board floor. He drew his robe closely about his tall figure, holding it partially over his face, his hands covered within the folds. In profound gloom the gray-haired prisoner sat there, without a stir for long hours and knew not when the day ended and the night began. He sat buried in his desperation. His eyes were closed, but he could not sleep. Bread and water in tin receptacles set upon the floor beside him untouched. He was not hungry. Venturesome mice crept out upon the floor and scampered in the dim starlight streaming through the iron bars of the cell window. They squeaked as they dared each other to run across his moccasined feet, but the chieftain neither saw nor heard them.

A terrific struggle was waged within his being. He fought as he never fought before. Tenaciously he hung upon hope for the day of salvation—that hope hoary with age. Defying all odds against him, he refused to surrender faith in good people.

Underneath his blanket, wrapped so closely about him, stole a luminous light. Before his stricken conscience appeared a vision. Lo, his good friend, the American woman to whom he had sent his messages by fire, now stood there a legion! A vast multitude of women, with uplifted hands, gazed upon a huge stone image. Their upturned faces were eager and very earnest. The stone figure was that of a woman upon the brink of the Great Waters, facing eastward. The myriad living hands remained uplifted till the stone woman began to show signs of life. Very majestically she turned around, and, lo, she smiled upon this great galaxy of American women. She was the Statue of Liberty! It was she, who, though representing human liberty, formerly turned her back upon the American aborigine. Her face was aglow with compassion. Her eyes swept across the outspread continent of America, the home of the red man.

At this moment her torch flamed brighter and whiter till its radiance reached into the obscure and remote places of the land. Her light of liberty penetrated Indian reservations. A loud shout of joy rose up from the Indians of the earth, everywhere!

All too soon the picture was gone. Chief High Flier awoke. He lay prostrate on the floor where during the night he had fallen. He rose and took his seat again upon the mattress. Another day was ushered into his life. In his heart lay the secret vision of hope born in the midnight of his sorrows. It enabled him to serve his jail sentence with a mute dignity which baffled those who saw him.

Finally came the day of his release. There was rejoicing over all the land. The desolate hills that harbored wailing voices nightly now were hushed and still. Only gladness filled the air. A crowd gathered around the jail to greet the chieftain. His son stood at the entrance way, while the guard unlocked the prison door. Serenely quiet, the old Indian chief stepped forth. An unseen stone in his path caused him to stumble slightly, but his son grasped him by the hand and steadied his tottering steps. He led him to a heavy lumber wagon drawn by a small pony team which he had brought to take him home. The people thronged about him—hundreds shook hands with him and went away singing native songs of joy for the safe return to them of their absent one.

Among the happy people came Blue-Star Woman's two nephews. Each shook the chieftain's hand. One of them held out an ink pad saying, "We are glad we were able to get you out of jail. We have great influence with the Indian Bureau in Washington, D.C. When you need help, let us know. Here press your thumb in this pad." His companion took from his pocket a document prepared for the old chief's signature, and held it on the wagon wheel for the thumb mark. The chieftain was taken by surprise. He looked into his son's eyes to know the meaning of these two men. "It is our agreement," he explained to his old father. "I pledged to pay them half of your land if they got you out of jail."

The old chieftain sighed, but made no comment. Words were vain. He pressed his indelible thumb mark, his signature it was, upon the deed, and drove home with his son.

"SWEAT"

by Zora Neale Hurston,

1926

It was eleven o'clock of a Spring night in Florida. It was Sunday. Any other night, Delia Jones would have been in bed for two hours by this time. But she was a washwoman, and Monday morning meant a great deal to her. So she collected the soiled clothes on Saturday when she returned the clean things. Sunday night after church, she sorted them and put the white things to soak. It saved her almost a half day's start. A great hamper in the bedroom held the clothes that she brought home. It was so much neater than a number of bundles lying around.

She squatted in the kitchen floor beside the great pile of clothes, sorting them into small heaps according to color, and humming a song in a mournful key, but wondering through it all where Sykes, her husband, had gone with her horse and buckboard.[1]

Just then something long, round, limp and black fell upon her shoulders and slithered to the floor beside her. A great terror took hold of her. It softened her knees and dried her mouth so that it was a full minute before she could cry out or move. Then she saw that it was the big bull whip her husband liked to carry when he drove.

She lifted her eyes to the door and saw him standing there bent over with laughter at her fright. She screamed at him.

"Sykes, what you throw dat whip on me like dat? You know it would skeer me—looks just like a snake, an' you knows how skeered Ah is of snakes."

"Course Ah knowed it! That's how come Ah done it." He slapped his leg with his hand and almost rolled on the ground in his mirth. "If you such a big fool dat you got to have a fit over a earth worm or a string, Ah don't keer how bad Ah skeer you."

"You aint got no business doing it. Gawd knows it's a sin. Some day Ah'm gointuh drop dead from some of yo' foolishness. 'Nother thing, where you been wid mah rig? Ah feeds dat pony. He aint fuh you to be drivin' wid no bull whip."

"You sho is one aggravatin' nigger woman!" he declared and stepped into the room. She resumed her work and did not answer him at once. "Ah done tole you time and again to keep them white folks' clothes outa dis house."

He picked up the whip and glared down at her. Delia went on with her work. She went out into the yard and returned with a galvanized tub and sit it on the washbench. She saw that Sykes had kicked all of the clothes together again, and now stood in her way truculently, his whole manner hoping, *praying*, for an argument. But she walked calmly around him and commenced to re-sort the things.

"Next time, Ah'm gointer kick 'em outdoors," he threatened as he struck a match along the leg of his corduroy breeches.

Delia never looked up from her work, and her thin, stooped shoulders sagged further.

"Ah aint for no fuss t'night, Sykes. Ah just come from taking sacrament at the church house."

He snorted scornfully. "Yeah, you just come from de church house on a Sunday night, but heah you is gone to work on them clothes. You ain't nothing but a hypocrite. One of them amen-corner Christians[2]—sing, whoop, and shout, then come home and wash white folks clothes on the Sabbath."

He stepped roughly upon the whitest pile of things, kicking them helter-skelter as he crossed the room. His wife gave a little scream of dismay, and quickly gathered them together again.

"Sykes, you quit grindin' dirt into these clothes! How can Ah git through by Sat'day if Ah don't start on Sunday?"

"Ah don't keer if you never git through. Anyhow, Ah done promised Gawd and a couple of other men, Ah aint gointer have it in mah house. Don't gimme no lip neither, else Ah'll throw 'em out and put mah fist up side yo' head to boot."

Delia's habitual meekness seemed to slip from her shoulders like a blown scarf. She was on her feet; her poor little body, her bare knuckly hands bravely defying the strapping hulk before her.

"Looka heah, Sykes, you done gone too fur. Ah been married to you fur fifteen years, and Ah been takin' in washin' for fifteen years. Sweat, sweat, sweat! Work and sweat, cry and sweat, pray and sweat!"

"What's that got to do with me?" he asked brutally.

"What's it got to do with you, Sykes? Mah tub of suds is filled yo' belly with vittles more times than yo' hands is filled it. Mah sweat is done paid for this house and Ah reckon Ah kin keep on sweatin' in it."

She seized the iron skillet from the stove and struck a defensive pose, which act surprised him greatly, coming from her. It cowed him and he did not strike her as he usually did.

"Naw you won't," she panted, "that ole snaggle-toothed black woman you runnin' with aint comin' heah to pile up on *mah* sweat and blood. You aint paid for nothin' on this place, and Ah'm gointer stay right heah till Ah'm toted out foot foremost."

"Well, you better quit gittin' me riled up, else they'll be totin' you out sooner than you expect. Ah'm so tired of you Ah don't know whut to do. Gawd! how Ah hates skinny wimmen!"

A little awed by this new Delia, he sidled out of the door and slammed the back gate after him. He did not say where he had gone, but she knew too well. She knew very well that he would not return until nearly daybreak also. Her work over, she went on to bed but not to sleep at once. Things had come to a pretty pass!

She lay awake, gazing upon the debris that cluttered their matrimonial trail. Not an image left standing along the way. Anything like flowers had long ago been drowned in the salty stream that had been pressed from her heart. Her tears, her sweat, her blood. She had brought love to the union and he had brought a longing after the flesh. Two months after the wedding, he had given her the first brutal beating. She had the memory of his numerous trips to Orlando with all of his wages when he had returned to her penniless, even before the first year had passed. She was young and soft then, but now she thought of her knotty, muscled limbs, her harsh knuckly hands, and drew herself up into an unhappy little ball in the middle of the big feather bed. Too late now to hope for love, even if it were not Bertha it would be someone else. This case differed from the others only in that she was bolder than the others. Too late for everything except her little home. She had built it for her old days, and planted one by one the trees and flowers there. It was lovely to her, lovely.

Somehow, before sleep came, she found herself saying aloud: "Oh well, whatever goes over the Devil's back, is got to come under his belly. Sometime or ruther, Sykes, like everybody else, is gointer reap his sowing." After that she was able to build a spiritual earthworks against her husband. His shells could no longer reach her. *Amen.* She went to sleep and slept until he announced his presence in bed by kicking her feet and rudely snatching the cover away.

"Gimme some kivah heah, an' git yo' damn foots over on yo' own side! Ah oughter mash you in yo' mouf fuh drawing dat skillet on me."

Delia went clear to the rail without answering him. A triumphant indifference to all that he was or did.

* * *

The week was as full of work for Delia as all other weeks, and Saturday found her behind her little pony, collecting and delivering clothes.

It was a hot, hot day near the end of July. The village men on Joe Clarke's porch even chewed cane listlessly. They did not hurl the cane-knots as usual. They let them dribble over the edge of the porch. Even conversation had collapsed under the heat.

"Heah come Delia Jones," Jim Merchant said, as the shaggy pony came 'round the bend of the road toward them. The rusty buckboard was heaped with baskets of crisp, clean laundry.

"Yep," Joe Lindsay agreed. "Hot or col', rain or shine, jes ez reg'lar ez de weeks roll roun' Delia carries 'em an' fetches 'em on Sat'day."

"She better if she wanter eat," said Moss. "Syke Jones aint wuth de shot an' powder hit would tek tuh kill 'em. Not to *huh* he aint."

"He sho' aint," Walter Thomas chimed in. "It's too bad, too, cause she wuz a right pritty lil trick when he got huh. Ah'd uh mah'ied huh mahseff if he hadnter beat me to it."

Delia nodded briefly at the men as she drove past.

"Too much knockin' will ruin *any* 'oman. He done beat huh 'nough tuh kill three women, let 'lone change they looks," said Elijah Moseley. "How Syke kin stommuck dat big black greasy Mogul he's layin' roun' wid, gits me. Ah swear dat eight-rock couldn't kiss a sardine can Ah done throwed out de back do' 'way las' yeah."

"Aw, she's fat, thass how come. He's allus been crazy 'bout fat women," put in Merchant. "He'd a' been tied up wid one long time ago if he could a' found one tuh have him. Did Ah tell yuh 'bout him come sidlin' roun' *mah* wife—bringin' her a basket uh pee-cans outa his yard fuh a present? Yessir, mah wife! She tol' him tuh take 'em right straight back home, cause Delia works so hard ovah dat washtub she reckon everything on de place taste lak sweat an' soapsuds. Ah jus' wisht Ah'd a' caught 'im 'roun' dere! Ah'd a' made his hips ketch on fiah down dat shell road."

"Ah know he done it, too. Ah sees 'im grinnin' at every 'oman dat passes," Walter Thomas said. "But even so, he use-ter eat some mighty big hunks uh humble pie tuh git dat lil 'oman he got. She wuz ez pritty ez a speckled pup! Dat wuz fifteen yeahs ago. He useter be so skeered uh losin' huh, she could make him do some parts of a husband's duty. Dey never wuz de same in de mind."

"There oughter be a law about him," said Lindsay. "He aint fit tuh carry guts tuh a bear."

Clarke spoke for the first time. "Taint no law on earth dat kin make a man be decent if it aint in 'im. There's plenty men dat takes a wife lak dey do a joint uh sugar-cane. It's round, juicy an' sweet when dey gits it. But dey squeeze an' grind, squeeze an' grind an' wring tell dey wring every drop uh pleasure dat's in 'em out. When dey's satisfied dat dey is wrung dry, dey treats 'em jes lak dey do a cane-chew. Dey throws 'em away. Dey knows whut dey is doin' while dey is at it, an' hates theirselves fuh it but they keeps on hangin' after huh tell she's empty. Den dey hates huh fuh bein' a cane-chew an' in de way."

"We oughter take Syke an' dat stray 'oman uh his'n down in Lake Howell swamp an' lay on de rawhide till they cain't say 'Lawd a' mussy.' He allus wuz uh ovahbearin' niggah, but since dat white 'oman from up north done teached 'im how to run a automobile, he done got too biggety to live—an' we oughter kill 'im," Old Man Anderson advised.

A grunt of approval went around the porch. But the heat was melting their civic virtue, and Elijah Moseley began to bait Joe Clarke.

"Come on, Joe, git a melon outa dere an' slice it up for yo' customers. We'se all sufferin' wid de heat. De bear's done got *me*!"

"Thass right, Joe, a watermelon is jes' whut Ah needs tuh cure de eppizudicks," Walter Thomas joined forces with Moseley.[3] "Come on dere, Joe. We all is steady customers an' you aint set us up in a long time. Ah chooses dat long, bowlegged Floridy favorite."

"A god, an' be dough. You all gimme twenty cents and slice away," Clarke retorted. "Ah needs a col' slice m'self. Heah, everybody chip in. Ah'll lend y'll mah meat knife."

The money was quickly subscribed and the huge melon brought forth. At that moment, Sykes and Bertha arrived. A determined silence fell on the porch and the melon was put away again.

Merchant snapped down the blade of his jackknife and moved toward the store door.

"Come on in, Joe, an' gimme a slab uh sow belly an' uh pound uh coffee—almost fuhgot 'twas Sat'day. Got to git on home." Most of the men left also.

Just then Delia drove past on her way home, as Sykes was ordering magnificently for Bertha. It pleased him for Delia to see.

"Git whutsoever yo' heart desires, Honey. Wait a minute, Joe. Give huh two bottles uh strawberry soda-water, uh quart uh parched ground-peas, an' a block uh chewin' gum."

With all this they left the store, with Sykes reminding Bertha that this was his town and she could have it if she wanted it.

The men returned soon after they left, and held their watermelon feast.

"Where did Syke Jones git da 'oman from nohow?" Lindsay asked.

"Ovah Apopka. Guess dey musta been cleanin' out de town when she lef'. She don't look lak a thing but a hunk uh liver wid hair on it."

"Well, she sho' kin squall," Dave Carter contributed. "When she gits ready tuh laff, she jes' opens huh mouf an' latches it back tuh de las' notch. No ole grandpa alligator down in Lake Bell ain't got nothin' on huh."

* * *

Bertha had been in town three months now. Sykes was still paying her room rent at Della Lewis'—the only house in town that would have taken her in. Sykes took her frequently to Winter Park to "stomps." He still assured her that he was the swellest man in the state.

"Sho' you kin have dat lil' ole house soon's Ah kin git dat 'oman outa dere. Everything b'longs tuh me an' you sho' kin have it. Ah sho' 'bominates uh skinny 'oman. Lawdy, you sho' is got one portly shape on you! You kin git *anything* you wants. Dis is *mah* town an' you sho' kin have it."

Delia's work-worn knees crawled over the earth in Gethsemane and up the rocks of Calvary many, many times during these months.[4] She avoided the villagers and meeting places in her efforts to be blind and deaf. But Bertha nullified this to a degree, by coming to Delia's house to call Sykes out to her at the gate.

Delia and Sykes fought all the time now with no peaceful interludes. They slept and ate in silence. Two or three times Delia had attempted a timid friendliness, but she was repulsed each time. It was plain that the breaches must remain agape.

* * *

The sun had burned July to August. The heat streamed down like a million hot arrows, smiting all things living upon the earth. Grass withered, leaves browned, snakes went blind in shedding and men and dogs went mad. Dog days!

Delia came home one day and found Sykes there before her. She wondered, but started to go on into the house without speaking, even though he was standing in the kitchen door and she must either stoop under his arm or ask him to move. He made no room for her. She noticed a soap box beside the steps, but paid no particular attention to it, knowing that he must have brought it there. As she was stooping to pass under his outstretched arm, he suddenly pushed her backward, laughingly.

"Look in de box dere Delia, Ah done brung yuh somethin'!"

She nearly fell upon the box in her stumbling, and when she saw what it held, she all but fainted outright.

"Syke! Syke, mah Gawd! You take dat rattlesnake 'way from heah! You *gottuh*. Oh, Jesus, have mussy!"

"Ah aint gut tuh do nuthin' uh de kin'—fact is Ah aint got tuh do nothin' but die. Taint no use uh you puttin' on airs makin' out lak you skeered uh dat snake—he's gointer stay right heah tell he die. He wouldn't bite me cause Ah knows how tuh handle 'im. Nohow he wouldn't risk breakin' out his fangs 'gin yo' skinny laigs."

"Naw, now Syke, don't keep dat thing 'roun' heah tuh skeer me tuh death. You knows Ah'm even feared uh earth worms. Thass de biggest snake Ah evah did see. Kill 'im, Syke, please."

"Doan ast me tuh do nothin' fuh yuh. Goin' 'roun' tryin' tuh be so damn asterperious. Naw, Ah aint gonna kill it. Ah think uh damn sight mo' uh him dan you! Dat's a nice snake an' anybody doan lak 'im kin jes' hit de grit."

The village soon heard that Sykes had the snake, and came to see and ask questions.

"How de hen-fire did you ketch dat six-foot rattler, Syke?" Thomas asked.

"He's full uh frogs so he caint hardly move, thass how Ah eased up on 'm. But Ah'm a snake charmer an' knows how tuh handle 'em. Shux, dat aint nothin'. Ah could ketch one eve'y day if Ah so wanted tuh."

"Whut he needs is a heavy hick'ry club leaned real heavy on his head. Dat's de bes 'way tuh charm a rattlesnake."

"Naw, Walt, y'll jes' don't understand dese diamon' backs lak Ah do," said Sykes in a superior tone of voice.

The village agreed with Walter, but the snake stayed on. His box remained by the kitchen door with its screen wire covering. Two or three days later it had digested its meal of frogs and literally came to life. It rattled at every movement in the kitchen or the yard. One day as Delia came down the kitchen steps she saw his chalky-white fangs curved like scimitars hung in the wire meshes. This time she did not run away with averted eyes as usual. She stood for a long time in the doorway in a red fury that grew bloodier for every second that she regarded the creature that was her torment.

That night she broached the subject as soon as Sykes sat down to the table.

"Syke, Ah wants you tuh take dat snake 'way fum heah. You done starved me an' Ah put up widcher, you done beat me an Ah took dat, but you done kilt all mah insides bringin' dat varmint heah."

Sykes poured out a saucer full of coffee and drank it deliberately before he answered her.

"A whole lot Ah keer 'bout how you feels inside uh out. Dat snake aint goin' no damn wheah till Ah gits ready fuh 'im tuh go. So fur as beatin' is concerned, yuh aint took near all dat you gointer take ef yuh stay 'roun' *me*."

Delia pushed back her plate and got up from the table. "Ah hates you, Sykes," she said calmly. "Ah hates you tuh de same degree dat Ah useter love yuh. Ah done took an' took till mah belly is full up tuh mah neck. Dat's de reason Ah got mah letter

fum de church an' moved mah membership tuh Woodbridge—
so Ah don't haf tuh take no sacrament wid yuh. Ah don't wan-
tuh see yuh 'roun' me at all. Lay 'roun' wid dat 'oman all yuh
wants tuh, but gwan 'way fum me an' mah house. Ah hates
yuh lak uh suck-egg dog."[5]

Sykes almost let the huge wad of corn bread and collard
greens he was chewing fall out of his mouth in amazement. He
had a hard time whipping himself up to the proper fury to try
to answer Delia.

"Well, Ah'm glad you does hate me. Ah'm sho' tiahed uh
you hangin' ontuh me. Ah don't want yuh. Look at yuh
stringey ole neck! Yo' rawbony laigs an' arms is enough tuh
cut uh man tuh death. You looks jes' lak de devvul's doll-baby
tuh *me*. You cain't hate me no worse dan Ah hates you. Ah
been hatin' *you* fuh years."

"Yo' ole black hide don't look lak nothin' tuh me, but uh
passle uh wrinkled up rubber, wid yo' big ole yeahs flappin' on
each side lak uh paih uh buzzard wings. Don't think Ah'm gointuh be run 'way fum mah house neither. Ah'm goin' tuh de white
folks bout *you*, mah young man, de very nex' time you lay yo'
han's on me. Mah cup is done run ovah." Delia said this with no
signs of fear and Sykes departed from the house, threatening her,
but made not the slightest move to carry out any of them.

That night he did not return at all, and the next day being
Sunday, Delia was glad she did not have to quarrel before she
hitched up her pony and drove the four miles to Woodbridge.[6]

She stayed to the night service—"love feast"—which was
very warm and full of spirit. In the emotional winds her domestic trials were borne far and wide so that she sang as she
drove homeward.

> "Jurden water, black an' col'
>   Chills de body, not de soul
>   An' Ah wantah cross Jurden in uh calm time."[7]

She came from the barn to the kitchen door and stopped.

"Whut's de mattah, ol' satan, you aint kickin' up yo' racket?"
She addressed the snake's box. Complete silence. She went on

into the house with a new hope in its birth struggles. Perhaps her threat to go to the white folks had frightened Sykes! Perhaps he was sorry! Fifteen years of misery and suppression had brought Delia to the place where she would hope *anything* that looked toward a way over or through her wall of inhibitions.

She felt in the match safe behind the stove at once for a match. There was only one there.

"Dat niggah wouldn't fetch nothin' heah tuh save his rotten neck, but he kin run thew whut Ah brings quick enough. Now he done toted off nigh on tuh haff uh box uh matches. He done had dat 'oman heah in mah house, too."

Nobody but a woman could tell how she knew this even before she struck the match. But she did and it put her into a new fury.

Presently she brought in the tubs to put the white things to soak. This time she decided she need not bring the hamper out of the bedroom; she would go in there and do the sorting. She picked up the pot-bellied lamp and went in. The room was small and the hamper stood hard by the foot of the white iron bed. She could sit and reach through the bedposts—resting as she worked.

"Ah wantah cross Jurden in uh calm time," she was singing again. The mood of the "love feast" had returned. She threw back the lid of the basket almost gaily. Then, moved by both horror and terror, she sprang back toward the door. *There lay the snake in the basket!* He moved sluggishly at first, but even as she turned round and round, jumped up and down in an insanity of fear, he began to stir vigorously. She saw him pouring his awful beauty from the basket upon the bed, then she seized the lamp and ran as fast as she could to the kitchen. The wind from the open door blew out the light and the darkness added to her terror. She sped to the darkness of the yard, slamming the door after her before she thought to set down the lamp. She did not feel safe even on the ground, so she climbed up in the hay barn.

There for an hour or more she lay sprawled upon the hay a gibbering wreck.

Finally, she grew quiet, and after that, coherent thought. With this, stalked through her a cold, bloody rage. Hours of this. A period of introspection, a space of retrospection, then a mixture of both. Out of this an awful calm.

"Well, Ah done de bes' Ah could. If things aint right, Gawd knows taint mah fault."

She went to sleep—a twitch sleep—and woke up to a faint gray sky. There was a loud hollow sound below. She peered out. Sykes was at the wood-pile, demolishing a wire-covered box.

He hurried to the kitchen door, but hung outside there some minutes before he entered, and stood some minutes more inside before he closed it after him.

The gray in the sky was spreading. Delia descended without fear now, and crouched beneath the low bedroom window. The drawn shade shut out the dawn, shut in the night. But the thin walls held back no sound.

"Dat ol' scratch is woke up now!" She mused at the tremendous whirr inside, which every woodsman knows, is one of the sound illusions. The rattler is a ventriloquist. His whirr sounds to the right, to the left, straight ahead, behind, close under foot—everywhere but where it is. Woe to him who guesses wrong unless he is prepared to hold up his end of the argument! Sometimes he strikes without rattling at all.

Inside, Sykes heard nothing until he knocked a pot lid off the stove while trying to reach the match safe in the dark. He had emptied his pockets at Bertha's.

The snake seemed to wake up under the stove and Sykes made a quick leap into the bedroom. In spite of the gin he had had, his head was clearing now.

"Mah Gawd!" he chattered, "ef Ah could on'y strack uh light!"

The rattling ceased for a moment as he stood paralyzed. He waited. It seemed that the snake waited also.

"Oh, fuh de light! Ah thought he'd be too sick"—Sykes was muttering to himself when the whirr began again, closer, right underfoot this time. Long before this, Sykes' ability to think had been flattened down to primitive instinct and he leaped—onto the bed.

Outside Delia heard a cry that might have come from a

maddened chimpanzee, a stricken gorilla. All the terror, all the horror, all the rage that man possibly could express, without a recognizable human sound.

A tremendous stir inside there, another series of animal screams, the intermittent whirr of the reptile. The shade torn violently down from the window, letting in the red dawn, a huge brown hand seizing the window stick, great dull blows upon the wooden floor punctuating the gibberish of sound long after the rattle of the snake had abruptly subsided. All this Delia could see and hear from her place beneath the window, and it made her ill. She crept over to the four-o'clocks and stretched herself on the cool earth to recover.

She lay there. "Delia, Delia!" She could hear Sykes calling in a most despairing tone as one who expected no answer. The sun crept on up, and he called. Delia could not move—her legs were gone flabby. She never moved, he called, and the sun kept rising.

"Mah Gawd!" She heard him moan, "Mah Gawd fum Heben!" She heard him stumbling about and got up from her flower-bed. The sun was growing warm. As she approached the door she heard him call out hopefully, "Delia, is dat you Ah heah?"

She saw him on his hands and knees as soon as she reached the door. He crept an inch or two toward her—all that he was able, and she saw his horribly swollen neck and his one open eye shining with hope. A surge of pity too strong to support bore her away from that eye that must, could not, fail to see the tubs. He would see the lamp. Orlando with its doctors was too far. She could scarcely reach the Chinaberry tree, where she waited in the growing heat while inside she knew the cold river was creeping up and up to extinguish that eye which must know by now that she knew.

Notes

INTRODUCTION

1. Edgar Allan Poe, "The Philosophy of Composition," *Edgar Allan Poe: Critical Theory*, ed. Stuart Levine and Susan F. Levine (Chicago: University of Illinois Press, 2009), 55–76.
2. Edith Wharton, "Preface," *Ghosts* (New York: D. Appleton-Century Company Incorporated, 1937), vii–xii, viii.
3. Kate Chopin, "On Certain Brisk, Bright Days," *The Complete Works of Kate Chopin*, ed. Per Seyersted (Baton Rouge: Louisiana State University Press, 1969), 721–22.
4. Anne Bradstreet, *The Complete Works of Anne Bradstreet*, ed. Joseph R. McElrath, Jr., and Allan P. Robb (Boston: Twayne Publishers, 1980), 177.
5. Patricia Okker, *Our Sister Editors: Sarah J. Hale and the Tradition of Nineteenth-Century American Women Editors* (Athens & London: University of Georgia Press, 1995).
6. Catharine Maria Sedgwick, "A Sketch of a Bluestocking," *Wielding the Pen: Writings on Authorship by American Women of the Nineteenth Century*, ed. Anne E. Boyd (Baltimore: Johns Hopkins University Press, 2009), 28–36, 35.
7. "Letter of 2 Feb. 1855," *The Centenary Edition of the Works of Nathaniel Hawthorne*, ed. William Charvat, Roy Harvey Pearce, and Claude M. Simpson (Columbus: Ohio State University Press, 1962), 308.
8. Fanny Fern, "A Bit of Injustice," *New York Ledger*, June 8, 1861, in *Ruth Hall and Other Writings*, ed. Joyce W. Warren (New Brunswick: Rutgers University Press, 1986), 318.
9. *The Journals of Louisa May Alcott*, ed. Joel Myerson, Daniel Shealy, and Madeleine Stern (Athens: University of Georgia Press, 1997), 22.

10. Rebecca Harding Davis, "When Shall Our Young Women Marry?," *Parry's Literary Journal (1884–1886)* 2, no. 12 (September 1886): 362.

11. Pocumtuck Valley Memorial Association. C. Yale to A. Fuller, January 25, 1873, box 26, Fuller-Higginson Papers.

12. Holly Jackson, "'So We Die before Our Own Eyes': Willful Sterility in The Country of the Pointed Firs," *New England Quarterly* 82, no. 2 (June 2009): 264–84, 265.

13. Charlotte Perkins Gilman, "A Suggestion on the Negro Problem," *American Journal of Sociology* 14, no. 1 (July 1908): 78–85.

14. Zitkála-Šá, *American Indian Stories, Legends, and Other Writings* (New York: Penguin, 2003), 91.

15. Gloria Anzaldúa, *Borderlands/La Frontera* (San Francisco: Spinsters/Aunt Lute, 1987), 79.

16. Melissa Marie González, "Resisting the 'Fatal Allurement' of Local Color: María Cristina Mena's Mexico in *American Magazine* and *The Century Magazine*," *Recovering the U.S. Hispanic Literary Heritage*, ed. Antonia I. Castañeda and A. Gabriel Meléndez, vol. 6 (Houston: Arte Público Press, 2006), 124–42.

17. Mary Chapman, "A 'Revolution in Ink': Sui Sin Far and Chinese Reform Discourse," *American Quarterly* 60, no. 4 (December 2008): 975–1001.

"CACOETHES SCRIBENDI"
BY CATHARINE MARIA SEDGWICK, 1830

1. The title is Latin for "mania for writing" and was a popular phrase in literary circles that may also be an allusion to Juvenal's seventh satire, "On Learning and Letters Unprofitable." Juvenal was a Roman poet active in the late first and early second centuries.

2. This quotation comes from Alexander Pope's "Dunciad," another literary satire published in 1728 about "Dunces in the Kingdom of Dulness."

3. This is a quotation from act I, scene II of William Shakespeare's *The Tempest* spoken by Miranda who, on seeing her lover, Ferdinand, for the first time, questions whether he is a spirit.

4. Georgics and pastorals are poetic forms concerned with rural life.

5. James Crichton (1560–1582) was a celebrated Scottish writer, philosopher, and intellectual who was murdered at the age of twenty-one. The 1652 fictionalized biography of Crichton by Sir Thomas Urquhart made much of his legendary genius in many fields and turned him into something of a folk hero.

6. The "erratic female lecturer" is likely Frances "Fanny" Wright (1795–1852), a Scottish American lecturer and reformer who became famous for the radicalism of her views.

7. "Coxcomb": foolishly vain—after the frill on a rooster's head.

8. Between 1830 and 1860, gift books became popular among middle-class readers in the United States. These were luxurious illustrated volumes intended to be given as gifts. Annuals were a kind of gift book advertised to periodical subscribers at the end of the year.

9. *The North American Review* was a well-respected literary magazine founded in Boston in 1815 that published poetry, fiction, and essays of a literary nature.

10. Atalanta is a figure from Greek mythology who was a skilled hunter and runner. An oracle prophesied that her marriage would be her undoing, so she agreed to marry only if her suitor could beat her in a footrace. Many suitors tried and failed, resulting in their deaths, but Hippomenes was finally successful after the goddess of love, Aphrodite, gave him three magic golden apples with which to tempt her.

11. "coup d'essai": first attempt.

12. A Saturday night book was a collection of religious reflections meant to be read in preparation for Sunday morning church services.

13. *Annals of the Parish* was an 1821 novel by the Scottish writer John Galt.

14. Cambridge is synonymous with Harvard College.

15. From Thomas Gray's "Elegy Written in a Country Churchyard" (1751). The poem is an elegy that considers the possibility of dying with unfulfilled potential.

16. Sophie von La Roche (1730–1807) was a German novelist notable for the financial success of her work. She was one of the most internationally famous female novelists of the eighteenth century.

17. The character of Meg Merrilies originally appeared in Sir Walter Scott's 1815 novel *Guy Mannering* as a fortune teller. Scott's character inspired an 1818 poem by John Keats that describes a "Gipsy [that] liv'd upon the Moors." John Keats, "Meg Merrilies,"

The Complete Works of John Keats, ed. H. Buxton Forman, vol. 2 (New York: Thomas Y. Crowell and Company, 1900), 218.

18. Ichabod Crane is the fictional protagonist of Washington Irving's 1820 story "The Legend of Sleepy Hollow." He is a schoolmaster, described as "tall, but exceedingly lank, with narrow shoulders, long arms and legs, hands that dangled a mile out of his sleeves, feet that might have served for shovels, and his whole frame most loosely hung together." Washington Irving, *The Sketch Book* (New York: James B. Millar & Co., 1884), 270.

19. Thomas Otway (1652–1685) was an English playwright best known for his tragedies and Torquato Tasso (1544–1685) was a popular Italian poet who was confined to an asylum later in life. His struggle with mental illness was the subject of a play by Johann Wolfgang von Goethe.

20. Isaac D'Israeli (1766–1848) was a writer and father of the first Jewish prime minister of the United Kingdom, Benjamin D'Israeli, who was also a novelist.

21. "dramatis personsae": the characters in a play or story.

22. "Blue stocking" refers to an independent, learned, politically active woman. The term originated in the Blue Stockings Society, an informal women's social and educational movement in England in the mid-eighteenth century. Blue worsted stockings, considered informal, came to symbolize the group's disregard for fashion and hierarchy. By the 1770s, the name came to apply to learned and especially literary women more generally.

23. Sir Walter Scott (1771–1832) wrote a series of twenty-eight popular historical novels set in Scotland that takes its name for the first in the series, *Waverley* (1814).

24. A blue ribbon would signify an identification with blue stockings; green signified fickleness.

25. The Tower of Babel is a story from the book of Genesis wherein the builders speak different languages and can't proceed with the construction because they cannot communicate.

26. Lancaster schools followed the pedagogical philosophies of Joseph Lancaster (1778–1838), a Quaker educational reformer who specialized in educating the poor.

27. Henry Cockburn, a Scottish judge and regular contributor to the *Edinburgh Review*, recalls Francis Jeffrey, editor of the *Review*, having made this remark to the famous bluestocking writer Elizabeth Hamilton (1758–1816): "I think it was to Mrs. Hamilton that Jeffrey said, in allusion to the good taste of never losing the feminine in literary character, that there was no objection to the

blue stocking, provided the petticoat came low enough down."
Lord Henry Thomas Cockburn, *Lord Cockburn's Works, Volume II: Memorials* (Edinburgh: A. and C. Black, 1872), 230.

28. *Legendary, Remember Me,* and *Token* are all titles of literary annuals.

29. "éclaircissement": explanation.

30. "c'est le premier pas qui coute": getting started is the hardest part. (Literally, only the first step costs.)

"LIFE IN THE IRON-MILLS" BY REBECCA HARDING DAVIS, 1861

1. This epigraph is a reworking of some lines from Tennyson's 1850 long poem *In Memoriam A.H.H.*

2. "Pig iron" refers to unrefined metal processed in pig trough–like molds. The method of iron refinement described in this story, using a reverberatory furnace, was widely used until the safer and less arduous Bessemer process was popularized in the late nineteenth century. By 1877, there were eleven Bessemer steel mills in the United States.

3. "rain butt": a vessel that collects rainwater for use.

4. *"la belle rivière"*: the lovely stream. This French phrase is an ironic, derogatory term for the industrial Ohio River.

5. "puddler": the worker responsible for stirring the iron in a reverberatory furnace—a notoriously dangerous and unhealthy job due to the fire, smoke, fumes, and difficulty of the physical labor. Most puddlers did not expect to live past their thirties.

6. Here Davis references a litany of popular ideological orientations: Egoism, the belief that one ought to act always in self-interest; Pantheism, the belief that God is to be found in all things; and Arminianism, an early Protestant evangelical movement based on the concept of free will.

7. "rolling mill": a mill that produced iron "rolled" into sheets or bars.

8. "picker": worker in a cotton mill who separates the cotton fibers for processing.

9. "feeder": worker in an iron mill who shovels the ore into the furnace.

10. "Begorra" is an exclamation that roughly means "by God!" and is stereotypically supposed to be a characteristic utterance of Irish people in nineteenth-century America.

11. "Vargent" signifies the Virgin Mary in the Welsh dialect of the quotation.

12. "Milesian" is a term used by medieval Christian writers to signify the Irish people in their origin stories; the descendants of King Milesius.

13. "flitch": fatty pork salted for preservation.

14. "molly": a derogatory term for an effeminate man. In the eighteenth and nineteenth centuries, "molly houses" referred to homosexual male gathering places.

15. *"sobriquet"*: nickname.

16. "cockpit": cock-fighting arena.

17. "korl": a calcium aluminum silicate that is the wasted byproduct of iron production, also known as "dross."

18. Farinata degli Uberti was an Italian aristocrat who is mentioned in Dante's fourteenth-century epic, *The Divine Comedy*, where he appears in canto X of *The Inferno* as a heretic confined to a fiery coffin for eternity. In life, Farinata was known for his rejection of the notion of an afterlife.

19. "bitumen": a crude coal used for fueling the fires.

20. "sinking fund": a portion of profit set aside each month for the paying off of debt.

21. Davis's narrator refers here to a trio of illustrious German philosophers whose works were common reading among the period's liberal Americans. Immanuel Kant (1724–1804) was known for his 1781 *Critique of Pure Reason*, a foundational work in German Idealism. Novalis was the pen name of Georg Philipp Friedrich Freiherr von Hardenberg (1772–1801), a German poet, novelist, and philosopher whose work also contributed to the German Romantic movement that predated Idealism. Wilhelm von Humboldt (1767–1835) was the founder of the Humboldt University in Berlin whose writings on the limits of state action influenced John Stuart Mill's 1859 *On Liberty*, a work that enjoyed an enormous popularity in 1860s America.

22. *"Ce n'est pas mon affaire"*: "That's not my business."

23. "'*Liberté*' or '*Égalité*'": Liberty, equality, and fraternity" was a phrase popularized during the French Revolution after a 1790 speech by Maximilien Robespierre. In 1870, it became the motto of the French Republic.

24. A passage in Charles Dickens's 1854 industrial novel, *Hard Times*, may have inspired this speech of Kirby's: "the multitude of Coketown, generically called 'the Hands'—a race who would have found more favor with some people, if Providence has seen

fit to make them only hands, or, like the lower creatures of the sea-shore, only hands and stomachs" (Charles Dickens, *Hard Times* [New York: Norton, 2001], 52).

25. *"De profundis clamavi"* translates to "Out of the depths I cry" from Latin—it is the first line of Psalm 130. "Hungry and thirsty, his soul faints in him" is a translation of Psalm 107, line 5 from the King James Bible.

26. "I am innocent of the blood of man" is from Matthew 27:24, while "ye did it unto me" is from Matthew 25:40. Kirby does have his quotations mixed up.

27. *"N'est ce pas"*: French for, in this context, "Aren't you?"

28. Saint-Simonians were followers of the founder of French socialism, Claude-Henri de Rouvroy de Saint-Simon (1760–1825). They called those who did not work "the idling class."

29. "Magdalens" is a euphemism for sex workers, based on Mary Magdalene of the New Testament.

30. Church creeds are statements of belief issued or adopted by religious authorities. Francis Bacon (1561–1626) was an English philosopher and scientist who is often considered the founder of scientific empiricism. He believed in drawing conclusions from observation and inductive reasoning. Johann Wolfgang von Goethe (1749–1833) was a poet, novelist, and philosopher who contributed to German Idealism. His work was influential to the American Transcendentalists of the 1840s and '50s.

31. Jean-Paul Marat (1743–1793) was a journalist and politician during the French Revolution whose newspaper *L'Ami du peuple* ("Friend of the People") sympathized with the Jacobins. Oliver Cromwell (1599–1656) served as Lord Protector of England from 1653 until his death. In the nineteenth century, he was popularized as a figure of progressive social reform for English and American Romantics after being celebrated in the works of the Scottish philosopher Thomas Carlyle (1795–1881).

32. In Luke 23:34, Jesus asks God for forgiveness for the Roman soldiers who crucified him: "Father forgive them, for they know not what they do."

33. "Frick" is from the Middle English "fricke" for "brisk."

"A WHITE HERON"
BY SARAH ORNE JEWETT, 1886

1. "bangeing": New England regional dialect for "hanging out."

"THE YELLOW WALL-PAPER"
BY CHARLOTTE PERKINS GILMAN, 1892

1. Any nervous condition experienced by women in this period was likely to be diagnosed as "hysteria."
2. "phosphates": a form of phosphoric acid that was marketed as a tonic for the treatment of nervous disorders in the late nineteenth and early twentieth centuries. High phosphorus levels in the body can be harmful, potentially causing calcium deposits in the organs.
3. "sticketh closer than a brother": from Proverbs 24 in the Old Testament.
4. "Romanesque": a style of medieval European architecture that predated the Gothic, characterized by stone arches, peaks, and turrets. "Delirium tremens": the most severe form of alcohol withdrawal; sufferers may experience altered mental states or even hallucinations.
5. Wallpaper paste at the time was made with flour and therefore prone to mold and mildew. Damp conditions could also cause the arsenical pigments frequently used in Victorian wallpaper dye to admit an unpleasant—even toxic—gas.
6. In the original *New England Magazine* publication, which this text follows, this is a question mark. Most subsequent editions replace it with an exclamation point.

"THE LITTLE ROOM"
BY MADELENE YALE WYNNE, 1895

1. Calico is a heavy woven cotton fabric that originated in southwestern India; chintz is a similar cloth also from the Indian subcontinent, distinguished by its frequent ornamentation with bold floral patterns.
2. The peacock was a popular motif with Arts and Crafts artisans such as Wynne. Peacocks appeared on jewelry, metalworks, wallpaper, fabric, and poster design throughout the period. The cover of the volume in which this story was published, designed by Wynne, features three peacocks.
3. "albums": a popular pastime for nineteenth-century middle-class girls and women, similar to a scrapbook. Such albums would contain drawings and verse as well as mementos and were often exchanged among friends and worked upon collaboratively.

4. "light-stand": a small table or pedestal for a candle or gas lamp, often containing drawers; "snuffer": a hand tool used to put out candles, consisting of a bell-shaped piece of metal.
5. "gilt-edged china": popular commercially manufactured dishes. Such commonplace plates would be at odds with Wynne's Arts and Crafts ideology. Wynne and Putnam used handmade dishes at their home in Deerfield.
6. "tarlatan": a stiff, open-weave cotton desirable as a window screen because it is translucent.

"THE NEW WOMAN"
BY BARBARA E. POPE, 1896

1. By "our schools," Margaret refers to African American vocational training programs, such as the one at Tuskegee where Pope taught. The scholar Jennifer Harris has suggested that Frank's unfamiliarity with this topic might imply an interracial marriage. Jennifer Harris, "Legacy Profiles: Barbara Pope (1854–1908)," *Legacy* 32, no. 2 (2015): 281–304.
2. "penwiper": a decorative and useful object found on a writing desk. A small piece of dark-colored cloth used to wipe pen tips would be incorporated into a representational design such as an animal or an article of clothing. Instructions for crafting penwipers and other small domestic objects were common fare in the periodicals of the time.
3. Dresden: a city in Germany renowned for the production of ribbon and lace from the seventeenth century onward; Dresden ribbon signifies quality.
4. "wheel": popular slang for a bicycle, often connected to the New Woman figure.

"SOULS BELATED"
BY EDITH WHARTON, 1899

1. *"Partenza"* means "departure" in Italian—an announcement like the English "All aboard!"
2. "galoshes": heavy rubber rain boots worn over shoes.
3. "parterre box": literally means "on-the-ground seats"; these were the most socially desirably opera boxes.
4. "Worth": the most prominent Parisian dressmaker of the period.

5. George Cruikshank (1792–1878) was a British caricaturist and illustrator best known for illustrating the works of the novelist Charles Dickens.

6. "copse": a small group of trees.

7. *"Je n'en vois pas la nécessité"*:"I don't see the need."

8. *"milieu"*: setting or environment.

9. *"tout d'une pièce"*: "all in one piece."

10. *"modus vivendi"*: way of living.

11. *"Table-d'hote"* translates to "the host's table" and was a way of referring to a price-fixed menu at European guesthouses.

12. *"Civis Romanus sum"*: a phrase used in Cicero's *In Verrem* (70 BC) as a plea for accessing the rights of a Roman citizen. Supposedly, uttering the phrase would grant travelers safety throughout the Roman Empire.

13. "front": a false hairpiece pinned to the front of the head. These were often made of a woman's own hair, collected over time from her hairbrush and collected in a "hair receiver," a small box.

14. "Christmas chromo": a highly colored holiday greeting card.

15. *"premier"*: a synonym for "seat" that also means "throne."

16. Jacques Doucet (1853–1929) was a French fashion designer who dressed celebrities like the actress Sarah Bernhardt.

17. "card-case": used to carry the visiting cards guests would leave at a house if their intended host was not in.

18. Henry Drummond (1851–1897) was a Scottish evangelist and writer.

19. Jean Henri Masers de Latude (1725–1805) wrote a 1787 memoir about his repeated escapes from the Bastille, a prison fortress in Paris.

20. *"noyade"*: a mass drowning.

21. "Bradshaw": the brand name of a series of travel guides and train timetables published from 1839 until 1961.

"MRS. SPRING FRAGRANCE"
BY SUI SIN FAR, 1912

1. "curio": rare art object. Mr. Spring Fragrance is likely an importer.

2. Alfred Tennyson (1809–1892) was an English poet. These lines are from *In Memoriam A.H.H.* (1850), an elegy Tennyson wrote on the death of his school friend, Arthur Henry Hallam.

3. *Chinese World* was a newspaper, also known as 世界日報, published in San Francisco from 1891 to 1969.

4. "li-chi," or "lychee": a small sweet fruit with a hard shell.

5. The note here in the original publication reads: "The plum blossom is the Chinese flower of virtue. It has been adopted by the Japanese, just in the same way as they have adopted the Chinese national flower, the chrysanthemum."

6. The Fifth Moon Festival, also called the Dragon Boat Festival or 端午節, is a traditional Chinese holiday that commemorates the ancient poet Qu Yuan with lavish festivities.

7. *The Gleaner* was a weekly Jewish newspaper in San Francisco started by journalist and rabbi Julius Eckman in 1857. It later became the *San Francisco Bulletin.*

8. "indemnity money": The Boxer Indemnity Scholarship Program (1908) was an Act of Congress that granted scholarship money to Chinese nationals wishing to study in the United States. The controversial program was funded through the excess balance of the indemnity fund China had given the United States in return for their aid in quelling the Boxer Uprising between 1899 and 1901.

9. "fallen in love with her picture": In the late nineteenth and early twentieth centuries, many Chinese men immigrated to the United States while single, only to later seek the services of a matchmaker who would find a suitable bride in China to be sent over to join him after the pair exchanged photographs.

10. "Tommies": young men, likely white.

"THE VINE-LEAF"
BY MARÍA CRISTINA MENA, 1914

1. "Malsufrido": The doctor's name means "impatient."

2. "tonsure": the part of a monk's head left bare on top by shaving off the hair.

3. "physicked": treated in the context of a medical practice.

4. Penitentes were a Catholic fraternal order that began in the early nineteenth century following Mexican independence from Spain. More generally, the word refers to repentant sinners.

5. Dr. Sangrado and Gil Blas are characters in the picaresque novel *Gil Blas* by Alain-René Lesage, published between 1715 and 1735. Dr. Sangrado is famously a quack.

6. "duenna": governess.

7. Bacchus is the Roman god of wine; Cupid is the Roman god of romantic love.

8. *"Chist!"*: Hush.
9. *"marqués"*: a nobleman of high rank.
10. *"Válgame Dios"*: an exclamation meaning "By God!"
11. "Lorgnette": a pair of reading or opera glasses held in front of one's eyes by a handle.
12. *"Válgame la Virgen"* is a variant of *"Válgame Dios"* that replaces God with the Virgin Mary.

"THE WIDESPREAD ENIGMA CONCERNING BLUE-STAR WOMAN" BY ZITKÁLA-ŠÁ, 1921

1. "Iye-que" translates to "recognize" in Lakota.
2. "Hinnu, hinnu" is a variation of "How, how!" in Lakota.
3. "White-Horse-Riders": the Sunkska Akanl Okolakiciye (in Lakota) were distinguished warriors and superior hunters. Most members chosen for the honor came from the Wablenecha, the Orphan Band.
4. Sitting Bull: Tȟatȟáŋka Íyotake, a Hunkpapa Lakota leader who lived from 1837 until 1890, when he was murdered by Indian police at the Standing Rock Indian Reservation.

"SWEAT" BY ZORA NEALE HURSTON, 1926

1. "buckboard": an open horse-drawn carriage.
2. "amen-corner Christians": the place in a traditional Black Church where the older members sit, especially women.
3. "eppizudicks": episodics; periodic attacks of ill health.
4. "Gethsemane": the garden where Jesus prayed before Judas betrayed him and he was crucified; "Calvary": the hill upon which Jesus had to bear his cross.
5. "suck-egg dog": an expression referring to a dog that steals chicken eggs on a farm; a nuisance.
6. "Woodbridge": a Florida town settled by Black laborers in the 1880s.
7. Delia sings about the Jordan River, which symbolizes deliverance in the bible.

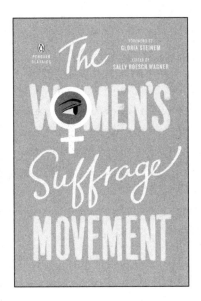

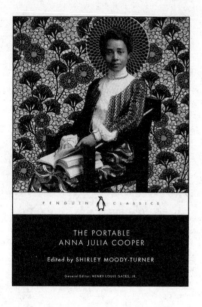

A Nation of Women

Edited with an Introduction by Félix V. Matos Rodríguez
Translated by Alan West-Durán

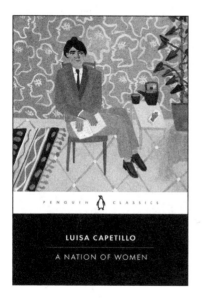

In 1915, Puerto Rican activist Luisa Capetillo was arrested for being the first woman to wear men's trousers publicly. The rebellious act elevated her to feminist icon status but overshadowed the significant contributions she made to the women's movement and anarchist labor movements of the early twentieth century. With *A Nation of Women*, Capetillo's socialist and feminist activism is given the spotlight it deserves.